# BILLY RAGS

# Praise for Ted Lewis

'Lewis is major' – **Max Allan Collins author of**
*The Road to Perdition*

'Ted Lewis cuts to the bone' – **James Sallis, author of** *Drive*

'A pulp-fiction triumph worthy of Jim Thompson or James
Ellroy. I can't remember the last time I turned pages so
eagerly... his work cuts to the bone, both literally *and*
metaphysically' – **John Powers, NPR's** *Fresh Air*

'One of the most coldly brilliant crime novels you will ever
read... a mesmerizing story of power, love, hubris and betrayal,
but, above all, the portrait of what one might call a tragic
villain... Complicated in plot, propulsive in its narrative pace,
beautifully structured, it is a book you'll want to read'
– **Michael Dirda,** *Washington Post* **on** *GBH*

'Ted Lewis is one of the most influential crime novelists Britain
has ever produced, and his shadow falls on all noir fiction,
whether on page or screen, created on these isles since his
passing. I wouldn't be the writer I am without Ted Lewis. It's
time the world rediscovered him' – **Stuart Neville**

'An example of how dangerous writing can really be when it is
done properly... By preferring to look the street straight in the
face instead of peeping at if from behind an upstairs curtain,
Ted Lewis cleared a road straight through the black jungle'
– **Derek Raymond**

'One of England's finest, but still most neglected postwar
writers' – **David Peace**

'His characters have no tenderness, the settings are bleak, but this isn't pulp fiction – it's real writing' – **Richard Preston, *Times***

'This is vintage British pulp fiction at its fast, furious and thoroughly sleazy best' – **Laura Wilson, *Guardian***

'The book is outstanding: Lewis… judges perfectly when to horrify the reader and when to hold back… But the book is also funny and zestful: Lewis's delight in his complex double-cross plot and low-life characters is infectious, and there is poetry in his stark evocation of Lincolnshire's desperate tattiness. It's equal parts suicide note and celebration of the human ability to find reasons to keep going' – **Jake Kerridge, *Daily Telegraph***

'The Brit noir masterpiece by the author of *Get Carter* has been reissued. It's well worth rediscovering' – **Robbie Millen, *Times Best Books of 2020***

'An intuitive study of fear, guilt, loss and the corruptive power of violence, sex and pornography that redefined the possibilities of psychological noir. A savage valediction for the smart-suited working class gangster' – **Nick Triplow**

'Aristotle when he defined tragedy mandated that a tragic hero must fall from a great height… but he never imagined the kind of roadside motels of James M. Cain or saw the smokestacks rise in the Northern English industrial hell of Ted Lewis's *Get Carter* – **Denis Lehane**

# BOOKS BY TED LEWIS

*All the Way Home and All the Night Through* (1965)
*Get Carter* (first published as *Jack's Return Home*) (1970)
*Plender* (1971)
*Billy Rags* (1973)
*Jack Carter's Law* (1974)
*The Rabbit* (1975)
*Boldt* (1976)
*Jack Carter and the Mafia Pigeon* (1977)
*GBH* (1980)

# BILLY RAGS

## TED LEWIS

NO EXIT PRESS

This edition published in 2022
by No Exit Press,
an imprint of Oldcastle Books Ltd,
Harpenden, UK
noexit.co.uk
@noexitpress

ISBN 978 978-0-85730-508-4 (Print)
ISBN 978-0-85730-509-1 (epub)

2 4 6 8 10 9 7 5 3 1

Typeset in 11.5 on 14.3pt Minio Pro
by Avocet Typeset, Bideford, Devon, EX39 2BP
Printed and bound in Great Britain by CPI Group (UK) Ltd, Croydon, CR0 4YY

MIX
Paper from
responsible sources
FSC
www.fsc.org
FSC® C171272

For more information about Crime Fiction go to crimetime.co.uk /
@crimetimeuk

# AUTHOR'S NOTE

This novel and its central character were originally inspired by certain actual events and by a real person. But it is a work of fiction: all the descriptions of prisons, convicts and their friends and relatives, prison officers and policemen are imaginary.

# INTRODUCTION
## by Nick Triplow

With *Billy Rags* (1973) and *Jack Carter's Law* (1974), Ted Lewis left behind the Humber landscape that had given his writing its distinct, edge-of-nowhere rawness. Written under pressure to repeat *Get Carter*'s success, these books are as close as Lewis would come to writing conventional crime novels. That said, moral certitude and sweet redemption are definitely not on the agenda.

*Billy Rags* is the story of professional villain, Billy Cracken, serving 25-years for armed robbery. A failed escape attempt sees him moved to E Wing of Aston prison, a high security fortress where criminal kingpin, Walter Colman, and his associates hold sway. Pitting himself against Colman and the prison system, Cracken's time is hard time and he hatches an audacious break-out plan.

Lewis's novel was based on the 1971 trial deposition of convicted armed robber and prison escapee, John McVicar, then in the first year of a 26-year sentence for robbery and firearms offences committed while on the run from Durham Prison's E Wing, the 'prison within a prison' that housed some of Britain's toughest inmates. The manuscript found its way to the desk of Lewis's literary agent, Toby Eady. Specifics are shady, but it seems the intention was for a part of the novel's advance to support McVicar's wife and young son on the outside.

Reviewing *Billy Rags* in the *Spectator*, Auberon Waugh praised Lewis's realistic depiction of 'ordinary, run-of-the-mill criminal psychopaths', while bending the conventions of traditional thriller fiction: 'Obviously, it is to Mr Lewis's credit as an artist that his book is extremely depressing and distasteful… scenes of sodomy and violence are described as they happen, neither more nor less.'

With a second roman à clef in mind, Eady brokered a meeting between Lewis and bank robber turned supergrass, Bertie Smalls – the project is rumoured to have been abandoned after one vodka-fuelled session. Instead, Lewis returned to the character that launched his career with the short story, 'Kings, Queens and Pawns', published in November 1973's *Men Only* magazine. A year later came *Jack Carter's Law*.

Lewis's first *Get Carter* prequel is set in the London underworld of the late 1960s. Carter hunts a police informer in the Fletchers' organisation. When he finds him, he'll kill him. Old loyalties break down as Carter's actions fuel old enmities.

In *Jack Carter's Law* there is no revenge for a murdered brother or exploited daughter. It is this absence of moral cause, writes Max Allan Collins, that makes *Jack Carter's Law* even 'tougher and more uncompromising' than its famous predecessor. Lewis delivers the comprehensive Jack Carter experience: the enforcer operating claustrophobic streets and grimy interiors of unfashionable London: low dives, smoky clubs and villains' flats; the insides of Ford Cortinas, fag smoke, sardonic asides, bent coppers, naked violence, and sex for money. And drink. A lot of drink.

By this time, Lewis was writing against the odds. Heavy drinking placed his marriage under strain. Yet his voice is unmistakeable. Characteristic preoccupations of violence, sex and obsession are rendered in first person, present tense narratives that leave no space between the reader and flashes of action. *Billy Rags* and *Jack Carter's Law* are timely reminders that when he was this good, Lewis made his own rules and dared you to look away.

Dear Sheila,

With any luck Ronnie should get this to you by Thursday. It had to come pigeon post on account of what I've got to say, as you'll appreciate. When you've read it, get rid sharp. What we are talking about is on, most likely some time over the weekend, but maybe Monday or Tuesday. Whenever it is, though, I'll be with you next week, darling. For Christ sake keep everybody else out of it. Only Ronnie knows and don't talk to him about it either, because you're not supposed to know and he might cop out, you never know. So just wait for the phone call, that's all you can do. I know you're feeling the same way as I am but it won't be long now.

See you soon
All my love
Billy

# PART ONE

I was glad I got Burnham. Not at first, and certainly not when I parleyed with the Governor, Captain Reece. He used to swish around the wing letting all the screws salute him; he and I had no difficulty whatsoever in identifying each other as enemies. He was shit-scared of me and he knew I knew it.

No, the thing I really liked about Burnham was the remarkable little trap-door in the top landing recess that led into the loft. I mean, I couldn't believe it. But what was more unbelievable was that nobody had done it before. A nickful of them and no one had doddled.

I remember saying to Toddy who was doing a ten-stretch.

'What they got in that loft Toddy? King Kong?'

'I'm not with you Billy,' he said.

Christ, I thought. I must be the only bright bastard in the whole nick.

'The trap-door,' I said. 'The trap-door on the landing recess. What's up there that stops anybody having a go?'

'I dunno,' he said. 'Can't say I've thought about it. You reckon it's worth a tickle, do you?'

Well, would I be talking about it if I didn't, I thought, but to Toddy I said:

'Tell us, Toddy, who are the chancers in this place? Who's ready and who's willing?'

Toddy gave me seven names, including his own.

'You're sure about that, are you?'

He knew what I meant because he said:

'No bother. They're all straight.'

So about a month after that conversation me and the seven others went through the trap-door after copping for the screws.

I'd plucked my one off the alarm bell, just in time.

We bundled them into a cell but we had to take off without tying them up because someone tipped a table up in the air that had a load of cups on it; but we all made it up through the opening. We scuttled along towards the end of the wing. As we ran Toddy said to Crump:

'You've got the rope, haven't you Crumpy?' Crumpy told him to fuck off but Toddy's voice had come out all fagwheezy and earnest and the fact that anybody on a doddle like this could forget the most important piece of equipment transformed the adrenalin pumping through the rest of us into hysterics, a sort of snorting giggle on the run. It was as if we were all running through apple trees with a farmer right behind us.

But when we got to the end of the wing I told them all where to start thumping at the roof and that channelled the hysteric energy in the right direction.

We smashed our way out through the tiles and Crump fixed up the rope and we all slid down it on to the ground and grouped together at the bottom of the outside wall. All except the strongest man in the nick; I stood apart and farther out from the others and began to swing the hooked rope to the top of the wall. I tried three or four times but it kept falling short.

Everyone began to look shitty and there was no doubt about it, the whole scene was very embarrassing: here we were out of the Security wing and standing by the wall in the dark without a screw in sight, with a rope and a hook and I just couldn't get the bastard up. After about eight tries a young chancer by the name of Gordon Harris said to me:

'For Christ's sake, man, give some other fucker a go, will you, otherwise we might as well turn it in right now.'

I slung the rope and the hook at him.

'All right, clever sod, you get it up then,' I said, and turned on Tommy Dukes who'd made the hook because I had to spin off my frustration and loss of face on someone.

I said:

'You stupid bastard, you weighted it all wrong.'

Tommy was so angry he couldn't speak. He just stared at me with his mouth open and his eyes bulging out at me as though I was strangling him.

'I told you the specification,' I said. 'Why didn't you do as I said?'

If he'd had the hook in his hand I think he would have put it over my head but before he could either say or do anything someone shouted, 'Screws'. At the same time the hook clattered and scraped down the wall and rang out on the concrete, sounding like a cell door sliding shut.

I turned round and looked at the screws. There were four of them, standing about twenty yards away, in the shadow of the main block, just watching us. I knew that the last thing they were going to do was to get in amongst us so I said to the others:

'Round the corner. We'll try there.'

We all took off like athletes at White City. The screws didn't move at first, either because the sprint start had startled them to death, or they knew something that we didn't.

We stopped again and had three or four more tries with the hook. By this time all the main prison cons were up at their windows, shouting encouragement at us but it didn't raise our game. The four screws appeared on the scene again so we took off towards the main gate.

But when we got there, Captain Reece was waiting to receive us, backed by a dozen or so more screws.

It's always hardest to lose when you think you've won. When I'd stood by the wall a few minutes back I'd thought it was just a formality. Now it was like being sentenced all over again; the same sick helplessness, the same desperate fighting feeling behind my eyes as the tears tried to get out, the same determination to show everybody you don't give a stuff.

Reece's piping voice floated through the night air.

'It's no good lads, the troops are surrounding the place. Come in quietly and don't let's have any trouble.'

You could tell from the tone of his voice he was feeling as shaky as we were. The screws didn't look too happy about it either. A few of them were holding riot sticks and Gordon Harris pointed at the nearest one of them and screamed at Reece:

'No trouble? What's he got a riot stick for, then? You're going to cosh us up, you bastards.'

The screw Harris had pointed at shifted the riot stick to behind his back and looked all sheepish. There was dead silence. Even the main block had gone quiet. The only sound was the far-off groan of a jet way up above the low night clouds.

'The bastards are going to cosh us up,' Harris screeched again.

Reece was beginning to look like a rabbit in a snare. He was frightened to say anything in case what he said triggered off the wrong kind of reaction but at the same time you could see he felt he had to say something as the screws were expecting it of him. But he didn't so the screw who'd shifted the night stick behind his back spoke in Reece's stead.

'Come on, lads, it was a good try.'

Everybody ignored him. We were all milling about just looking sick. Freddie Simpson said to no one in particular:

'I can't believe it. I can't believe it. I really thought we'd made it.'

Reece sounded in just as bad a state when he singled me out.

'Cracken. Come on lad. It was a good try but you may as well go in.'

He must have thought he sounded coaxing, but to me it was just grovelling.

I stepped to the front of our group.

'They don't want to go in,' I said.

This was just what Reece didn't want; grandstanding. It would load the atmosphere even more against him.

'They'll go in if you go in,' he said.

I turned round slowly and began to walk away. I was too depressed to play out a scene for the benefit of the main block. I didn't have any particular place to go, it was just that I wanted to walk away from the whole fucking issue.

As I walked I was vaguely aware of Reece trotting behind me trying to kid me about how I could get them all back inside. Then I became aware of a different voice. I stopped and turned round. Gordon Harris was still holding the hook but Freddie Simpson had picked up the rope and was making a loop out of it.

'I am going to hang you, you Welsh mountain goat. This is all your fucking fault.'

I realised he was talking to Reece about two seconds before Reece did. Reece's jaw dropped and his eyes went glassy but the words he'd been saying still kept coming out as though his brain had nothing to do with his mouth and he started circling round me, with Freddie following him holding the loop and Harris trailing behind carrying the hook. It was the weirdest bloody thing you've ever seen. I mean they went right round me, two full circles, Reece staring at them shit-scared and yet burbling on to me as though nothing was happening, Freddie creeping after him like Quasimodo mumbling how he was going to fucking hang him and Gordon Harris poncing along behind holding the hook, looking like a spare prick at a wedding. And Freddie would have done it if he could, he had that look, it was all the grief of not being over the wall twisting him up inside and all he could see was Reece between him and the other side of the wall.

For Freddie's sake I had to break it up so I shouted across to the others: 'Let's go back the way we came out.'

It took a minute or two to sink in because everybody had been fascinated by Freddie and his rope trick but I walked over to the main group and past them towards the spot where we'd dropped down. Reece just naturally followed after me and Freddie and Harris dropped the rope and the hook and ran past Reece to join the others who had already begun to follow me to the spot. When we got there Toddy cocked his head at the roof and said: 'Why not give the troops a show?'

I nodded. Anything that would pour a little more crap over Reece's head.

Reece had got back a bit of the military style he'd lost round by the gate. He'd certainly taken a big swallow because he walked over to us, his chin sticking out at right angles to his scraggy neck; he'd obviously decided that the time had come for him to take matters firmly in hand.

But everything shattered for him again when he saw the rope strung up and everybody climbing back up it to the roof of the wing. Toddy and I were the only two left on the ground when Reece got close to us.

'Come on, Billy,' said Toddy, offering me the rope. 'No ranks always last.'

He was only doing a twelve.

'After you, Toddy,' I said. I wanted to see what Reece would do, whether he would make a grab for me if he saw I was left on my own.

Toddy went up the rope. I could see from Reece's face that he was thinking about it, and so could everybody else. Death or glory, he was thinking.

He was probably writing the headlines himself: 'Governor

tackles Cracken single handed; courageous action foils attempted break.' Except that the part the press wouldn't put in was the two broken arms and the two broken legs that Reece would finish up with if he tried anything.

Reece was very close to me now. The screws and the cons were all watching Reece, to see if he'd do it, and I was looking at him too, letting my eyes tell him that I knew he never would, not in a million years.

Then I just gave him a smile that described how pathetic he was and I turned my back on him and swung away up the rope.

Afterwards a screw told me: 'He should never have let you get away with it. He should never have let you get up on that roof.'

I scrambled over the top of the roof and stood up. The air was cold and fresh and above me the clouds were breaking up slightly and through the breaks crystal stars were still and remote, winking blankly at this pointless charade. I looked over the wall into the street. Besides the troops and the police, there were about a hundred people standing around, faces upturned, waiting to see what the animals would do next. What would it be? Swinging from branch to branch or scratching under the armpits. I wanted to spit on them. I looked at the lads. A few of them were so sick they couldn't whip up any enthusiasm for a demonstration but Freddie and Toddy and Harris began to rip the slates off and smash the woodwork and tear the tarpaulin underneath. Scrambled words drifted up into the night air from the loud hailers. The lads just carried on dismantling the roof. Then they got the spotlight on us and began to unwind the hoses.

'They're going to squirt us,' Harris said.

With that he hurled a tile down towards the plain-clothes police who were standing in the nick yard, looking up with those po-faced expressions they all have. The tile shattered in front of them and they all stepped back, slowly, in perfect time with each other, like a load of bloody chorus girls.

Harris picked up a tile and so did Toddy and me and we began a barrage down into the yard.

This time the boys in grey overcoats lost their symmetry and scattered like so many bits of broken glass. Flash guns started going off. The police were popping from inside the nick, the press from outside. The press were wasting their time as we were fifty feet up but the police photographers were only fifteen yards away from the bottom wing so I tried to cover my face every time they took a picture.

The heroes down below finally got the hoses going but the power was too weak to dislodge us. Deliberately so. They couldn't risk the scandal of one of us finishing up in the street with a broken back. That gave us back our confidence. Freddie eased himself to the edge of the roof.

'I can piss harder than that,' he shouted.

If he'd been better hung he'd have given them a demonstration.

We kept the tiles winging down for a couple of hours. Then the group inside the nick gave over with the hoses and just left us alone. Our audience down in the street started to drift away. Without any attention the situation began to pall.

'Well, I don't know about anybody else,' I said, trying to detach my damp clothes from my skin, 'I'm fucking freezing.'

Toddy sank down on the ridging.

Harris flung a tile out into the night as hard as he could and then relaxed completely, sagging down next to Toddy.

'Bastards,' he said. 'Bloody sodding bastards.'

'We've got to go down sometime,' Toddy said.

'Come on,' I said. 'Let's go down. If we stay up here much longer somebody might miss us.'

Toddy pretended he found it funny and got up and swung himself down through the hole.

When we got back to the trap-door, Reece was waiting in the recess. He watched me all the way as I climbed down and

21

he watched me as I scrubbed my tarred hands in the wash-basin. He was back in command again. Or so he thought. The exhibition he'd made of himself outside was just another memory for him to distort.

A half-decent bloke called Greaves, the chief screw, walked me back to my cell.

'Well that didn't get you very far, did it Billy?' he said.

I shrugged.

'It was only the hook that done us,' I said.

'I reckon you're on two months' chokey for tonight.'

'It was worth it seeing Reece mess himself.'

Greaves didn't say anything to that. He didn't have to. He didn't say anything to the lads who were calling their congratulations and commiserations as we walked the block, either. I just grinned at them all, well-braced as I walked, coming the old swagger, but when Greaves shut the cell door behind me I lay on my bed and I could have thrown up I was so depressed. There'd been a chance. A real one. All that had happened was that someone had ballocksed up the hook. I lay there and I could still smell the freshness of the night air and hear the soft surge of the town and see the warm orange of the strings of lights on the main roads that led out of the town. I didn't sleep for a long time because I kept concentrating on the sounds and sights and smells of the evening so that I'd have something to exercise my mind on during the inevitable chokey that was to come.

The day before the visiting Magistrates' Board turned up to smack our hands because of the escape I said to Toddy: 'Have you ever noticed the way everybody bulls up for a scene like the Board?'

'Sure I have, Billy. Standard practice.'

'It may be standard practice for you and the rest of the fucking cons in the place but you can leave me out of it.'

'How do you mean, Billy?'

'The way they all go down there. Polished and pressed. It's disgusting. Like they're going to a party.'

'So what about it?'

'Wait until tomorrow, Toddy,' I said. 'I'll give the sods bulling up.'

I'd always been a great one for walking around in my underpants in the Boobs. It's a marvellous demoraliser of the spit and polish union to which all screws are fully paid-up members. And after getting myself all wound up by all the anxious pleasers I realised that the interview with the Board was an occasion when underpants were *de rigueur*.

So the next day I went to meet the Board just wearing my underpants enhancing the effect with my hair *en brosse* and about two weeks' growth on my face.

The local worthy couldn't believe his eyes when I sauntered in. Neither could his secretary: her eyes and mouth registered Full House disgust.

Reece affected a wash-my-hands-of-it-all expression but I knew he'd be burning slowly for the next day or two.

Then the Chairman read out the charges and told me off in a voice full of tact and kindness appropriate to dealing with the abnormal. So just to show him he hadn't got me weighed up wrong I acted a bit spare as though I hadn't understood very much of what he'd said so he repeated it all over again carefully enunciating every word and pausing after the long ones. I never had the heart to keep it up second time round so I gave him a nod or two just to encourage him and then pleaded guilty. Reece just stared into space, but even though he wasn't looking at me he couldn't see anybody but Billy Cracken in front of his eyes.

So we did our chokey and after two months everybody came off except me. I was the only one that got put on a confined-to-cell rule. Not even Freddie got that one and he'd threatened to hang the sodding Governor.

I tried a new tactic with Reece. Instead of ignoring him, I tried to talk to him as he came to my cell door, just to throw him. But all the time I talked he just looked into my cell at me with this expression of contempt on his face and when I'd finished he just smiled his smile and walked away without saying anything. I marked him up one point.

But the next time I went out on Exercise I refused to go back in. Six screws gathered round me and there was the usual little drama.

They set me and I set them but it was up to them to make the first move and that was never going to happen. The Chief Screw came out and bawled at them to take me in but he was wasting his breath so to save face he said: 'For Christ's sake Cracken don't be a cunt. What do you think this'll get you apart from the 'flu? All I've got to do is double them up and then even you won't have any choice.'

'All right, Chief,' I said. 'I'll come in now because I'm on a hiding to nothing out here. But if I'm not moved inside three days I'm going to smash one of your screws for you. I won't give him any chance. Because nobody's giving me one.'

With that I walked through the bunch of them and back inside.

Two mornings later a screw unlocked my cell and said: 'Get your kit packed up, Cracken.'

I looked at him. I knew I was going but screws make a point of telling you as little as possible just to keep you down so I said: 'Going? How do you mean going?'

'What I say,' said the screw. 'You're on your way.'

'Where to?'

'Just pack up, Cracken. Then maybe you'll find out.'

The screw's name was Melchett. He'd been down on my list since the first week. But now I'd never get the chance.

'You're a very lucky screw, Melchett,' I said. Melchett just looked at me. He knew what I meant. And so because he knew

24

he was safe he relaxed and leant against the cell door and fished out a cigarette.

I began to sort out my odds and ends.

'Hope you don't suffer from homesickness,' Melchett said.

I ignored him.

'Where you're going'll make this seem like home sweet home.'

I picked up my stuff and whirled round quick as if I was going to cop for him. He dropped his cigarette and leapt out into the corridor. I grinned at him.

'Right,' I said. 'Let's go down.'

I walked out into the corridor.

'What's up, Billy?' Toddy said from behind his door.

'I'm off on my holidays.'

'Somewhere good?'

'Reece's booked me for the Riviera.'

'Give Brigitte one for me,' called Freddie as I passed his door.

'Send us a postcard,' said somebody else.

'If I've time to write,' I said.

We walked downstairs.

Reece was waiting at the bottom with about fifteen screws. We all walked out into reception. It was like a state visit. While I was signing the private property book Reece went into another room and I heard him say: 'Why isn't he wearing a jacket?'

Some screw mumbled a reply and Reece said: 'I want him wearing a jacket when he goes out of here.'

A couple of seconds later a decent sort of screw came into reception holding a prison jacket.

'Billy,' he said, 'put this on.'

I straightened up.

'You must be joking,' I said.

'Come on, Billy,' he said.

'Tell silly ballocks to put it on himself.'

The screw went back into the room where Reece was and

there was some more muttering and about four of them came back out and the same screw holding the jacket said: 'You've got to put it on. Otherwise the Governor's ordered us to make you put it on.'

'Oh, well,' I said, 'that's all right then. Now we know where we are. This way there'll be no misunderstandings.'

I backed off into a corner and shaped up. I look the business when I shape up, hard eyes and everything, it's one of my best effects. The screws walked towards me but they weren't too keen to get where they were going. There was a bit of manoeuvring and then Greaves who had been watching from the doorway of the room where Reece was, walked to the screw who was holding the jacket and plucked it off him in disgust and went back into the room. I heard him say very emphatically: 'He won't wear it, sir.'

The edge in his voice was to let Reece know that that was that. There was a pause while they faced each other out and then Reece said something I couldn't catch.

Greaves came back out looking weary of the whole fucking world, put the cuffs on me and handed his half of the cuffs over to one of the police officers who'd come to fetch me.

I got in the back of the car, a copper on either side of me and one up front beside the driver.

Reece came out and stood next to Greaves to watch us drive off. Just before Greaves closed the car door on us I leant across and said:

'Where are we going, Greavesy?'

Before Greaves could answer Reece stepped forward and stared in at me. The veins in his head were almost throbbing enough to knock his hat off. He just couldn't help himself because he snapped: 'Broadmoor.'

The car drew away. We never went to Broadmoor. We went to Aston.

But even the piddling victories available in the nick have to be paid for one way or another. Two and a half years later, a couple of days after I'd been recaptured, I had to talk to a PO about a visit.

In the course of the conversation he casually remarked: 'Oh, by the way, I was talking to an old friend of yours on the phone yesterday. Captain Reece. He asked to be remembered to you.'

They always win in the end.

*The new kids are beginning to settle down. Cocksure set of little bleeders. Playground hardly room to move, they're pushing and shoving and running all over the place. Soon be time to show them who's top. Who's king. Who's Bozo.*

*Grey cloud streaks across the water puddle sky and shatters broken with footstep running.*

*A new kid stops in front of me.*

*'Hey, is it you?' he says.*

*I stop. Johnny Stretch and Arthur Easton stop too, two steps behind me, like they should.*

*'Is it you though? Is it you that's called Billy Rags?'*

*The excuse. The chance. Now I'll show them.*

*'Who told you to say that?'*

*The yukker makes to dart but only his legs move flailing nowhere because his shirt collar's in my fist.*

*'Who?'*

*'Don't.'*

*Tears.*

*'Who?'*

*'Him.'*

*A nod of the head to Bas Acker. Bas. The rival. The only one worth fighting. I'd found that out my first week. Two years above me. But that didn't matter. I'd cracked him easily, publicly, quickly. I was top. That was what counted. I'd weighed it up: you were popular if you had no peers. You did everything best. Best at fighting, best at footballing, best at cig-carding, everything.*

The better you were, the better you were liked. And if you were liked, you could do as you liked. And everybody did things for you. You were a king. It was easy. And now Bas had given me the excuse to prove it all over again, to the new lot.

I dragged the yukker over to where Bas Acker was standing with his mates. Johnny and Arthur followed behind.

'Now, boy,' I say to Bas. 'This yukker says you told him I'm called Billy Rags.'

Bas glances at his mates who in turn wait to see what he's going to do.

He hasn't any choice.

'What if I did?'

'Take it back, that's what.'

'What if I don't?'

'You'll see.'

Bas doesn't say anything. I say to the yukker: 'My name's William Cracken. What is it?'

'William Cracken.'

I slap him round the head.

'What is it?'

'William Cracken,' he says, through tears.

I slap him again.

'Leave him,' says Bas Acker.

'Oh yes?' I say. 'And what if I don't?'

Now he's no choice. Bas steps forward. I let the yukker go.

'Fair fight, boy?' I say to Bas.

'Fair fight.'

'Leather him, Billy,' Johnny says.

I step forward.

'I will,' I say. 'Just like last time. And next.'

After the fresh air it's the smell that gets you. Even though I'd been inside the police car breathing in the BO of my four travelling companions, it had been like sniffing Paradise compared to the smell of E wing. It hadn't been up more than three years, but the smell was there. They must mix it in with the concrete.

E wing was an L-shaped block of cells. The two gates leading into it were on the bottom landing on either end of the L. When I arrived there were about twenty-nine normal prisoners scattered around on the top three tiers. Apart from three sex cases: Strachey, Hopper and Rose.

Of course, these were kept separate, but they were there.

There was no work. You either stayed in your cell during the day or were split into one of two rooms where you sat around chatting. There was a piddling little exercise yard that people often didn't bother to use for the statutory hour a day. And from six to nine there was television. The only other facility was weight lifting or weight training every week night from six to seven-thirty. Which was something I marked down for when I got out from behind my door.

Which was where I spent my first month at Aston.

But just the same when I got from behind it I'd sorted out everything there was to be sorted. I'd got all my information through my door in the form of notes from Walter Colman via a tame screw called Fussey.

Walter was the first person I went to see the day they unlocked my door.

When I appeared in the doorway of Walter's cell he was half-lying, half-sitting on his bunk reading a *Playboy* magazine that was without its cover. I thought: knowing you Walter, you'll be reading the interview or an article on the proliferating dangers of a data bank society, not studying the bums and knockers.

He didn't look much different since I'd seen him last, except that this time he didn't have a tie on. The shirt was nice, pale yellow with a tabbed collar, and the trousers were sharp and beautifully pressed, obviously the bottom half of one of his old business suits.

His hairline had receded a bit, but he'd combed it across instead of back so that his forehead didn't show too much. He still had his sideboards and at the back his hair was barbered just the way he always wore it, just tickling over the edge of his collar. Except for a slight pursing of the lips there was no expression on his face at all as he read the magazine. His eyes were blank and his face was flat and motionless as ever.

I tapped on the cell door.

'Anybody at home?' I said.

Walter looked up. For a split second the deadness stayed on his face and then he grinned and got up off the bunk, but his eyes were blank and cold. Walter's eyes always were: excepting when he was shooting volts through someone's ballocks.

'Billy,' he said, taking hold of my hand. 'You're out, then.'

'That's right, Wally,' I said, gently pulling my hand away from his. 'They finally decided to open the cage.'

'Sit down,' Walter said, indicating the bunk. 'Have a snout and tell me the news.'

I shook my head.

'I've been sitting down for the last bleeding month,' I said. 'And funnily enough nothing very much has happened to me.'

'No, what I meant was,' Walter said, offering me a snout, 'tell me about Burnham.'

I took the snout and Walter lit us up. I leant on the edge of his writing desk and he lay down on his bunk.

'I saw about it in the papers,' Walter said, 'but tell us what really happened.'

I shrugged.

'That's all in the past, Wally, I don't really want to talk about it.'

'Suit yourself.'

'You tell me your news,' I said.

It was Walter's time to shrug.

'A few changes in the offing,' he said. 'Or so I hear.'

'Like what?'

'They're talking about a proper exercise yard being built. And they're fixing up a wrought-iron shop on the ground floor.'

'That should be fun,' I said.

'Yes,' said Walter.

Outside across the landing, four cons broke into laughter at something or other. The sound echoed up to the roof of the block.

'And what else?'

'What else?' Walter blew smoke out into the air. 'Nothing, only that we get a new Governor shortly, together with his new assistant who'll be responsible for this wing.'

'I can't wait.'

Walter smiled slightly.

'You seem quite content, Walter,' I said. 'I mean, sort of at peace with the world and all that.'

'Not much sense being any other way, Billy, really, is there? I mean, with my card.'

I put my cigarette out in his ashtray.

'How's business?' I said.

'Can't complain,' he said. 'We show a profit.'

'You must be fucking rolling in it,' I said. 'If it's anything like I remember.'

'That was quite some time ago,' Walter said. 'We've expanded a bit since then.'

'I bet you fucking have. What happened at the trial? I mean, you must have done a deal for them to leave the other operations alone.'

'The way of the world, Billy,' said Walter. 'Justice must be seen to be done. We were too much in the public sector to be absolutely watertight on that one.'

'Don't tell me you took a chance, Walter. I mean, not you and Tony.'

'Let's say our inside man at the top had a lower tolerance level than we'd bargained for.'

'That man being Braben.'

Walter didn't say anything.

'Who is now off the force.'

No answer. The penny dropped.

'That's why they only clobbered you on the one operation,' I said. 'That's why they only went for you and Mavis. They wanted Braben. And you gave him to them.'

'Retired of his own accord, so I believe,' Walter said.

There was a short silence. I looked at Walter and Walter looked at the ceiling. A lump of ash dropped on to his shirt, but he didn't attempt to brush it away. Which was very unlike Walter.

'You know,' he said, almost as if he was talking to himself, 'I reckon if we'd knocked off Franklin, I mean, actually finished him off, as opposed to what we did do, I don't think I'd have got my card marked anything like as big. Or Mavis. I really don't.'

I didn't say anything to that. I knew all about Walter and Mavis when they went to work on someone and that was one reason why Walter and I would never be bosom pals. Amongst various other things.

'So,' I said. 'Now you're leading a baron's life.'

'It's different in Security. Not like the other wings. Less of a hassle to make your points. There's no petty stuff. All big fish together. Who wants to prove anything? We wouldn't be here in the first place, would we?'

'You'd call Strachey and Hopper and Rose big fish, would you?'

'We never see them, so consequently we never think about them.'

'I hope we never do,' I said. 'I don't want to have to go back behind my door because of that filth.'

'You know, Billy,' Walter said, 'that's always been your

32

trouble. If you don't mind me saying so. You're always on the boil. Never know how to relax. Never been able to sit back and accept things.'

'And that's what you're going to do, is it, Walter,' I said. 'Sit back and accept things. For the next twenty-five fucking years?'

Walter didn't like that one. He raised himself up on his elbows.

'Do you know where you *are*, Billy?'

'Yes,' I said.

'Well, there it is. I can't be plainer, can I?'

'You mean to say that with all your bread and influence you're calling this place the end of the line?'

He shrugged.

I looked at him.

'Do me a favour,' I said.

He didn't say anything. I picked up the magazine from his bed.

'Lend us your *Playboy*, Wally,' I said. 'After all, you've got plenty of time in front of you to finish it.'

'*Cracken.*'

*Soft shafts of afternoon sunlight slide through the slow swirling chalk dust in the quiet classroom.*

*I pretend not to hear Copley's voice. Johnny Stretch and the others begin to buzz at the prospect of a Cracken diversion.*

'*Cracken? Somebody pinch him, will you, just to make sure he's still with us.*'

*Copley always tries to turn this kind of thing into a joke if he thinks it's going to get out of hand. He's one of the easiest of the lot to play up.*

*The buzzing gets a little louder.*

'*Quieten down, class,*' *he says.*

*I stay as I am, hunched forward over my desk as if I'm concentrating on my book. The class goes quiet again. Copley* is forced to walk down the aisle of desks to where I am sitting. I take no notice of him.

'Cracken?'

I sit bolt upright in my chair, nearly causing my desk to topple over, acting as though I've been startled out of my wits. The class bursts out laughing. Copley steps back a foot or two in surprise.

'Yes sir, sorry sir,' I say, like a soldier on parade.

Copley tries to recover his poise.

'Cracken, I was attempting to communicate with you. But somehow I didn't seem to be meeting with much success. Do you think you could explain why?'

'Pardon, sir?'

'Why didn't you answer?'

'Sorry, sir, I can't hear you very well. You haven't lost your voice have you, sir?'

Copley is on the verge of fetching me one but he manages to restrain himself.

'Out to the front of the class, boy,' he says in what he imagines to be his no-nonsense voice.

'Sorry, sir,' I says, wrapping my handkerchief round my finger, and wriggling it about in my ear. 'I think I've gone deaf.'

This is too much even for Copley. He grabs my arm and drags me to the front of the class and with his free hand he scrambles his wooden ruler out of the drawer in his desk. He moves his grip down to my wrist and holds my hand out in front of me.

'Now, boy,' he says, 'we'll see if this won't improve your hearing.'

But as he swishes the ruler down I jerk my hand out of the way not only causing him to miss but also to over-balance slightly, so that he has to let go of my hand to steady himself on the edge of his desk.

'Sorry, sir,' I say. 'My hand slipped.'

The class roars with laughter.

'Quiet!' shouts Copley.

'Won't let it happen again, sir.'

*Copley grasps my hand again and furiously brings the ruler down seven or eight times, completely out of control, haphazardly hitting my knuckles, fingers, wrist, anywhere. But I make his lack of control even more unbearable for him because all the while he is raining blows on me I just keep looking him straight in the eyes and smiling as though he's not having any effect on me at all.*

When Moffatt and his assistant Creasey took over you could hardly say the earth shook. Nothing changed and nobody took much notice of them. But I sensed that Moffatt was watching us and most of what he saw he didn't like. I was on to his game straight away; he was giving it a week or two to sort us out and after that we could expect a few new rules to stop life from becoming one long dreary round.

I found out about the first innovation one night while I was working out with the weights. The gym was empty until Terry Beckley, who was on a fifteen for armed robbery, came in and squatted down on a bar-bell and watched me for a while.

Terry was twenty-two. I'd got his form from a mate of mine while I'd been outside. He was one of those characters who always seem to have some private joke going on inside their heads. Whenever you bump into them they always look as though they've just seen something very funny and you always have the feeling that when you say something to them it reminds them of what they were laughing at in the first place. But this mate of mine who'd known him on the outside had been full of bad news about him. He'd once seen Terry do his pieces on an old billiard hall cowboy called Harold Pearson just because Harold had tried to save the game by accidentally-on-purpose moving the pink to get a better angle. Now, according to my mate, Terry wasn't exactly short of a bob or two at the time and Harold whose eyes for the game were no longer as good as they should be, and not being a superannuated man, was reduced in his old age to living off the leftovers at the all night pie-stands. But on the occasion of his tournament with Terry he must have thought he was in luck because apparently even a blind man playing with an eel for a cue could have beaten him.

But Harold hadn't been able to resist brushing a cuff against the pink and Terry had taken him apart and finished up by putting Harold's fingers on the edge of the table and giving them one with the stick.

But tonight Terry was his usual grinning self.

'What is it, Billy?' he said. 'Planning to walk through the walls? Like Superman?'

I let the weights go and picked up my towel and draped it round my shoulders.

'You've got muscles on your muscles,' he said.

'Never know when you might need them,' I said. 'Got a snout?'

'Naw,' he said. 'Right out. Got some news, though.'

'News?'

'There's something else to look at in the TV room.'

'How do you mean?'

'Moffatt's invited Hopper and Rose out to watch TV.'

I stared at him.

'You're joking,' I said.

'Rose had more sense,' Terry said, 'but Hopper's out there now, looking for a friendly face. Course, with Strachey, it's different. He's going to be allowed to see "Watch with Mother" during the day.'

'How long's Hopper been up there?'

''Bout an hour.'

'And nobody copped for him?'

Terry shook his head.

'Well, I hope they have before I get up there,' I said. 'Otherwise I might wind up behind my door again.'

I went into the shower and ran it cold. I thought about

Hopper. Just Terry saying his name had been enough to tie my stomach up in knots.

I'd been in the nick at the time he'd made the papers. Usually I avoided reading stuff like that, but this I'd read and I'd been shocked to tears, the kind of tears that pop out of your ducts when grief chills the skin on your face. The bit that had affected me really badly had been the part where the father of one of the kids had found his own daughter where Hopper had left her. I could imagine myself standing over the body, looking down at what Hopper had done to it, done to something that had once belonged to me.

I towelled myself down and dressed and walked upstairs to the TV room.

I stood in the doorway and looked round the room.

Hopper was sitting near the door with his screw, well apart from the rest of them. The others, eleven or so of them, were sitting in a semi-circle around the room. Everybody was watching TV as though they'd never seen it before. Not one of them was cracking on to Hopper. It was as if he wasn't there. Maybe they were ignoring him because none of them wanted to go behind their doors. Or because just to acknowledge his presence would make them sick to their stomachs. But whatever the reasons I wasn't standing for this. I looked at Hopper who was staring hard at the box. He didn't look more than seventeen, let alone twenty, with his fair hair brushed straight back and his bony cheeks and the straggling bumfluff along his top lip he looked like something out of a sepia photograph around nineteen-fourteen. He was sitting bolt upright, his hands gripping his kneecaps.

The only person who'd cracked on to my being in the doorway was Terry Beckley who'd fixed himself up with a place next to the TV so that he'd have a good view of my entrance.

'Turn it off, Terry,' I said. 'He's not watching that.'

Terry was well pleased to do something. He promptly stood

up and turned it off and grinned his grin in Hopper's direction.

The room was so quiet it could have been empty. Everybody was looking at Hopper. I began to wind them up.

'You got any kids, Tommy?' I said to Tommy Dugdale. Tommy inclined his head slightly and massaged his bald spot with the flat of his hand.

'Yeah, Billy,' Tommy said. 'I got a little girl.'

'What sort of age is she, Tommy?'

'She'll be nine next birthday.'

'That's nice,' I said. 'Nine. Nice age that.'

'Pretty little thing, she is,' Tommy said. 'Golden curly hair. She really loves her terrible old daddy.'

'I bet she does.'

'Don't know what I'd do if anything was to happen to her.'

'I know what you mean.'

I turned to Dave Simmons.

'What about you, Dave?' I said. 'You've got a couple, haven't you?'

'That's right, Billy. Twins. Little crackers they are.' He fished a small leather envelope out of his breast pocket. 'Did I ever show you the snaps?'

'Don't think you did, Dave,' I said, walking over to him. I stood behind his chair and bent over him.

'That's outside the house with the missus,' Dave said, handing me a photograph. 'And this one's at Margate with their Auntie Annie. They had a week there last year.'

'Nice,' I said. 'You seen these, Terry?'

Terry joined me behind Dave's chair.

'Charmers,' Terry said. 'Aren't they, Billy?'

I looked across at Hopper.

'Just his type, I would have thought,' I said.

'Bit old for him,' said Ray Crompton. 'Too much for him to handle.'

'Probably prefers them with nappies on,' said George Hodge.

38

'Do you like them in nappies?' said Des Walker.

'Lovely feller, really,' said Terry.

'A charmer.'

'Just loves kiddies.'

'Do anything for them.'

'To them.'

'Which bit do you like best? Before or after?'

'Or in between?'

'The bit with the bayonet, I should think.'

'When they're crying for their mummies.'

'They should have given him to the father.'

'They should have cut his fucking balls off.'

'Maybe somebody will.'

Hopper's face had gone the colour of ice cream and his head was flicking from speaker to speaker like the swivel head on a ventriloquist's dummy. Everybody was worked up ready to explode. It was written all over their faces. I was waiting for somebody to trip it so that I could screw the first two knuckles of my fist into Hopper's neck.

While everybody had been calling out, the screw had stood up and put himself between Hopper and the rest of us, but now there was fear on his face because he knew that once we moved there would be absolutely nothing at all that he could do to stop us.

One or two of the boys made movements as if they were about to stand up. The screw said: 'Out, Hopper. Back to your cell.'

Hopper stood up as though he was on strings and ran out of the room.

'He's crying,' somebody said. 'The rotten little bastard's crying.'

The screw gave us as long a look as he dared and then followed after Hopper.

'Fuck it,' I said, belting the back of Tommy Dugdale's chair.

'Billy, that was a victory,' said Benny Beauty. 'No one got nicked. Gordon will be sick about the whole thing.'

'We should have had him,' I said. 'We will next time.'

'Once, when I was in Leicester,' said Ray Crompton, 'there was a feller called Cliff Reid who was down for it, and so what everybody did was to fill up their mugs from the tea-room boiler and they let him have it that way.'

'Here, that's not half bad,' said Terry. 'That's a little beauty.'

'If we were to do that,' I said, 'everybody would have to be on it. Nobody not carrying a mug.'

'What about the lads down on the Twos?' said Ray. 'Are they in?'

The Twos were well pleased it wasn't on their plate. You could tell. There was an atmosphere of wary elation about them, like frightened kids in a classroom when only one of them was responsible for putting the tintack on teacher's seat but knowing that they'd all cop for it in the end.

I wandered down to the Twos during the day and the only one who openly committed himself to the plan was Walter, who was a bit of a Twos denizen. I had my own ideas about that one: knowing Walter, he'd sussed that he didn't have to push so hard on the Twos as he would on the Threes. There were more starry eyes downstairs.

'So it's the all off tonight, Billy,' Walter said.

'Yes,' I said. 'Coming up are you, Walter?'

'I'll be there,' he said.

'Anybody else?'

'Everybody likes the idea.'

'So?'

'You never know.'

'I do,' I said.

Walter folded up the newspaper he'd been reading and leant forward, looking me in the face. The usual limpness had gone. The skin on his face was stretched tighter over his skull.

'Listen, Billy,' he said. 'You know what would be better?'

'Tell me, Walter?'

'Not boiling water: boiling fat,' he said. 'It clings.'

He clawed his hands across his face in imitation of the effect his idea would have. He was really living the part.

'Oh, that's lovely, Wally,' I chivvied. 'And we'll all end up with another five apiece. It's like saying I haven't got enough bird, please give me some more.'

Walter relaxed again.

'What's the difference?' he said. 'We won't exactly get a weekend in Brighton for the water.'

Oh, so you've considered that one, I thought. I wonder if we *will* be seeing you tonight, Walter.

I got up and left him on the Twos.

That night there were no weights. All the Threes men came out holding their mugs like testimonials of intent. Everybody took their places in the TV room and waited. Three-quarters of an hour later and there was no sign of Hopper.

Benny Beauty said: 'Maybe he's had the sense to stay behind his door.'

I shook my head.

'Maybe he has but not Moffatt,' I said. 'I'm on to him. He's not going to be beat in his first week. He'll have Hopper down here even if he has to parcel him up.'

We waited some more. Nothing happened. Then about eight o'clock Sammy Chopping from off the Twos stuck his head round the TV room door.

'Hopper's on the Twos,' he said. 'They've fetched him in there.'

'So why tell us?' I said. 'What the fuck are they doing about it down there?'

'I dunno,' said Sammy.

'Fuck all, that's what,' I said, getting up. 'I knew those sods would chicken out.'

41

I could tell everybody was pleased at seeing the ball out of their court and that not one of them wanted to make it down on the Twos so I cleared off down there on my own.

Both TV rooms were situated on the outside corner of the L, one below the other. I walked past the door of the Twos' room. The room was empty except for Hopper and his screw.

I went straight to Walter's cell. There were about five of them in there muttering about it. I stood in the doorway.

'What's happening then?' I said.

Everybody except for Walter looked a bit sheepish.

Walter said: 'We're just working out the best way of approaching it.'

He didn't like it. It was written all over his face. He didn't like the new boy coming down to his floor and embarrassing him in front of his little enclave, making him look like a chicken for not being first in with a mug.

'What's to work out?' I said. 'You just go in and you do it.'

One of them said: 'It's not that easy.'

'Listen,' I said. 'None of you cunts offered to come upstairs and help us, did you? Not when you thought you'd get away without being in it. So now it's down here, and it's all yours. Boiling water in the boat.'

'At the same time, Billy,' said Walter, liking it less and less. 'I don't see anybody from the Threes funnelling down here.'

'What am I then, Walter? A fly on the fucking wall? I'll stand for the rest of them.'

And this was the part that Walter liked least of all. I turned away from the cell door and all of Walter's brood just automatically got up off their backsides and went to get their mugs. Walter had no choice but to follow after them as though the general exodus had got something to do with him.

While the others from Walter's room went to fetch their mugs, I sorted a few more malingerers from out of their cells and went off on my own to the Twos' TV room to wait for them to assemble.

But when I got there the room was empty except for Benny Beauty who was sitting back in his armchair smoking and watching television as though there was nothing on except the TV set.

'Where's Hopper?' I said.

Benny blew out smoke. He didn't take his eyes off the TV.

'I told him to fuck off else he'd get hurt. He's banged himself behind his door.'

'What did you tell him that for?'

'I'm not with you?'

'I mean, you knew what the plan was. For Christ's sake, man. How can we do the ponce now?'

'Oh, that,' he said. 'Yeah, well, Billy, but who wants to get nicked for that, eh? I mean, the way you're going about it, you'll get *everybody* nicked. If it's got to be done it's got to be done but it's better this way.'

I was beginning to get it.

'Who says it's better?' I asked.

'Well, Billy, there's only you here, so *everybody* must say it's better.'

Yes, I thought, but they daren't say it to me. Walter's organised this one. Just to trim a bit of weight off me.

Footsteps sounded in the corridor behind me. Just the one pair. Walter's. He appeared next to me in the doorway carrying his mug.

'Where is everybody, then?'

'Don't you know, Walter?' I said.

Walter tut-tutted.

'Everybody dropped out, have they?' he said.

'Everybody but us, Walter,' I said. 'That's what it looks like.'

'Pity,' he said. 'Still, there'll be another time.'

But there wasn't. The next day Moffatt installed a set on

the Fours, just for the use of the sex-cases and no one else. Everybody got steamed up about it, and the new catch phrase was, 'The Governor does like a sex-case.' But the same people who got steamed up were the same people who'd swayed in Walter's wind and left themselves out of actually doing anything about Hopper.

Of course, I never let on to Walter that I'd cracked it. That's what he would have liked. I was just the same as ever. But we both knew what it was all about; it was either him or me. For the time being there was just one consolation as far as I was concerned: that inside Walter's rubber mind he knew who it was going to be in the end.

*Sitting at the table next to the window, the street sounds drifting up unheard, my elbows boring into the green dust of the corduroy table cloth, the pages of my mother's library book brilliant in the window's sunshine. The clock ticks and a fly buzzes and the dust itself hums with silence. The cocoon is complete. The book wrapped round me like a blanket. Till tea time I belong to no one but myself and the book is me till then.*

*But I'd forgotten Linda.*

*The door opens and the sound of her voice strives against the rattle of the handle and the crash of the woodwork, the entrance of her tiny body propelled forward on the kitchen sounds behind her.*

*'Billybillybilly,' she shrieks. 'Billybillybilly.'*

*'Clear off.'*

*'I want to come in.'*

*'I'm reading.'*

*'Read to me, Billy.'*

*'You wouldn't understand it.'*

*She runs to the table and cuddles close to me.*

*'Go on, Billy, read me a story.'*

*Mam comes into the room to get her cigarette.*

44

'Go on, Billy, read to your sister.'

I push Linda away.

'Go on, get out of it,' I tell her. Then to Mam: 'Dad can read to her when he comes up.'

'Your father'll be too tired. He has a long day.'

Yes, a long day, I think. Half past six in the morning when he opens the shop till nine o'clock at night. Then away to the pub. He doesn't even come up for his dinner any more.

'Is Dad coming up today, Ma?' Linda says. 'Is he coming up?'

'He's a very busy man, your father,' she says as she goes back into the kitchen.

I recognise the tone of voice and I recognise her expression. She's going to defend him, to tell us how hard he works, that if it wasn't for Dad we'd be across the road in the Buildings with the rest of them, that he only thinks of us, that she, Mam, has a lot to be thankful for, but although she says the words in the right tone of voice the final effect is different, as though she has been referring to herself, not Dad, and by referring to herself she's having a go at Dad, by letting us know that she's only defending him for our sakes, because that's her duty, as Mum, *even though she has a lot to put up with*, she puts us first, *even though* he won't. And yet she's said none of this, but it's all there.

Of course, the final underlining will be the mentioning of the drink. I wonder how she'll work it in today? Yesterday it was easy for her. Dad had asked for some to be brought so she'd asked me to go, given me the jug, trying to hide her distaste but not trying hard enough, so that I'd see in her face what she wanted me to see, how noble she was trying to be secret, how noble in comparison to the man downstairs behind the counter, rocking quietly on his feet staring back in time to the years of his childhood in the heather, becoming more silent as each drink burns down into his stomach.

I wait, staring at the page, while Linda slides her hot arms round my shoulders, pressing close to me and gently rocking, as if she is trying to sway me off my seat without my realising.

'Billy,' she says, 'read to me from the book; tell me the story.'

In the kitchen the kettle boils and hot water gurgles into the tea pot. A pause for brewing then two cups are filled and the tea is stirred and Mam says: 'Billy, will you take this down to your Dad? He'll be ready for a cup by now.'

So that's what it is today. An unwanted cup of tea, to demonstrate to me again what is happening downstairs behind the counter.

I loosen Linda's arm and cross the room and take the cup from Mum and open the door to the stairs and edge my way down past the cardboard boxes and the Vimto crates and the Craven 'A' cartons and at the bottom I open the door that leads into the shop.

Dad is standing in the dusty sunlight, his head bowed, his arms rigid, his knuckles quietly grinding into the counter top. The shop is as hushed as a church.

I walk over to the counter.

'Dad,' I say. 'Mam's sent your tea.'

Only the head moves, slightly, in my direction.

I put the cup and saucer down on the counter. I look into Dad's face. His eyes are on the tea and his head begins to shake slowly from side to side.

I walk back to the stairs' door and close it behind me and as I go back up the stairs I hear the sound of the cup and saucer as they are swept from the counter down on to the floor.


In prison, you never get tired. You can always sleep; but that's because you use sleep as an ally, to shorten consciousness, to defer thought. Lots of cons make a career of sleeping. Always on their pits whenever there's a chance, hoping their nap will carry them closer to the gate and farther away from the subsequent awakening. But that kind of sleeping is easier during the day, when it's light, because you can see what it is you want to shut out, but at night, in the dark, when there's nothing to look at, it's harder to sleep because the imaginary outside images are brighter in your mind than the grey realities of the day.

The mistake most cons make is to try to fight the pictures in their minds, to black them out with sleep. But that never works. It's better to approach the problem from the opposite direction, to make the pictures even brighter, bring them into sharper focus, move around in them, stage manage them, make them work for you as an alternative reality, tire out your mind by trying to make the unreal real and giving the shadows form.

This is what I used to do. I'd pick on an event, just something at random, then I'd start with the time of day the event took place, remember the light, the colour, the temperature. Then the location, and the same with that, down to the last detail. Then the people who were involved, colour eyes, colour hair, colour clothes, style, cigarettes, drinks. Then I'd tie everything together and move through the same scene from the beginning to the end, saying all that was said and acting all that was done in my mind, endlessly going back to the beginning to make sure I'd got it all right. And not always events on the outside. Sometimes I'd take the characters I mixed with every day and go through them, head to toe, mannerisms, histories, conversations, and check them out against my memory the next day, to see how well my mind was working, to make sure the nick wasn't softening up my brain. That way I knew my outside memories could still be trusted.

For instance, I'd take Benny Beauty.

Benny.

The hair; black, jet black, a bit gyppo, especially with the style, too-long Tony Curtis, greased inches thick, freezing the dandruff, the fore-peak always stuck to his forehead, the tops of his ears thrusting up behind the motionless comb-strokes. And the brass ring on his left ear lobe, the colour of the wax inside. And his eyebrows, jet black again but flecked with grey, almost off-white, at the edges. His eyes, black-blue, sleepy lidded, the bags underneath bulbous and wrinkled. The nose, flat and shiny, lips fat and skin-cracked pursing forward above the cleft chin, almost Cypriot in its depth and darkness. The heavy hands, muscular, like the rest of his body, just on the verge of being too fat. His movements slow, always relaxed, almost tired.

He'd nailed a man called Cecil Foster to a tree in Epping Forest, Benny had. On orders, of course. The brief had been to show Foster's backers that Benny's backers were only good for a laugh for so long. But the method had been left to Benny himself. So Benny and two of his freelancers had sorted Foster out of his club in Meard Street on a Saturday night and taken him up the A11 to the forest and given him the message Benny's way. They'd left him far enough into the forest for him not to be found for a couple of days.

The case had made all the nationals. Someone had grassed on Benny and normally Benny's backers would have been able to get him off but this time someone on the law advised them against so they'd given Benny away and stayed out of it themselves. I know how glad Benny's backers must have been when he got maximum security.

Or I'd take somebody like Ray Crompton. Ray was more difficult than Benny. When you first thought about Ray you saw a face without features, hair without colour, a body with only two dimensions. But when you concentrated, really pulled everything together in your mind, you realised that after all there was something that gave you a hint of some kind of personality, and that something was his mouth, and the only thing special about that particular feature was that it hardly ever moved, not even when he spoke. It was hard and small and straight and it told you everything you needed to know about Ray. It was the mouth of a man who could wait for revenge on an unfaithful wife. Which was what Ray had done. He'd had a firm in Birmingham that had been doing very nicely until his number two, a man called Jackie Smails, had started pumping up Ray's wife every Wednesday afternoon. Ray's wife had been the usual, but Ray apparently had never seen it. They never do. To Ray she'd been the perfection every man always wanted; perfect except to everyone else who didn't have to use bifocals. It'd taken Ray even longer than usual to find out what was going on under his nose. When he did of course he had Jackie Smails reduced to little bits, but left just alive enough to remember the pain for the rest of his invalid life. Of course this threw the shits into Audrey, Ray's wife, and she must have started packing her cases the minute she heard about Jackie. But Ray had got to her before she could clear off. And to everybody's surprise, not the least Audrey's, he'd done absolutely nothing about it. Never even mentioned it. Come home, had his dinner, watched TV, taken Audrey upstairs and given her the usual pumping up. Got up the next day, had his breakfast, went out, back in the evening. The same thing for a month. Audrey couldn't believe her luck. So naturally she'd turned it on all the more, given him the ever-loving bit twenty-four hours a day, and according to Ray she'd been even better than ever in the pit. So after about a month or so Ray had suggested a weekend in London, a kind of second honeymoon, taking a couple of open cheques instead of luggage so that Audrey could do a bit of kitting out. The Saturday, he took her round all the shops and let her have whatever she fancied. One item he'd chosen for her himself, and that had been a French lace negligée. In the evening he'd taken her to dinner at Quaglino's and then they'd gone back to the hotel and she'd put on her new negligée and they'd got into bed and Ray had taken this razor out of his pyjama pocket and cut her face so that she was all one gaping mouth. Then he'd taken her over to the mirror and made her look at what he'd done and then he had put the razor to her throat and still forcing her to look he'd drawn it across her flesh until there were two new mouths instead of one. Then he'd sat down on the edge of the bed and smoked a cigarette and watched her until she was dead. That was the kind of man Ray Crompton was.

I used to go through this kind of mind-exercising with all the cons. I'd done it in every nick I'd ever been in. It helped to pass the night away. And recently, since my last caper, it had become more and more necessary.

It helped keep away the thoughts of Sheila. And the kid.

*The shop is warm with morning sun. Dad sits at the counter, the paper spread out in front of him. Next to him, discarded, waiting for me, is the crisp new copy of the* Hotspur. *I take it from the counter and go and sit down on the stairs. Today is the final episode of Montana Mike, the boy with a past. It's the most fantastic story I've ever read. Mike is being hunted for a murder he committed under extremely extenuating circumstances, but in spite of this he lives by his own code of great fairness and integrity.*

*I read the final episode. Mike is killed, sacrificing his own life to save that of Marshall Ned Rutter, the man who has been hunting him, although each respected the other. I read the episode again, unable to accept Mike's death, unwilling to give up the world set out on the sweet smelling newsprint. I feel depressed. A sense of loss and anger at returning to the real world of my parents clouds my mind. Mike is dead. I wish I was. Dead that way, nobly, everyone acknowledging the outlaw's natural nobility, everyone sad at his passing.*

*I hadn't felt so unhappy since the day I'd finished* Wuthering Heights.

'Here, Billy,' Ray Crompton said to me. 'Heard the latest?'

I was squatting by my pit doing my stomach exercises.

'No,' I said, not moving. 'What's that, Ray?'

'About the gear.'

'What gear?'

'Our gear. Listen. Prison shoes, shirts and trousers to be worn at all times. Overalls only to be worn to work.'

I stood up.

'Oh, Christ,' I said. 'What for? What the fuck's that to do with security?'

'Maybe Moffatt thinks he won't hear us if we get on the roof in our baseball boots.'

'And what about Creasey? What's his answer?'

Ray shrugged.

'Has anybody put it to him?'

'I don't know.'

I swore. It wasn't just the fact that the prison stuff was less comfortable than our own gear. It was the idea behind it; just one more method of reminding us of where we were and what we were. This was nothing to do with security. It was an attack on our identities.

I walked to my door and looked out. Creasey was making his rounds, flanked by a couple of screws. I strolled out of my cell and stood in their path.

'Back inside, Cracken,' said Bastin, the senior screw.

'Permission to speak to Mr Creasey,' I said, taking my fags from my overall pocket.

'No smoking when you address the assistant governor,' said the other screw. I lit up. The screws looked at Creasey but he ignored them and said:

'What is it, Cracken?'

'About these regulations, sir.'

'Which regulations are those?'

'The regulations relating to dress, sir.'

'Yes?'

'Well, I mean, do they stand?'

'Regulations are usually meant to stand, yes. That is, in my experience.'

I looked Creasey up and down. Considering what he was, he was quite a reasonable fellow. I didn't dislike him, any more than I could dislike a brick in the prison wall. The fact that from time to time he allowed a certain dry humour into his conversations with the cons meant that at least he didn't regard us as being entirely without any kind of humanity. But he was what he was, and that being so, he wasn't going to get out of this one so easily.

'What exactly is the purpose of the new rules, sir?'

Creasey looked at me for a moment before answering. I knew what he was thinking; being reasonable, he knew that there was no purpose to the new regulations. They were just regulations. But that was something he could never admit to me. At the same time he knew that any of the dozen or so answers he could let me have wouldn't go down at all well, either. So to avoid getting into a losing battle he attacked:

'Is there something in the new dress regulations you disapprove of, Cracken?'

'Only that everybody's happy enough with things as they stand at the moment, sir.'

Of course, I shouldn't have said that. That really let him in.

'Perhaps that's why they're to be enforced. As a reminder to everyone that happiness is not the main aim of this establishment.'

He began to walk by me. The two screws were grinning all over their faces. And that kind of thing I can do without.

'Sir,' I said.

Creasey carried on walking away.

'Sir,' I said. This time my voice rang round the gallery.

Creasey stopped and half-turned. I put on my innocent face.

'Hope Mr Moffatt knows what he's doing.'

Creasey's face went black. He strode back to where I was standing.

'What did you say?'

'I said I hope Mr Moffatt knows what he's about. I mean, happiness isn't the main purpose of this establishment, is it? On either side.'

'Meaning precisely what?'

I shrugged.

'Cracken,' Creasey said, lowering his voice in inverse proportion to his anger, 'we have your file. From time to time we even read it. Not a lot in it, really, as far as any remission's concerned. But at the moment it's an open file. It would take very little to close it.'

I smiled at him. He turned away again and marched off.

'So now what?' said Ray Crompton.

'So we keep asking Creasey why the new regulations.'

'What for?'

'So that eventually he'll get so sick and tired of the same bleeding question that he'll pass the buck on to Moffatt and Moffatt will have to answer us himself.'

'Where will that get us?'

'I dunno,' I said, going back into my cell. 'But at least we'll have the satisfaction of getting Moffatt on the spot.'

I sat down on my pit. The bastards. They'd do anything to remind you what you were. Well, maybe we could remind them back.

Suddenly a thought struck me, and for a moment I didn't feel so bad.

'Here,' I said to Ray. 'Does Walter know the news?'

'I don't know,' said Ray, getting it and beginning to smile. 'I don't think so.'

I smiled back.

'Walter'll take it especially hard,' I said. 'All that mohair going to the wall.'

'Why don't we go and tell him?' said Ray.

'Just what I was thinking,' I said.

So we kept on at Creasey until the buck was finally passed. Moffatt called a meeting.

The meeting was set up in one of the living rooms on the end of the wing. Moffatt kept us waiting for a good twenty minutes before he showed up. Eventually he swept in flanked by Creasey and Bastin, the chief screw. Bastin whipped up a wooden chair and the Chief sat down, self-composed, almost prim, waiting for the murmuring to stop. Creasey and Bastin stood either side of him, slightly to the back, like advisers to the king.

Moffatt was in his mid-forties, slim, about five foot ten inches. He was a bit like Walter in the care he took with his clothes. His suits were nothing like as expensive as Walter's but because of the way he wore them and looked after them you could hardly notice the difference. Outside, he wore snappy, Sinatra-type felt hats that gave him a misleadingly rakish effect; in fact he was an extremely self-controlled, unyielding man, a man who didn't care very much for other people and cared less about what they thought of him.

When all the rhubarb subsided, Moffatt flicked at his knee to remove the non-existent fluff and said:

'I have called this meeting to enable you to put to me any questions that might clear up misunderstandings or confusion arising from the new orders which come into effect next Monday.'

Of course, he knew there wasn't any confusion. Just objections. So it was apparent how the meeting was going to turn out.

There was a short silence after Moffatt's first statement. Then the first con rose. Eddie Brooks, fifty-eight years old, four years to run, preferred it inside to out, a screw pleaser.

'Only one thing, sir,' he said. 'The shoes. My feet aren't too good and the baseball boots ease them up a bit for me. I mean, is that section absolutely, er, compulsory?'

Moffatt clicked his fingers and Creasey leant forward and gave him a copy of the regulations. Moffatt's fingers snapped the paper into some kind of authoritarian stiffness and he made a scene of flicking his eyes up and down the list as if he couldn't immediately find the relevant section.

When he finally chose to discover it he read it out, word for word, then looked at Brooks. Brooks said: 'Yes, sir, I know what it *says,* but...'

'If you know what it says you know what it means. So in that case it must be perfectly clear to you that prison shoes will be worn at all times.'

'Yes, sir.'

Brooks sat down. Terry Beckley stood up.

'Sir,' said Terry, 'is there any particular reason why we have to wear prison shoes? As opposed to what we usually wear.'

'The rules are laid down by head office. It is not my function to justify them.'

'Yeah, right, but you don't *have* –'

Moffatt cut right through him by reading out the regulation again. When he'd done that he said:

'Does that seem clear to you, Beckley?'

'Yes, sir.'

'Then there's no problem.'

Terry sat down. After that other cons stood up and talked, their expressions ranging from disobedient apologetic to outright defiance but nobody got anywhere at all. Moffatt listened to them all but he never answered anybody. He just read out the appropriate regulation and that was that. You bloody bastard, I thought. This was nothing to do with head office. In fact the Council For Penal Reform had recommended that Security Wing Prisoners should be regimented as little as possible. Dress had been specified as one area in which they should be given some choice.

I sat there and stared into Moffatt's face. The only emotion he was showing was a mild arrogance, described in the way he moved his head from speaker to paper to speaker. But underneath I knew how he was feeling. He was practically creaming himself with this power he had. It was almost orgasmic. Moffatt, one man, could sit on a wooden chair in front of a load of hard cons and say no to every single one of them. Nothing anyone could do about it. He was tense with the pleasure of it. If everyone had gone silent all at the same moment we could have heard his heart pumping the joy around his body.

More and more, the cons around me were allowing Moffatt's tactics to frustrate them into thoughtless reputation-making rhetoric, something I wanted to stop; Moffatt had got enough out of them. It was time for me to ask my question.

'You're absolutely rigid about the dress regulations, Governor?' I said.

Moffatt gave me a long look. He was probably wondering whether or not to ask me to stand if I'd got something to say him him.

'Yes,' he said. 'I am. Absolutely.'

I stood up.

'In that case,' I said, standing up, 'there seems no further point in continuing the mystery.'

This, with the exception of free-thinkers like Walter, was what the other cons needed. A lead to a piece of positive action, something to latch on to, a move to self-assertion. Leaving the meeting was just the job.

Everybody began to shuffle out, the noise growing and flowing out into the corridor, drowning the noises the Big Three were making about not having given us their permission to leave.

Outside Walter drifted towards me through the crowd.

'So there we are, Billy boy,' he said, looking very unhappy indeed. 'The bastard's sticking.'

'Can't you un-stick him, Walter?' I said. 'I would have thought if anybody had the muscle, you could.'

'If I go for this then it's likely to cock up everything else,' he said, not liking the question. 'I have to spend my money very carefully these days.'

'What you saving up for, Walter? Your old age. Or your holidays?'

Walter didn't answer. At that moment I knew I was on to him. The bastard had already made his plans. That was why he didn't want to use any influence in this area. It was stretched tight enough already. And whatever they were, he was keeping his plans to himself. For which you couldn't blame him. There were always too many cons with flaps for mouths, whichever nick you were in. But knowing Walter, safety and secrecy wouldn't be his only motives for keeping things to himself. The power thing would be just as important. Sitting around in his cell, day after day, watching the different cons turn up at his door, hopeless, brave sometimes, sometimes eating shit for a good word or a favour from Walter, Walter knowing that they would always be in, but that one day he would be out, and that even in their moments of deepest despair, they'd still admire number one, Walter, the number one that got away.

But I didn't want Walter to know that I'd got any of this weighed up and worked out. For him to know that I was on to him would make things that little bit harder for me when I discovered the ways and means to get myself out. Because if he thought I might screw up anything for him by doing a fast moonlight he'd pull all the strokes he knew to keep my ankles tied to my bunk.

So I let it pass and turned to Tommy Dugdale and said: 'Well, what about it Tommy? What's the answer to this one?'

'Dunno, Billy. We either take it or we don't take it and what's the fucking point of taking it?'

'Right,' I said. 'So we show that cunt Moffatt that he can't ride twenty-six winners past the post all at the same time.'

'What you got in mind, Billy?' Walter said, glad to be out of the earlier bit of facing-out.

'A demo,' I said. 'A real one. A barricade. Somewhere they can't boil us out of without taking the building to bits.'

'Where, Billy?' Tommy asked.

'The annex,' I said.

Walter looked at the floor and thought about what I'd said.

'You've got some idea of how to get in there, Billy?' Walter said.

'I've got ideas of how to get in and out of every fucking where in this bastard nick, Walter,' I said. 'It's just that there's no point to demonstrating it with that thing all around the outside they call a wall.'

Walter wriggled that statement in and out of his mind, wondering if it meant that I'd weighed everything up and decided that I'd have to get myself moved to another nick before I tried to take off. Which was what I hoped he'd think. He must have been fairly chuffed with the speech because he brightened up and stopped looking at the floor and decided to indulge my idea for the demo. But at the same time he had to make a gesture that reminded the others of who Walter was as far as the nick's structure was concerned so he said:

'Why don't we all go and chew it over down my cell,' he said, putting a hand on my shoulder, implying that he would be the decider, he would yea or nay whatever I had to tell everybody. I went along with it because I didn't mind Walter scoring his petty points to keep himself going. My satisfaction would be much deeper, much more lasting, the day I went over the wall without him.

*'Come in, Cracken.'*

*The Headmaster steps aside to let me through the door. His study is hushed and dusty, sound-proofed by books. Instead of* going behind his desk, he perches on the edge of it, hands thrust in the pockets of his trousers. He asks me why I was fighting; I don't want to tell him. He'd never understand. He can't see why it is right to hit someone who insults you. He can't see that it's the only answer. Pride is the motive. To deny pride, to back down, devalues self. But he insists. So I lie to him. I blame myself entirely. I tell him it was all my fault.

When I've finished there is a long silence. Then the Headmaster stands up. He begins to wander around the room, deep in thought. Then he speaks. There is no anger. Just a kind of pained bewilderment, laced with an indefinable kind of sympathy. He asks me about my mother, the effect my behaviour is likely to have on her. He asks me why, in view of my academic record, do I have to spoil things by letting myself down in this way. Everybody expects great things of me. When I go to the Grammar School, he would like not only to recommend my academic strengths, but also my personal ones. Beneath it all, he knows, I am a nice boy, full of good, a credit to my mother, potentially an influence for good in my year, throughout the school, a hero, supported by my class, my athletics, my position in my class. What he can't understand is why, when I have all these advantages, I should spoil them with my aggression, when after all, I could go far, be a credit to my family, and to the school, and to him. Why should I let them down, when they expect so much?

His words are worse than the cane, cutting far deeper. The sentences touch on deep-embedded nerve-ends, fraying, releasing unexplainable tears, less controlled than if the cane had caused them, causing him to offer consolation, which only makes me feel the worse. I sob out my promises to be better, to try, to be a paragon from this day on, but later, when the tears have dried, I resolve another way. No one can touch me. No one has the right. No one pulls that one on Billy Cracken. No one has the right.

Sunday night. Almost quarter past eight. I stood in my door, smoking and looking across the landing. Opposite me was the door to the TV room. Ray Crompton was standing there, leaning against the jamb. There was no one else at their doors or on the landing. We must have looked like a couple of bookends.

Prison noises filtered through from the other wings but on our wing there was no sound at all.

Then at quarter past eight, dead on, Dave Simmons strolled out of his cell and across the landing and down the stairs. Ray and I stayed where we were, looking at each other or at the empty stairwell. Then, a minute or two later, we heard the sounds we'd been waiting for. Two sets of footsteps coming back up the stairs. Dave on his way back with the PO. In five minutes time we'd be on our way.

The annex was a new two-storey building grafted on to the end of the wing. The bottom half housed two visiting rooms and the PO's night room. On the second storey there was a chapel and the office. The second storey could only be reached by passing through a steel gate on the end of the Twos. This gate opened into a small passageway about twelve feet long. Half way down the passage, on the left, was the door to the office, and on the other side of the passage was the door to the chapel. The office was our objective. The plan was to get into the office and erect a barricade. We would use the massive altar and the rows of chairs from the chapel, and the four big steel filing cabinets in the office and if we could use all this to seal off the passage we would be virtually impregnable as the windows of the chapel and the office were barred and bullet-proofed and there was no other way into the passage except through the steel gate.

We decided to have the demo on the Sunday night before the Monday morning the new regulations came into force; all we'd had to do was figure out a way to get beyond the steel gate ourselves.

All the cells were fitted with piped radio, similar to the type they have in hospital; you plugged earphones into the mains and you got one or other of the stations, whichever happened to be on at the time. And that was determined by the main radio that was housed in the office. If someone wanted the station changed they'd get the PO to take them through the steel gates and up into the office. While whoever it was was changing the station the PO always left the gate open until he brought the con back and only then he'd close it and lock it behind them.

So the idea was to get Dave Simmons to ask for a change of station. Dave had been selected for drawing the PO in to retune the wireless as this was a regular late night touch of Dave's. On this particular occasion we'd worked it so that nearly everyone had filtered into the Twos TV room. Everyone except for a few of the lads we'd stationed in cells on the Twos just to spread the load a bit. And, of course, Dave, and Ray, who was to tip us the wink.

The idea was to wait until the PO had unlocked the gate and gone through to the other side with Dave and then for us to make a mad dash across the catwalk. The ones in front would grab the PO and take his key and sling him out while the others were streaming in. Then we'd lock the gate. The screws outside would have to go away and find another key because we'd have the only one on the wing. But by the time the screws had come back we'd have got our barricade built. The whole bastard wing bar one out of reach. Untouchable. The only character who wasn't in was Harry Read, the joker who'd knocked off three fuzz in Harrow. A real brave bastard he turned out to be. A mate of his had put round the word that Read was in bed with bronchitis. So consequently nobody had bothered to ask him if he was in. But on Saturday morning I decided to do some recruiting. I'd been to see him in his cell. He was sitting up in bed, smoking, talking to Ian Crosbie, a little Vaseline-arse who was in for croaking his boyfriend with the sharp end of a chisel. Crosbie had always been a subject for speculation amongst the rest of us because the line went why put someone in the security wing when he couldn't knock a hole in a pair of tights. However, Crosbie'd skittled when I'd arrived. I'd told Read that we were planning to make one the following evening, everybody in, was he with us? His face'd gone chalk white. God knows what he did to his underpants.

'Tomorrow night?' he'd said, as if he was really trying to fit it into his schedule. 'Tomorrow night?' Head-shaking. Chin-shaking. 'I don't know, Billy. I don't know if I'll be all right.'

I turned it a bit.

'What do you mean, all right?' I said. 'You look all right to me.'

That made him turn even paler.

'I'll try, Billy,' he said. 'Course, I'll try.'

He tried all right. He must have had the quickest relapse any bronchial sufferer ever had. It's a wonder they never rushed him off to hospital. He kept his door shut and his head under the sheets for the next two days. Somebody who took his grub in for him on the Sunday evening said he still wasn't capable of coherent speech. So much for the brave fuzz-shooter.

But Read was the only one. Apart from the sex-cases, and they didn't count.

When Dave sauntered out of his cell to cotton the PO I got that marvellous singing gut feeling I always got on capers like this one. These were the kind of moments you lived for, especially in the nick. The feeling was so great it was almost dangerous: at a moment like this it didn't matter what happened to you before or after the moment. Only the moment itself mattered. The tension, the assertion, the tangible danger. Before this kind of moment you were like a guitar with its strings slackened off. Then you moved into the moment of danger and you became tight, strung with the purpose and the risk, aware of every muscle and every nerve in your body, but in control of everything, thoughts progressing through your brain with the cool purity of spring water stroking subterranean rocks.

The minute I heard Dave and the PO begin to climb the steps I lit up a snout and began to stroll across the landing to the TV room. Half way across I saw the two of them rise up from the Ones, Dave's face blank and white, the PO looking at me with that stare they all have. I flicked the match away and strolled into the TV room. Inside, it was a scene to remember.

It was as if they were at the starting flag in a seaside handicap, crouched out of sight of the screws on the landings. Ray had given them the wink that Dave had gone to get the PO because now they were holding the buckets of water and trays of bread puddings and boiled eggs and fruit and cheese all wrapped in towels and Christ knows what else that had previously been hidden under the TV room chairs. When I drifted in past Ray every eyeball in the place swivelled on to me. They all stood there, slack-jawed, poised like wankers, clutching their provisions to their chests, ready for the all off. Still, I don't suppose anybody fancied being last through that gate.

About now Ray should have told us that Dave and the PO had gone through the gate and that the gate was open and that now was the time to go charging out of the TV room. But he didn't. Instead Ray said: 'They've gone through but he's locked it. The bloody bastard's locked it.' Ray turned round to face into the room. Nobody had moved. The poses were still struck as if nobody had grasped the significance of his words. Ray struck a pose himself, chest forward, arms supplicant, knees knocked, arse stuck out and said again in a kind of low shriek:

'The bastard's locked it.'

Everybody melted and a few characters sank down into chairs, trying not to look too relieved. Everybody was looking at everybody else.

'We can't call it off now,' Terry said.

Nobody replied. Walter began to pace up and down in the middle of the room.

'Come on,' Walter said, 'what are we fucking about for? This is no good. We've got to get into that office.'

He was having a bout of resolution tremens. I'd seen this kind of thing before, back in the old days: red face, wild staring eyes, clutching fingers, the words coming out all wrong because his mouth was stiff with frustration. But again nobody said anything.

'We'll – get – in – that – office,' said Walter.

He looked as if he was about to dash out and grapple the gate off its hinges.

'Leave it out, Walter,' I said, 'you'll nouse it.' I appealed to Walter's cousin. 'Dennis, for fuck's sake calm him down, will you?'

Dennis took a grip of Walter and said:

'Wally. For fuck's sake.'

Walter carried on gurgling out words until I cut him short by saying:

'Look. The gate's locked. So somebody's got to come out of George's cell and claim the PO on the way back.'

George's cell was the one nearest the gate.

'I mean,' I said, 'Dave can't do it, can he?'

Dave was about eight stone nothing. Everybody knew that Dave couldn't pull it. But nobody volunteered to take Dave's place. Before the situation became too embarrassing Ray turned back to the door. Everybody focused on Ray's back.

'They're coming out,' Ray said. 'He's locked it.' I listened to the footstep sounds clanging across the landing. 'The PO's staying at the gate. I think Dave's going to have a listen.'

The footsteps got closer. Dave passed by the doorway on the other side of the landing.

'I'm just going to test it, Ray,' Dave said.

For form's sake Ray said: 'Make sure you get it right, then. I'm sick and tired of you fucking that wireless up.'

Dave went into his cell. Ray said: 'The gate's still unlocked. The PO's standing by for Dave's OK.'

There was only a minute or so to decide what to do. Everybody could feel it slipping away from them. It was out of the question to try to rush the PO as he and Dave were going in or out: we were about fifteen yards from the gate and we would have to bundle across the catwalk to get at him. It was just no go: screws get very quick at sticking keys in locks. Basically it was all down to what I'd suggested earlier: one of us had to cop for the PO. Walter knew it, and he also knew who it had to be to do the copping.

'Billy,' he said, 'you do it, will you? You've got the sense. Someone else is bound to fuck it up.'

I'd known it would be down to me all along but I let Walter think his appeal to my vanity had tipped the balance; the more Walter felt he had me, the better it would be for me later on when I screwed him.

'All right,' I said, 'I'll go down and spring him when Dave brings him out again.' I turned to Tommy Dugdale. 'Tommy, you grab his keys and lock the gate after I've pushed him out.'

Tommy agreed to the nomination. A second later Dave came out of his cell and walked over to the TV room door and said:

'He's locking the poxy gate now I've checked it.'

From behind Ray I said: 'For fuck's sake, tell him it's not right and go back in and fix it again. When you come out grab him to stop him locking it again. I'll be right on you as you do.'

Dave couldn't back out with all the eyes in the TV room on him.

'You're sure?' he said.

'I'll be there, Dave. Don't worry.'

Dave nodded. Then he walked off back to the gate. When Ray told me that Dave and the PO had disappeared into the office I left the TV room and strolled down to George's cell which was about eight feet from the catwalk.

It suddenly struck me as I got near to George's cell; there wasn't a sign of a screw on the landing. I looked up. The Threes were deserted as well. But there was no time to sort the implications because I heard Dave and the PO start to leave the office.

I dodged into George's cell. Lenny Monks was waiting in there with him. Their eyes nearly dropped into their trays of bread pudding.

'What the fuck's happening?' George said.

'Change of plan,' I said.

'So what's –'

'For fuck's sake, George.'

He shut up.

The footsteps stopped. The keys jingled. Then the lock was turned. Now the door was open.

I pounded out of George's cell screaming my bloody head off. The screaming had the desired effect; the PO froze and stared at me as if he'd never seen anything like it in his life. I was vaguely aware of all the other cons streaming out behind me but I was so intent on my own business that the racket they were making was as faint in my ears as the sound of the sea in a conch-shell.

Dave grabbed the PO. Then the PO unfroze and with hardly any trouble at all threw Dave off his back. Dave hit the floor kidneys first. All the breath flew from his body. But luckily Dave had chopped the PO's wrist with a canteen knife before he'd wrestled him and the PO had let go of the keys which were attached to his belt. The PO scrambled for them and he was half way to the lock when I got to the gate. I didn't slow down. I angled myself and grasped the bars and kept going. The edge of the gate smashed the PO's forearm against his chest. He turned green but I'll give him this, he still tried to make it. He grabbed one of the bars with his free hand just as I hit the gate, so he didn't go over the way I'd intended. Instead he clung on to the gate and tried to pull himself up even as I was coming through it. He was wasting his time. I twisted round the gate and picked him up by his middle pinning his arms to his sides. I slammed his shoulders against the wall.

'Behave your fucking self,' I said. 'Don't forget your nice supper's waiting for you in the oven.'

By now the others were stampeding across the catwalk. Tommy was first through the gate and began to rip the keys from the PO's belt. Everyone started pouring through the gate, faces like hysterical gargoyles. When Tommy had got the keys I began to push the PO out. I've seen films of salmon swimming upstream against a strong current and that's just how the PO went through that gate, swimming. Any help I gave him was superfluous. I doubt if he'd ever wanted anything as badly as he wanted to get through that gate before it was locked. His arms were flailing against the surging cons as if he was trying to do the breast-stroke.

As the last of the cons were getting in and he was getting out I saw the vanguard of the heavy mob streaming down both sides of the landing towards us, the big riot sticks in their hands. The feeling I'd had a few minutes earlier had been right: the demo had been leaked. That's why the screws had been evacuated from the Twos. They must have been waiting in the visiting rooms all evening.

We pushed the gate to. The PO was reeling all over the landing, dazed and dishevelled, just like a drunk out of Laurel and Hardy. The screws charged past him, spinning him round all over again. Tommy turned the key in the gate just as the heavy mob hit it, jabbing their sticks through the bars at us. They were sick. They looked like a bunch of gorillas in a bramble bush, jab-jabbing away, screaming out our names, squeezing every inch of their arms through the bars.

Behind me, the altar came rocketing out of the chapel. I had to nip to one side as six of the lads propelled it along the passage and slammed it into the gate. One of the screws got his arm broke in the process and fell to the floor, screaming. Some of his mates dragged him off. I squeezed past the lads who'd brought the altar and left them to cheer the screw with the broken arm.

Everybody else was working in the office so I went into the chapel and set about smashing up the furniture in order to buttress the back of the altar. Soon the whole passageway was wedged up with steel filing cabinets, tables, furniture; even the doors had been ripped off the office and the chapel and jammed in amongst the rest of it.

It would have needed a tank to get down that passageway. The screws were still pissing about with their sticks. One of them came back with a key but by that time it was too late. Walter had ripped some metal piping off a wall and had broken himself off a bit and was waving it at the screws. He was having a rare time; his face had all pursed up and the veins were wriggling in his forehead.

'You cunts,' he screeched. 'You're the thickest fucking screws in the country! Thicker than the fucking Filth!'

'You've got to come out sometime,' one of them yelled.

Walter picked up the seat of a chair and winged it at the gate. All the waving arms withdrew for a second. Walter got the rest of the lead pipe and broke it up into short lengths and organised a five-handed poking-militia just in case the screws got too ambitious. I made myself conspicuously absent from all this and got on with feeding furniture to Benny Beauty who was stacking everything he could shift on to the barricade. After about half-an-hour it was almost up to the ceiling but there were plenty of gaps and passages and you could climb through the middle to get from the chapel to the office or vice versa, no trouble.

The screws kept digging and poking at the stuff by the gate but that would get them nowhere.

I crawled through the barricade and into the office.

*Lying by the edge of the football field, Potter, Jarrow, Clapson, and me. Warm summer sun fills the sky and beyond the school buildings there is the buzz of lunch-time traffic.*

'What you doing tonight, Billy,' Potter asks.

'Pictures, I expect,' I answer.

'What's on at yours?'

'Street With No Name. Richard Widmark.'

'Seen it. Saw it at ours last week. Dead good. He gets mown down at the end.'

'All right, don't tell us about it.'

'It's dead good, though.'

*We fall silent. On the opposite side of the pitch, walking slowly round the perimeter, is Derek Arnatt, arm in arm with Anita Dent; they started going with one another the end of last week.*

*They turn the angle where the corner post is and walk another straight line towards the goal posts.*

'Look at them,' Clapson says. 'Love's young dream.'

'Gordon MacRae and Doris Day,' says Jarrow.

'Wait till they get on this side,' I say. 'We'll give them a calling at.'

*They turn by the next corner flag and walk towards us. I can tell that Arnatt is already embarrassed, dreading the gauntlet, but not daring to turn back.*

'Do you reckon they're off to the bushes?' Clapson says, loud enough for them to hear.

'Naw,' says Arnatt. 'You don't do things like that when it's True Love. That'd spoil it.'

'Or when your dad's a copper,' I say. 'That'd never do.'

*Anita Dent's face is crimson.*

'Here, Arnatt, how many villains did your dad catch last

night?' calls Jarrow. 'Twenty-six or was it twenty-seven?'

'Forty-nine,' says Clapson. 'That's where he gets his name from. PC Forty-nine.'

'Forty Eight and a Half,' I say.

Arnatt stops and turns to face us.

'All right, clever sods. Now pack it in,' he says.

'I thought that's what you were going to do in the bushes,' I say.

The others burst out laughing.

Arnatt takes a few steps towards us.

'I'm telling you,' he says.

'What?' I say.

'Shut up or I'll shut you up.'

'What he means is he'll tell his Dad,' says Clapson.

'No point,' I said. 'His dad's even a bigger ponce than he is.'

Arnatt lunges forward and tries to pull me up off the grass but I grab his blazer and pull him to the ground, next to me.

'So that's what you want, is it boy?' I say.

'Go on, Billy,' says Clapson. 'Murder him.'

Arnatt and I stand up. Clapson and the others move away to give us room.

'Come on then,' I say to Arnatt. 'You first. Put one on me.'

Arnatt lashes out with his right and tries to land it on the side of my head but I parry the blow with my forearm and punch him hard in the chest. I am well set on my feet and there is a lot of weight behind my punch but it doesn't have the effect I expect it to have. It rocks him all right, but it doesn't seem to hurt him very much, and while I am considering this he has given me a left and a right to the head. Stars burst and he hurls himself at me, toppling me. I try and roll out of the way but I'm not quick enough and he jumps astride me, punching as he lands. I stretch up my arms to pull him off me but his blows scythe down my arms and I take punch after punch on my head. I thrash about and try to arch my body but I can't dislodge him. He has *a furious strength I didn't expect. I know I'm tougher than he is, I know I can beat him. Yet he is winning and I'm unable to do anything about it. All my mates are watching, and a crowd is growing. I hear someone shout from across the pitch, 'Billy Cracken is getting a beating.'*

*Tears of frustration well up in my eyes and I am weakened by the fear of losing.*

*'Do you give in?' breathes Arnatt, pinning my arms to the ground. I shake my head and more blows clang down on me. The tears roll down my cheeks and the watchers think it's because I'm hurt but they don't know the real reason. Suddenly Arnatt jumps off me. I don't move straight away because his action has surprised me. I raise my head. Arnatt is walking away, proving to the crowd that he has finished with me. Anger and frustration rush through me and I get up and rush after him. Voices cry out and Arnatt spins round and grabs hold of me before I can throw any punches and hurls me to the ground. This time I don't get up. The humiliation has left me too weak to carry on. The rest of the crowd begins to drift away.*

*Except for Potter and Jarrow and Clapson.*

*They know better than to try and help me up.*

The office was eighteen feet by twelve. Most of the twenty-two were inside it. The noise was deafening. Everybody was talking at once. The radio had been turned on full blast. Records and files and papers and smashed furniture were scattered all over the floor and most of the cons were down on their hands and knees sorting through the mess trying to find their own records. Those who'd already found them were systematically tearing them up and throwing the shreds of their lives up into the air, creating their own little blizzards.

When Ray Crompton saw me come into the office he waved a thick file above his head.

'Here, Billy,' he said. 'I've got yours here.'

I took the file off him and put it on the window sill. Out of the way.

'There's Hopper's as well,' Ray said.

I picked up that one and did the same as I'd done with my own.

Over by the window, Walter was talking on the phone.

'It's Walter Colman,' he said. There was a pause. He looked at me and grinned. 'Honest,' he said down the phone, 'it's right. Listen, if you don't believe me. I'll tell you about the last time we met. Right? Fine. It was the Turk's Head, am I right? Middle of last March. You'd got a message from the Filth that they were out for me so you come along and give me the information in return for me giving you the exclusives if they ever sort it, right? Also you want me to phone you every week from wherever I am so you can let me know what the Filth's up to. And you put a few misleading paras in your rag so's the Filth's legging it all over Manchester. In return for a deposit of two grand and fifty a week till I'm nicked. Right? So who else could it be?'

He raised his eyes to the ceiling.

'All right, I'll give you the number and you can phone back. But make it quick before they tumble, otherwise you'll miss all the juice.'

Walter put the phone down.

'That cunt's about as trusting as my lawyer.'

'When he rings back tell him Billy Cracken sends his best,' I said.

The pandemonium was getting worse. Some of them were so excited that I thought maybe they were going to start rolling about the floor in ecstasy. Every so often there'd be a scream from the passageway and a load of cons would rush out to repel boarders but it would always be a false alarm and they'd shuffle back in and take it out on what was left of the furniture.

Then Moffatt came on the scene.

Everybody except Walter, who was talking to his reporter,

crammed outside to the barricades and began to volley him off.

'You cunt, Moffatt, you heap of shit, you fucking egg, you wanking motherfucker.'

It was like the Anfield Kop. Everybody screaming all at once, all the animal hatred and frustration focused on Moffatt who was standing out there like a referee putting down the names in his little notebook. But the roar of abuse didn't stop and even Moffatt couldn't take it for very long. He had as much chance of negotiating a settlement as the public hangman. So he stopped trying to promote his stock and retired. Some of the cons stayed at the barricade after Moffatt had gone. I led the others back into the office. Walter was still on the phone.

'For Christ's sake,' he screamed at us as we all bundled back in. There was quiet for a moment or two but the hysteria was too great for the racket to be kept down for very long. Walter gave up and I took over the phone and gave the reporter a few facts and then Walter had a word with him. We soon got bored with this so we swallowed the reporter and Walter phoned up his bird, Chloe Raines, the pop singer.

Then everybody began to queue up for the phone so that they could ring up their birds or their old ladies or anybody else they could think of. I felt a bit out of it because I couldn't ring Sheila as her Mum wasn't on the phone then and I couldn't remember anybody else's number. Then 'Don't stop de Carnival' came on over the radio and somebody turned the volume up full blast and everybody began to dance and laugh and shriek and join in with the song. Walter stood by the telephone, clapping his hands in time to the music and jigging up and down, his eyes flicking from con to con, looking like a benevolent gargoyle watching the antics of a group of animated garden gnomes. One of the cons was screaming down the telephone.

'Well fucking well go and find her,' he shouted. 'And don't come back without her.'

The scene depressed me. There they all were, dancing like cakewalkers, as if they were pissed, as if they were free, as if they'd really done something great. And it was nothing: they wouldn't even be doing this if it hadn't been for me. And there was Walter on the other side of the room, clapping them along, the benevolent dictator, joining in like the boss at the firm's office party, determined to prove he was one of the boys. I watched him through the swirling bodies. He made me sick. He thought he was number one. But to be number one you had to stand alone. And that was something Walter could never do. He couldn't be content with being top of the pyramid. The rest of the pyramid had to be made up of Walter-lovers. And he couldn't see how they were only Walter-lovers because he wanted them to be. If he'd wanted them to be the other way, they'd have been the other way. It wasn't as if they were all frightened to death of him. Some were, but they were frightened of their mothers' shadows as well. The others were kissing Walter's arse for what they could get out of him, inside and out. They knew Walter liked appearing large, so if they stuck their tongues right up his crevice then they could rely on him to keep them and their families in the jam. The cons who couldn't give two fucks for Walter could be picked up one-handed. But my advantage was that I was the only con in the nick with the strength to pick them up. And the other greasers were more frightened of me than they were of Walter: I had nothing to give them but my clenched fist, and in the short run, that was more persuasive than Walter's stocks and shares. So when the time came for me and the handful to go over the wall, the only con in the nick without a clue would be Walter. Moffatt would know before he did. Poor old fucker. But it was his own fault. It was evident that Walter's plans only included Walter. The benevolence stopped at the wall. The only pity as far as I was concerned was that I wouldn't be around to see the expression on Walter's face.

But that was in the future. This little diversion had to run its course before I could get on to that one.

Walter caught me looking at him. He stopped clapping and gave me a look that said both you know and I know that really they're all behaving like a bunch of cunts but what can you do, people like us, we've got to go along with the rubbish, makes them feel important when people like us get stuck in with them.

I smiled. Walter was even using his technique on me. He wanted me on his team. That would give him even more credibility with the rest of them. As well as it being easier for him to keep on eye on me. But that was the difference between Walter and me. I didn't need a team. I didn't need to be on a team. There was no reason. I could get along on my own.

Walter began to move across the room. Then the lights went out and the radio went off and the room went dead quiet except for the con who'd been using the telephone. His aggrieved voice cut through the blackness.

'I've been cut off,' he said. 'The sods have cut me off.'

*Frobisher House. A youth club in Canning Town. Inter-club boxing, ours against Mill Road Club. Both clubs are well supported and the rivalry is sharp and rowdy. The full sound carries through into the dressing-room and pumps the adrenalin round my body. I know I'm going to win my bout. There's no way I can lose. I feel too good. As I walk down the aisle all my mates give me the big cheer. This is what it's all about. Knowing you're going to fulfil what everybody expects of you. Expressing publicly what you're capable of doing.*

*I'm down against a good boy called Barry Croft. He's a slow mover but slow to anger as well, composed, unwilling to let my aggravations draw him into danger. So I have to wait for my moment, filling in the first round by snapping in as many lefts as I can get through his guard.*

*The bell goes and I sit down in my corner and give the wink* to my mates in the front row. Then a stillness in one of the characters in the crowd catches my eye. I have to look twice to make sure. I can't believe it. My father. His eyes are shining in a way I've never seen before. Full of pride and admiration. I just can't believe it. How did he even know I was boxing?

The bell goes again and I throw myself into the fight. I've never boxed so well before, relaxed, even more convinced of the final outcome. I try to get the decision inside the time but that doesn't work out. Croft just closes up and walks away from the rest of the fight. But the decision is mine and after the fight I look for my father but he is no longer in the crowd. Perhaps he's gone to the dressing-room to wait, so we can walk home together and talk about the fight. But there is no sign of him. Outside. That's where he'll be. He'd rather wait outside in the rain than have to hang about talking to people.

I hurry to get changed but as I'm changing a mate of mine sticks his head round the door and says: 'Your old man told me to tell you he's had to go on somewhere and you're to go on home with your mates.'

I sit down on the bench. Why couldn't he have waited? Why couldn't he have let me walk with him, even just as far as the pub?

When I get home I wait up for him. He comes in solid and goes straight to bed. He doesn't even nod at me as he comes through the door. Just straight through into the bedroom without saying a word.

Later, as I lie in bed, I can hear the dry sound of his snoring from their bedroom. The sound goes on and on and I want to get out of bed and smash my fists into his stupid open mouth again and again so that the rattling sound might stop for good.

The candles flickered.

I was sitting on the floor with my back to the wall, my file open on my legs in front of me. Most of the other cons were sitting the same way, leafing through their files, calling out the choice bits.

The screws seemed to have packed it up for the night, but we'd worked a rota system to keep the barricades covered. The reason the lights had gone out was because the slag of a reporter had phoned through to the Governor after he'd got what he wanted out of us and told Moffatt about the phone calls. That way his paper got two stories.

I looked at my file. It was about the size of the *New Statesman* and about a foot thick. It must have weighed ten pounds. It made a lot of confetti when I eventually tore it up. Which is about all it was worth. It was incredible. Nearly everything in it was speculative and unsupported by facts. I expected to learn something about myself, some analytical insight that might have shed some light on my motives, but all I discovered was what the great British public already knew via the newspapers. I was just another thug. A bit more spectacular than most, but just a thug. It made me sick. These people had put me in the same cell in different prisons for a total of almost ten years and they were the experts and this was their testament. Just another thug.

But the worst part in the file concerned the padre. I was registered as an atheist, but one day he'd barged into my cell full of assurances that he hadn't come to try to convert me, just to see 'if I was all right'. We'd had a chat for about a quarter of an hour but I'd hardly told him a thing, certainly nothing about my private life. But he'd got enough out of that quarter of an hour of conversation about prison generalities to knock up a nice neat little report confirming my irrevocable criminality; quite a juicy little tit-bit lying in the middle of my file, there for any nosey screw to browse through.

But I wasn't the only one he'd put on file.

Ray Crompton said: 'Here, would you fucking believe it? That bastard Tailby's been going at me from behind his collar.

It's all down, what I told him about Maureen and me. About our business.'

'And me,' said Terry. 'He's made me out to be a right cunt.'

Tommy said: 'He's just been working as an assessor. It's all down here about how in his opinion I'll be back on the old tickle once I'm out and that the Governor should take this into account whenever I come up for review.'

'Christ, I'll shit all over him when I see the fucker,' said Dave.

'Why wait?' said Terry.

'How do you mean?' said Ray.

'Well we need a karsi, don't we? What's wrong with his fucking chapel? It's the next best thing to shitting over him.'

Tommy stood up.

'Funny you should say that,' he said. 'I've been meaning to strain the greens.'

He got up and walked over to the door.

'Anyone for tennis?' he said.

Everybody cheered and those who could stir their bowels followed Tommy into the chapel and for the next five minutes the chapel echoed to the groans and farts and laughter of half a dozen cons. The rest of us in the office cheered each new noise and somebody remarked that it was a pity the wireless Tannoy had been disconnected as we could have put one over the air and dedicated it to Moffatt.

While all this was going on, Walter's cousin, Dennis Colman, who was sitting next to me reading Walter's file suddenly burst out laughing.

'What's got in your trousers?' I said.

He kept on laughing.

'Come on,' said Walter. 'Let's all share the joke.'

Dennis wiped the tears from his face.

'Walter,' he said. 'Have I got news for you.'

'What are you talking about?'

Dennis handed the file to me.

'Oh, John,' he said, 'you've got to read this about Walter. You know that screw he was always saying was a good 'un? Well, he was slipped in. The screw was planted.'

Walter stared at him.

'Don't look at me, Walter,' Dennis said. 'It's all down in the file. You've been screwed by a screw.'

He burst into laughter again. I began to read the bit he was on about. The screw that Walter had been cultivating, getting a sympathetic ear for the travails of his life, had been slipped in a couple of months before Walter had arrived in this nick. The screw had been given the brief of getting Walter's confidence and reporting to Moffatt whatever he could find out. The assessment he'd made was encouraging: 'Colman is self-centred... completely unrepentant... feels everybody is fair game to be used and has no qualms about using them... continually trying to establish a relationship with me and enlist my agreement with his running down of the staff...' And so on. I read all this out while Dennis fell about. Tommy and Ray and Terry had returned from the chapel and they augmented Dennis' laughter but the rest of the cons didn't know quite how to react. Walter couldn't stand having the piss taken and he had a long memory. Except for Dennis and Tommy and Ray and Dave and Benny Beauty and me the cons were all watching Walter's face to see which way he was going to bend.

It's the only time I've seen Walter speechless. He was too astonished to be angry. He took the file from me and sat down near a candle and read through the screw's report as if he was reading a foreign language, shaking his head as if he couldn't make any sense out of the words.

I said: 'I thought your screw was too good to be true, Walter.'

'So did I,' said Dennis. 'I mean, how many times did I say just that, Walter?'

For once Walter was unconcerned about his image. He was talking to himself, as if he was on his own.

'I can't believe it,' he said. 'I just can't credit it. Imagine it. All the time he was coming into my cell he was at it.'

'Never mind, Walter,' I said. 'You can't swallow everybody.'

Walter's face went black. Then he picked up his file and flung it across the room.

'Cunt,' he said.

Whether it was me or the screw he was referring to wasn't quite clear.

'Here, Billy,' said Ray, 'let's have a look at Hopper's file.'

I got the file and passed it over to Ray. I'd been thinking about reading it myself but I'd put off opening it up for one reason or another.

Ray took the file and began to leaf through it. I lit up a cigarette and watched Walter as he stood by the window and looked out into the black night, not seeing the night at all, just seeing the face of his tame screw and no doubt imagining the designs he would work on it if he ever got the chance.

'Jesus,' Ray said, softly.

I turned to look at him. He let Hopper's file sag gently across his knees.

'What's the matter?' I said.

Ray shook his head.

'This,' he said, indicating the report.

'What about it?'

Ray carried on shaking his head.

'It's just… I don't know… I can't.'

Tears appeared at the edges of his eyes. I took the file off his lap. It was open at Hopper's deposition, his statement to the police.

'What's that, Billy?' Tommy said.

'Hopper,' I said.

'Read it to us,' Tommy said, his voice quiet and serious.

'Well,' I said. 'If you want.'

I began to read. I didn't want to read it, let alone read it out loud, but it was as if somebody else was reading it, not me, somebody with a voice like a railway station loudspeaker, reading without emphasis or emotion, just droning on like a bored teacher on a hot summer afternoon. But even the voice that seemed to be outside of myself had to stop when in the text it occurred that Hopper had sliced into one of the little girls with razor blades when she'd refused to go down to him, and all the time she'd been calling for her Mummy but her Mummy never came and it was five hours after Hopper had used the razor blades he'd finally killed her. And then he'd turned to the other little girl who'd had to watch everything.

I think I must have stopped in mid-sentence but nobody asked me to go on. I put the file down on the floor beside me. I didn't have to look into any faces to know how everybody was feeling.

Just five minutes with him was all anybody wanted.

The picnic was never the same after that.

*All I feel about him, looking at him, dead, in the coffin, is how like him yet unlike him he looks. The features are exactly the same as they were in life, the same distances, the same arrangement. But at the same time he looks like no one I've ever met before. A face passed in a crowd, unreal, making no contact. But that is all I feel. As I stand there I can hear my mother sobbing in the other room. The sound irritates me. Why doesn't she stop? It's just a useless irritating noise, empty; the grief is for her lost life, not his. Later Linda comes to my bedroom. She stands by the bed, crying, asking to get in with me, but I pretend to be asleep, and eventually she goes away.*

I awoke at quarter past six.

I sat up and the file paper I'd used to cover myself with slid off me and rattled coldly on to the floor. Grey morning light filtered through the barred windows. Ray was lying next to me and the smell of his feet drifted into my nostrils. I got up and went out of the office. I lit a cigarette and leant against the corridor wall. There was no sound out on the landing. Most of the screws would be in their pits, stoking up for the events of the coming day. We'd hardly heard from them at all during the night. The odd cowboy had thrown rocks up at the office window, but that had brought them no joy, except the pleasure of seeing our candle-lit faces squashed up against the glass.

I blew out smoke and it hung on the motionless air. I thought about something Dennis had said the night before. At the time it had made me smile not because of what he'd said but because before his current sentence he'd only done six months inside and it would hardly give him a wealth of experience about his subject. But now, thinking about it in the daylight, Dennis had been quite sharp about the situation. He'd made his remarks shortly after a sing-song Walter had organised. The favourite number had been *Maybe it's because I'm a Londoner*, and Walter had been in his element, beating time with his fist, exhorting those who were sick and tired of the song to join in at the tops of their voices. But when even Walter had no longer been able to keep the Scouts' atmosphere going, most of the cons had taken to wandering round the room like characters in search of a director, smashing up any remains of furniture still big enough to break, sticking bits of wood and metal in their belts like pirates, cursing the screws and the Governor and their mates and their wives and their mothers. It was during this aimlessness that Dennis had said to me: 'Look at them, Billy. They're not up to it. They're not equal to this situation.'

'How do you mean?'

'They're a lot of piss artists. Before this, to hear them talk, you'd have thought they were all fucking Prime Ministers. "I did this, I did the other, when I was on so and so's firm, and with that I said..." all that fucking cobblers. But they're a fucking joke. They don't know how to handle fuck all. They're just winding themselves for nothing. They've convinced themselves that they're in control. There's no reality to them any more. They've done too much bird. Even Walter's acting like a fucking infant.'

I hadn't agreed and I hadn't disagreed. I hadn't known Dennis long enough to commit myself with him.

'I'll have a bet with you, Billy,' he'd gone on to say. 'Right now, all those that are roaming about are feeling stalky. That's half the reason they can't sit down. They're being pulled round by their pricks. Inside half an hour there'll be some action, no worry.'

He had been right. I'd seen it happen before when there'd been a mixture of excitement and fear and frustration. Once when I'd been on a driving job with two heavies and the truck we'd been waiting for had been ten minutes late and we'd all been in danger of getting nicked just sitting by the kerb waiting, one of the heavies had slipped his hand in his pocket and given himself one just to get the tension out of him. And it had been the same with the cons during the night. Three of them had started crowding that Vaseline-arse Ian Crosbie who didn't mind a bit but appreciated that those hard-cases, Monks, Climie and Ford liked it with rough stuff and so he'd put on a bit of a show of resisting. But before it'd gone very far I'd faced them out of the office and into the chapel because that kind of game is inclined to make me want to hurt somebody. Badly. A few of the others had drifted out with them to watch but when they'd all come back into the office afterwards only Monks and Climie had had the guts to look into my face and then not for very long.

I threw the cigarette down on to the floor and turned and had a look at the barricade.

But beyond the barricade there was something much more interesting to look at.

Two people had come out on to the landing. One was a bastard of a screw called Swain.

The other character was Hopper.

He was carrying a bucket and a floor cloth.

Swain's voice echoed up and down the levels.

'All of it, Hopper,' he said. 'And I want it looking good.'

Hopper put the bucket down and got down on his knees and dipped the floor cloth in the bucket.

'Not there,' said Swain. 'You can do that afterwards.'

Hopper looked up at him.

'I want you to do the catwalk first. No sense in doing all this and going over there and then walking your mucky feet back over what you've already done.'

Hopper's head swung round towards the gate. I stood stock still.

'What, over there?' he said.

'That's right,' Swain said.

'But what about them?'

'What about them?'

'Supposing they come out?'

'They won't come out,' said Swain. 'Why should they, now they're in? Besides, the gate's locked. So get on with it.'

I didn't wait to listen to any more. I dodged back into the office and shook Ray and Tommy until they were awake.

'Hopper's coming to the gate,' I said.

Now all the sleep fell away from their minds.

'To the gate?' Tommy said.

I nodded, then explained what was going on. There was a silence. Eventually Ray said: 'It's a trap.'

I nodded again.

'That's right,' I said.

Another silence.

'So what do we do?' Tommy said.

'What do we want to do?' I said.

More thoughtful silence.

'It's chancey,' Ray said.

'That's right,' I said.

'But worth taking,' said Tommy.

'Right,' said Ray. 'How else are we going to get close to him?'

'Right,' I said. 'And if we're claimed, so what?'

'We're not staying here forever,' said Tommy.

'That's what I thought,' I said.

'So what's the form?' Ray said.

'One of us goes to the gate when's he's over the catwalk, taking the key with us. Clear a little space to give us room to manoeuvre. Chat to Hopper for a bit. Then when he's in the best position try and haul him inside. At which point the other two come and give the other one a hand, and in the event of a trap we organise Walter's pokers to beat back the heavy mob.'

They both agreed.

Between us we woke up the others. Of course Walter was all for rushing out and claiming Hopper on the landing. I sometimes wondered how Walter had managed to become such a rich man. But he saw it our way when we told him that he was to be king of the pokers.

As it was our plan, Tommy, Ray and me drew for who went on the landing. I'd volunteered but the other two wouldn't have it: everybody wanted to be first to lay a hand on Hopper.

So Tommy ambled out on to the landing and sorted his way through the barricade.

Ray and me stayed in the background in the gloom near the office door and the rest of them stayed in the office, ready for the action.

The minute Hopper heard Tommy sorting through the barricade he got to his feet, standing like a hare poised for flight. But Tommy just got to the bars and lit a snout and rested his elbows and said to Swain: 'Where is everybody, then? Everybody given up, have they?'

'That's right, Tommy,' Swain said. 'You're too big and brave for us. We've decided you'll just have to stay in there forever.'

'That's all right, then,' said Tommy. 'At least you won't have to work so hard.'

'That's what we thought. When you've all starved to death it won't be a job for us any more.'

'I can see that,' Tommy said. 'Course, there's still plenty of room if you want to get anybody else off your hands.'

Hopper began to back away towards the catwalk.

'What's the matter with you, Hopper? Finished that floor already?'

Hopper turned to look at Swain.

'Who told you to get up off your knees?' said Swain. 'Get down and get finished. If you stop once more I'll open the cage and let them have you.'

Hopper got down again and began to swab the floor. Swain stayed on the other side of the catwalk, watching.

Tommy turned his attention to Hopper.

'We had an interesting evening last night,' Tommy said.

Hopper didn't look up but he was trembling like a leaf.

'Should have been there. We got the records out and had a party.'

While he'd been talking Tommy had taken the key out of his pocket and gently slipped it into the lock.

'We all read out our party pieces. Everybody had a go. Really is a pity you weren't there. Because yours was by far the most interesting. Really, I can't remember when I last enjoyed such a good read.'

Tommy flicked his cigarette end through the bars and into Hopper's bucket. Hopper stared hypnotised into the water. That was when Tommy made his move. And Ray and me made ours.

Tommy swung the gate and grabbed Hopper by his hair. Ray and I scrambled through the barricade to get to the gate but the minute Tommy stepped out six screws appeared from either side of the gate. They'd been there all the fucking time, just holding their bloody breath and waiting.

Tommy didn't have a chance. Three of the screws claimed for him while the other three pushed their way inside the gate. But I'll give Tommy this, he didn't let go of Hopper. Still clutching Hopper by the hair he tried to swing him round towards the gate just in case any of us could get to Hopper and haul him in. But Ray and me had the other three screws on our hands and there was nothing we could do about it.

In front of us I could see the rest of the screws racing across the catwalk towards the gate. I chopped off one of the screws inside the gate and Ray was sorting another and the third didn't have a chance at all because Walter and his clubmen had got to us and they finally had someone to ease their tensions on.

We bundled the screws out and met the second wave through the bars but they didn't last very long because the position was exactly the same as when we first got in. A lot of fucking good their hide and seek had done them.

I stood back and watched Tommy after the screws had been chucked out. Before they gave him the stick he got his boot in Hopper's face and the other one across Hopper's fingers. But he just wasn't able to get the one in where it mattered. Hopper had pulled it again. I thought: there'll be a third time. There's got to be a third time. Then it'll be us who are lucky. Not Hopper. Not next time.

*I'm sitting in the café with Howard and Johnno. Early evening sunlight warms the Formica of the table top. Empty espresso cups are huddled together at tables and to make room for Howard's invisible blueprints of the coming job.*

*'This point's the really tricky bit,' he says. 'Getting on the roof's a piece of piss. A doddle. The skylight'll be nothing, either. It's just the drop from the skylight to the stockroom floor. We can only guess at the height. But we've got to be careful because the*

walls are no thicker than the wallpaper. Next door, as I say, they're always up. The old bat never sleeps. She probably wanders about all night just waiting for something like this to happen. I remember when we used to neck round the back in the alley she was always sticking her head out of the window and bawling at us. She could hear a Durex slipping on at fifty paces. So, as I say, it's just the drop down. Nice and soft and we'll be all right.'

'How much do you think there'll be?' Johnno asks.

'He doesn't cash up till tomorrow. Wednesdays and Saturdays he stacks it away. So if we go tonight there'll be two days' worth in the till. A chemist, could be anything. He's got four staff on so he's doing all right. Won't be less than two ton. Four could be nearer the mark.'

Johnno whistles.

'Christ,' he says. 'A ton each. Just think of it. Up West with a ton in your pocket.'

But I'm not thinking of the money. I'm thinking of the climb, the drop, the actual job.

The café door opens and in walks Tony Jackson, all suited up and ready for some kind of action. He comes over to our table and sits down.

'What's on, Tony?' Johnno asks. 'Who is it tonight?'

'Sharon Cross. Three hours of finger at the Essoldo. And tonight she'll really be a goer now she's got her results.'

'Results?' I say.

'You know. School Cert. She got all she went for so she'll be chuffed to NAAFI-break tonight.'

'When did they come through?' I ask.

'This morning. Didn't you get yours, then?'

I shake my head.

'Got mine. Sharon told me. They posted them up at school. As expected, one hundred per cent successful.'

'How do you mean?'

'Didn't get any.'

*I want to ask him if he knows what my results are. But I don't want to seem interested in front of Johnno and Howard. Not that I'll have done any good. I deliberately threw the exams. They weren't important any more. But now the evidence of my failure will be public. I feel depressed with shame. I can't help thinking of the waste, knowing what I could be like. But it was a choice, deliberate and calculated. And tonight, climbing to the roof of the chemist's shop, the choice will be vindicated by the way I'll be feeling then. But right now, all I can think of is the dusty sunny exam hall, and the way Mr Bradley kept looking at me as I sat back and watched everybody else scribbling away. The feeling then was good, and afterwards everyone clustered round my boldness. But now the feeling is different. The scene has gone sour.*

*I look at my watch. Six hours to the job. If only the crowd from school could be around to admire this one.*

*

On the third day, the Home Office showed up. They sent up a man called Hepton. This was good news in more ways than one. First it meant that the Home Office had concluded that Moffatt wasn't up to getting us out. Which made Moffatt look bad and us feel good. Second, Hepton was straight, according to Terry, who had known Hepton when he'd been a Governor. Straight, principled and fair. So the Home Office were worried, worried enough to ease us out with someone we'd tumble to.

When Hepton appeared Terry was elected spokesman. The rest of us stayed in the office and listened to the dialogue. Hepton's words were the best we could hope for; while he wasn't prepared to bargain with us, he'd read our statement of grievances and he assured us they'd be given very serious consideration. He hinted that the longer we stayed in the less serious the consideration would be. But everything about Hepton's words and the way he said them pointed to what we already knew: they badly wanted us out, whatever the terms.

When Terry came back from the barricade we all had a parley.

'The way I see it,' I said, 'if we go out under Hepton where Moffatt failed, then we'll have made Moffatt look bad. We wouldn't be going out under threat or by Hobson's choice. We'd be going out reasonably and rationally, in fact behaving the dead opposite to the way Moffatt's behaved to us. This can only improve whatever chances are going at the Home Office as far as them looking into Moffatt's policies are concerned. And besides, there's a terrible hum drifting over from the chapel and speaking personally I don't think I could take another four days' worth. No, as far as I'm concerned now's the time to negotiate.'

Walter said: 'Yeah, all that's fine, Billy, it's all fucking lovely, but how do we know Hepton's playing it straight? We'll get clobbered once we set foot outside of here.'

'No, no, Walter,' said Terry. 'I'm telling you: Hepton's straight.'

Walter mumbled for a while about getting clobbered but when we put it to the vote he voted with the fors. There were eighteen fors, four abstentions and against were Monks, Climie and Ford but they were head cases and didn't really count.

So that was it. Terry went back to the barricade and negotiated us a meal and no loss of privileges. We went out to a battery of magistrates and screws formed in threes, but Moffatt wasn't there.

We stripped, bathed, changed our clothes, went downstairs to the hot-plate and got ourselves a dinner and went back to our cells to eat it. A few of the screws had been round the cells smashing record players and ripping letters and photographs and burning private towels, that kind of thing. They'd been sensible enough to leave me out.

Although the screws must have tried hard to get us all done for assault, in fact only Dave and two others were given the arbitrary honour of copping for that one; the visiting commission was tempering justice with common sense; they didn't want a backlash against the sentences. In fact they even had the nerve to accept Terry's explanation of how he came to be in the office. Terry was first one up in front of the commissioners and he told them that he'd just come out of his cell and got caught up in the mad rush and despite trying desperately to disentangle himself he'd been carried along in the tide and once in the office the rest of us hadn't let him go. Nobody on the Board believed a word of it but Terry got acquitted; the commissioners would appear straight and just men on the paper on which the minutes were taken.

Apart from the token assault charges the rest of us were done for mutiny and destruction of government property and we got forty-two days behind our doors and the equivalent loss of earnings. We all kept our cell privileges such as wireless, newspapers, tobacco, etc. It was the most toothless sentencing any of us had ever been dished out. Almost a seal of approval on our actions. Nobody could get over it. Particularly the screws. They weren't just mystified, they were fucking furious.

So they retaliated with about the only weapon they'd got left in their armoury; the three-man unlocking rule at meal times. The food was kept downstairs on a hot-plate and normally you were taken down in threes and you brought your food back to your cell. There were a number of gates between the cells and the hot-plate and normally these were left unlocked until everybody had been there and back. But now the screws locked and unlocked every gate on the way there and on the way back with each trio of prisoners. And they took their time doing it. This effectively dragged out meal times to about one and a half hours and it worked out that about three-quarters of us got lukewarm food. To me it was a case of beggars not being choosers. We'd got off light and easy and I figured forty-two days of lukewarm food was neither here nor there. But not

Walter. He elected to register his protest by going on a hunger strike. For the privilege of being starved I can do all sorts of wonderful things such as chin screws, smash prison property, generally be a pest, but to do it voluntarily is just squandering my seed. But it was one out all out and so I included myself in. The wing was on hunger strike. And a lot of bloody good it was too. I've never seen screws so happy. There was a sparkle back in their eyes and a fresh jingle in their key rings. Their wives or boyfriends could never have had so much attention. Sometimes when they opened my door and asked me if I was coming for my grub and I told them I wasn't they'd stand there for a moment, grinning, savouring the sheer delight of the situation.

For about three days I never really minded; self denial is good for the soul and when that line of thinking palled I took consolation in the longevity of the rats who were starved one day out of three.

I let it drift on another couple of days and then I mounted a propaganda campaign. The trouble was we'd committed ourselves to acting over this cold food run-around and we couldn't start eating spaniel over it and do nothing. I wanted to institute some kind of retaliation system against the screws like putting a pot of shit over their heads on a one a day rota basis. But a hunger strike is nice and safe and predictable; the heavy mob aren't going to slip into your cell one morning just because you're starving yourself. So a lot of the cons saw the strike as the lesser of a lot of other evils they could get sucked into. Or worse evils that they wouldn't be able to deliver on; for the weak, not eating was something they could do. It didn't really matter if they never reached their goal. So long as they stuck it out no scorning fingers would disturb their lives. Cold food or not eating at all were preferable to scorning fingers as far as the weak cons in Nick Society were concerned.

We only exercised in threes and fours and to reach everyone

I had to go round the cells and talk through the doors. It was like trying to juggle with mercury balls: no one would come off unless everybody else did. Of course, Walter was the staunchest of the lot, seeing as he'd fetched up the whole bloody idea. He was responsible so he would be the one to come off last. He was revelling in it.

On the sixth day I'd managed to get a provisional Yes from everybody except Walter. I'd left him till last, hoping to shame him out of his minority, blackmail him with a unanimous front. But when I reached his door he got up to his window and started yelling: 'Dave, Tommy, Benny?'

I heard them all answer. I yelled at Walter.

'Wally, listen, everybody wants to…'

But Walter ignored me and shouted to the others:

'You're all staunched up, are you? Not weakening?'

Like a shibboleth of loyalty they all chorused back exactly the opposite to what they'd told me.

'Good,' Walter shouted back. 'We'll show them they won't beat us.'

So Walter bonded it off. You had to hand it to him. He was a propagandist in his own right.

When he'd finished he came over to his door.

'That you, Billy?' he said.

'As if you didn't know, Wally,' I said.

'What's your trouble, Billy?'

'You just undid three days' work in two seconds.'

I walked away and left him at his door. Of course, what most of the others didn't know was that one source of Walter's strength was the appeal visits he was having. His bird would come up and force sandwiches on him.

'Now you eat them, Wally,' she'd say.

'No, Chloe, I can't, I'm on hunger strike, in I?'

'You eat them or I'll force them down your bleeding throat,' she'd say.

And so Walter would reluctantly eat. She'd been well pruned. I was indebted to Ray for this piece of information. He specialised in Wally watching.

Still, the strike had some compensations. Twelve of the cells overlooked one of the main prison paths and once the strike had got under way we'd gone completely anarchic and we'd get up at our windows and volley off anybody who used the path. Moffatt only took one dose of it and afterwards carefully avoided that path. It must have been quite hairy, having twelve screaming, cursing, starving maniacs turning their attention at you. The priest got his, the doctor, and every screw without exception. The best was when it first started. Someone would spot a screw and volley him off and the screw would get indignant and shout back in his very best official snarl: 'Get down from that window!' The response would be instant and massive. Everyone would dive to their windows and rain a deluge of abuse on him. The screw's mouth would hang open in astonishment and then he'd scuttle out of sight in case he got into trouble for starting us off. Also the prison work parties had to be re-routed as we'd shout out all sorts of contradictory orders that had everyone marching in different directions.

On the eighth day they came round and weighed us. I got the shock of my life. I'd lost twenty pounds in body weight. I couldn't get over it. My muscles were being squandered to subsidise Walter's fantasies. By this time he was really out of his mind: he expected the Home Office to send up another director and when he came Walter was going to hold out for conjugal visits. The success of the demo had really gone to his head.

'We're doing ourselves a lot of good, Billy,' he told me. 'All this publicity is getting us a lot of sympathy.'

I'd given up arguing with him. It only seemed to lend substance to his irrationality.

So, in the end, I decided to eat. But in such a way that it

camouflaged my weakness by upping the stakes in the real issue – the test of endurance. I did it by changing my protest tactics into a sphere that few of them could emulate and that being the case it wouldn't damage my name.

In other words, I decided to have a tear up.

But first I pulled all the die-hards. I told them: 'I'm going to eat tonight and tomorrow morning at breakfast I'm going to perform. You're the starvers who think it's great not eating. Fine. Well, I followed you for eight days and in the morning I hope you follow me in and make one after I've made mine.'

I told each of them this separately. No one condemned me to my face or said anything I could have taken offence at. So that was that part of the scheme taken care of.

It's an odd thing about fasting: after five days the hunger pains stop and then you feel a bit depressed and then even that comes and goes. People who at three and four days were craving to come off were now, at eight days, completely convinced of their cause, and of the value of what they were doing. It was almost a form of hysteria.

That night I went and got my tea and Ray and Tommy and Terry followed suit. There were no sounds from Walter as we passed by his door.

The next morning I went downstairs to get my breakfast. There were about five screws lounging around by the hot plate. They all gave me a look that was meant to say fancy that. Big Billy isn't so tough after all, he's the first to come off. But their expressions soon changed when I tipped over the hot plate and threw all the breakfast everywhere. When I'd done that I went to the remains of the previous day's grub and did the same with that. One of the screws was ambitious, either that or he just didn't think, because he made a move to go for me. But when he saw he was on his own he braced himself and stayed with the ranks.

The whole landing was awash with custard and tea and

porridge and soup. Someone must have rung the alarm bell because by the time I'd finished there were about fifteen screws standing in the middle of the wing, all looking at me across the swill. Upstairs everybody was wise to what I'd done and they were all banging on their doors. With the possible exception of Walter.

I backed off down towards the end of the wing till I was opposite the punishment cell. None of the screws said anything. After about a minute the PO turned up and picked his way round the edge of the swill.

'You try and grab me,' I said, 'and I'll break your fucking jaw.'

The PO held up his hands.

'No, no, Billy,' he said. 'I'm not going to do anything like that. Are you away to your cell now?'

'No,' I said. I pointed at the punishment cell. 'You're going to have to put me in there.'

'You're being silly, you know,' the PO said.

'You know how silly I am,' I said.

The PO looked at me for a moment. Then he went back to the bunch of screws. A few of them were fingering the straps on their sticks. I thought, well, you're committed now.

I stood there for another five minutes. Nothing happened. I picked up a loose orange from off the floor and ate it. Then the PO came back.

'Look, Billy,' he said, 'we're not going to put you away. You can stand there till the Governor comes in if you like. It's up to you.'

He paused, looking at me calmly.

'So why don't you just go away to your cell?'

I knew what his meaning was: I could go back now, no trouble, or I could try to sort out fifteen screws with sticks. I didn't feel so tough at that moment, what with the effects of the hunger strike and the thought of all those bad bastards just waiting to get at me with their sticks. So I turned my back on them and went back upstairs to my cell. Everybody was shouting out for me to tell them what had happened. I told them that I'd come back up because I'd felt silly just standing there with none of the screws making a move for me. When I got behind my door I broadcast the fact that I'd be performing again tomorrow and for the rest of the day I sang, 'What have all the starvers done?' to really get up Walter's nose.

About eight o'clock that evening my door opened and the biggest screw in the nick stepped in.

'Pack your kit, Cracken,' he said. 'We're moving you over to the other side.'

'You're sure about that, are you?'

'Cracken,' he said wearily, 'you're going to be moved whichever way you go. I've orders to move you with whatever force is necessary and there's a doctor and a magistrate out there acting as witnesses.'

The screw moved out of the way of the door. There were screws everywhere. The doctor and the magistrate were standing by the railings.

'Why just me?' I said to the screw.

'Don't worry. Some of the others are going as well.'

The others were Walter, Tommy, Ray and Benny. We spent the night in the strong box over there. The next morning I got an ordinary cell in the main prison, on the bottom landing away from Walter and the rest. I settled down to read and make the best of it. I never spoke to anyone and I never saw anyone I knew. I would pace up and down on a patch of ground near the hospital for half an hour in the morning and half an hour in the afternoon. To the cons I was a bit of a tourist attraction. They had to line up outside my door before going to labour and I'd hear them saying, 'Christ man, twenty-three years... I'd top myself... I couldna do it... he doesn't look different...' and so on. Sometimes, when I was slopped out late, I'd have an audience and I used to ham it up a bit. It's hard to resist a bit of free ego stocking.

After about a week a running battle developed over the original cause of the demo. I'd come over to the main wing in plimsolls, overalls, shirt, vest, pants and socks and every now and again a funny little screw would casually open my door and try to check off a little clothing list he'd have in his hands.

'Just a stock check,' he'd say. 'Have you got a tie, shoes…'

That word.

'Look, pal,' I'd say, 'don't come in here with your silly little list. I've got exactly what I need.'

'I'm only checking what you've got.'

'Yes, I know, and I'm not bothering anyone so don't force any animal tactics on me. I'm not wearing shoes, ties or greys.'

In the main wing of any prison escape risks have to put their clothing, knives, spoons, razor and mirror on their chairs outside their doors. Naturally this rule applied to me. One morning the door opened and the chair was pushed quickly inside and then the door was slammed shut. The swiftness of the operation was ominous.

I got up and had a look. On the chair was a nice new pair of shiny black shoes and no plimsolls.

I picked up the shoes and stuffed them out of the window. Then I waited to get unlocked. But they let me stew for a while and didn't unlock me until it was time to slop out.

The screw who'd shoved the chair round my door was standing by the recess. I walked over to him.

'Take my plimsolls, did you?' I said.

I didn't raise my voice. I just asked him nice and quiet. The screw stretched his neck a bit as if his collar was a bit too tight for him.

'No, I never took them,' he said. 'Never even knew you had any.'

'You fucking well took them, you cunt,' I said, still nice and quiet and polite.

The screw began to sweat. I gave him a long smiling look and went back to my cell. When you've got them frightened enough to lie you've got something to kid yourself with.

The next time I slopped out, I slopped out barefoot. As I went out of my door I saw that the shoes had been put back. I picked them up and flung them across the landing. As I came back out of the recess a decent screw called Dickinson came up to me.

'What are you walking about like that for, Billy?' he said, looking at my feet.

I told him I'd had my plimsolls nicked and that I couldn't wear shoes.

'Well, we can't have you walking about like that,' he said. 'I'll get you a pair of slippers. What size do you take?'

I told him and he came to my cell half an hour later with a pair of slippers. But the next day Moffatt ordered that I should have my exercise stopped unless I wore regulation shoes. So I stayed in my box and I didn't move out of it for a week. Not until the Home Secretary visited the nick.

When a couple of screws visit you and tell you that the Home Secretary wants to see you you're justified in telling them to fuck off. But it was right. The Home Secretary had been over in the Security Wing and had asked Moffatt what had happened to me. Moffatt must have told him because the Home Secretary requested my presence.

I hadn't shaved for about four days and they don't like to see it. With all the bird I'd done it had got to be a habit. But you've got to make some sort of a show for a Home Secretary, so I brushed my hair even though it was cropped almost to a stubble.

I went out, slippers flopping on the tiles. The screws showed me into a small office near my cell.

The Home Secretary was sitting behind a small plastic table, facing the door. Moffatt was sitting to his left, in the corner, legs primly crossed. The Chief stood by the door to my right.

Moffatt said:

'The HS is visiting us, Cracken. He's decided to see you.'

I didn't look at Moffatt. I just looked straight ahead at the Home Secretary.

'Thank you, sir,' I said, making it clear my remarks weren't addressed to Moffatt.

'Sit down, Cracken,' said the Home Secretary. All genial and open. 'Is there anything you'd like to talk to me about?'

'Well, yes sir, there is as a matter of fact.'

'Well, that's what I'm here for. You can say what you like. No one will stop you.'

He grinned encouragingly. Moffatt re-crossed his legs.

'I know that it was wrong what we did, sir, having the demo and that, but we hadn't any choice, had we? I mean, what's the point of trying to enforce regulations that your own council's recommended for the chopping block? In any case, they weren't even enforced by the previous Governor.'

I went on a bit in that vein and the HS never argued the toss. Nobody could. Moffatt had been gauntlet slapping and the demo had been a direct result. But I wasn't deluding myself about the HS. He was more interested in getting some first hand experience of prisoners than debating the merits of the mutiny.

When I'd finished he leant back in his chair and said: 'I stand by the Governor.'

I didn't say anything.

'In many respects,' he said, 'this situation is similar to an industrial dispute where both sides have dug in and stubbornness is only making matters worse. But of course the Governor was fully within his rights to issue those orders and my department and myself back him up to the hilt. Nobody wants to see you chaps with sentences like yours locked in your cells for long periods of time but what else can we do when you behave like this? Everybody finally gets on to me and I have no choice.'

'I realise that, sir,' I said, 'but, I mean, all of us are cooped up together in the maximum security wing, and business like stupid regulations is bound to set something alight.'

'The dispersal policy will go some way to remedying that particular problem.'

'Ah, now sir, if I may say so, a maximum security prison is more realistic. Where people like us are able to breathe.'

All the time we were talking Moffatt was sitting seething.

The Home Secretary looked down at the table top.

'What *do* you do all day, Cracken?' he said.

'Me, sir?' I said. 'I'm in my cell, reading.'

'What, all day?'

'Yes sir.'

'Why all day?'

I didn't look at Moffatt but I knew he was staring at me fit to burn me up.

'Well, sir, the Governor won't let me go out on exercise.'

Moffatt had to speak now.

'Wait a minute, Cracken,' he said. 'Tell us *why* you're not allowed on exercise. Tell the Home Secretary about your refusal to wear the shoes as issued.'

I couldn't believe my luck. Moffatt had shot himself in front of the Home Secretary.

I said: 'I don't suppose the Home Secretary wants to hear about my shoes, Governor.'

'What's this about, then?' said the Home Secretary.

Moffatt was committed now.

'Cracken was issued with a new pair of shoes. He threw them out of the window, refusing to wear them. That's why he's not allowed out on exercise.'

The Home Secretary looked at Moffatt and then at me, taking in the Governor's venom and my own contempt.

'Well, come on, Cracken,' he said. 'Tell me about the shoes.'

There was the trace of an amused smile on his face.

Well, he had asked, and you don't look it in the mouth when it comes.

'He's just trying to make me look bad, Mr Home Secretary,' I said. 'I came over here from E wing wearing a pair of plimsolls which I'd worn for weeks without anybody objecting. Then a week ago a warder pinched them off my chair when I'd put it outside my door. The shoes were put there instead. I admit I stuffed them out the window, but, Jesus, these kind of tactics, well, hardly the kind of games so-called responsible people are supposed to play. I mean, are they?'

The Home Secretary found this all highly amusing.

'Is that right?' he asked Moffatt. 'Were they pinched off his chair?'

Moffatt passed it on to the Chief.

'I merely gave the order for him to be issued with a new pair of shoes,' Moffatt said. 'What happened, Chief?'

The Chief was having a bit of a smile-up, too.

'Well, yes, quite frankly, they were taken off his chair in the manner described, yes,' he said. 'Because, to be honest, I knew he wouldn't give them up if he was just asked.'

'That's not the point,' I said. 'There are ways of doing these thing and there are ways of *not* doing them. I mean, that's the kind of trick we're supposed to get up to.'

'If you can't...' Moffatt began, but the Home Secretary cut through him.

'Cracken,' he said, 'I'm not in the habit of asking prisoners favours. But will you do something for me?'

'Yes sir, of course.'

'Will you wear your shoes if they're given back to you?'

'Yes sir, of course I will.'

I knew he'd meant my plimsolls. So did Bastin. But Moffatt missed the point completely. Pedantic as ever, he snapped out:

'Yes, of course. If he wears his shoes he can go out on exercise.'

'Good,' said the Home Secretary, looking down at the table top.

There was a short silence while the Home Secretary, Bastin and myself thought one thing and Moffatt thought another.

Moffatt was finished now. That was obvious. He didn't know it. He probably never would. But it was clear that the Home Secretary was going to implement a few subtle changes, via Creasey probably, that would only filter through to Moffatt if it was absolutely necessary that he should be made aware of the changes. I got the feeling that it would never be absolutely necessary. Moffatt would just be kept happy until such time had elapsed that he could be respectably moved on.

That afternoon I got my plimsolls back and went out on exercise. The day was bright and sunny and by the hospital the flowers rocked from side to side in the slow warm wind. I stood in the shadow of the wall and looked up at its edge and beyond and watched the fluff-ball clouds drift across the kodak-blue sky and I thought about the park near where Sheila and Timmy and me had lived before this last lot. It's funny how good weather works your memory. I thought of the swings and Timmy's laugh as I pushed him higher and higher, right up into the sky, the chains clanking, Sheila calling 'Be careful', Timmy laughing louder and louder, the goodness of the feeling of my own strong arms thrusting against the swing with the warm sun glinting on the warm iron and the squeaking of the joints and Timmy's little hands gripping tight as life itself.

I lay down on the grass by the hospital. So I'd screwed Moffatt up. Fine. For a moment there it had been great, a triumph, virtue rewarded. A victory to be savoured and passed on and absorbed into the false brightness of prison mythology. And the very fact that for a while I'd counted the victory as amounting to some kind of importance now described to me only the slackening of my own grip on my scale of virtues. I was like one of the cons Walter's cousin had described on the demo as suffering from too much bird. The victory was purely relative. Six months ago it wouldn't have been worth piss in the wind to me. Now I was stoking up on small glory.

I lay on my back and lit a fag. That way I couldn't see the wall or the hospital or any of the other hospital buildings. There was just the sky and the drifting clouds and the weight of the warm earth falling away beneath me.

I'd spent seven of the last ten years inside. The longest time all at once had been eleven months, the time before this last lot. I'd missed the first year of Timmy's life.

Only twenty-two years and seven months of this one to go.

I stood up and looked at the wall.

*The wall is dark against the night sky. Now and then clouds slide slowly over the face of the moon. Beyond the wall is the building, its rooftops just visible over the wall's lip.*

*'Are we going over, then?' says Jackie Robinson.*

*'That's why we came, isn't it?' says Tony Cook. 'No point in coming, otherwise.'*

*We are standing outside the approved school they've left recently. Earlier, in the cellar club, after the Bennies had been taken, they'd started talking about the school, about the lads they'd left behind, how great they were, how I should meet them.*

*We all shin up the wall and drop down the other side. Silence. The huge building is lit only at two windows. It is still and solid and its outline makes me shudder. All those kids in there, enclosed, regimented.*

*'That's Derwent's window,' says Jackie, nodding at one of the lights.*

*'The bastard,' says Tony.*

*We are about to move towards the building when a downstairs light is switched on. We freeze. A door opens and light pours out into the night. Someone comes out and walks round the corner of the building, out of sight. We turn and run and make it back over the wall.*

*'Bloody bastards,' says Tony. 'I bet it was Derwent.'*

*'Bound to be,' says Jackie. 'The sod never sleeps.'*

*We walk the streets until it is time for Jackie and Tony to turn off. We arrange to meet in the club up West again tomorrow. I look at my watch. I reckon that it will take me at least two hours to walk home. By that time it will be five-thirty in the morning. But I never make it. On my way home the Filth stops me, inspired by my Teddy Boy clothes. I am searched, and they find my file, my offensive weapon. Later I am conditionally discharged, but that doesn't matter to me, one way or the other. The important thing is that now I'm one of the boys, and that now I can start to rise above them. I have the first of my credentials.*

When I got back to E wing things had changed. Everything was different.

The wing was definitely under new management. Gordon was still there. Naturally. But it was Creasey who was running things. Everything was sweetness and light. The whole thing was a different place.

It almost made you think twice about making it over the wall.

For a start, the wing had been almost cleared. We were left six-handed. The only three left from the original lot apart from me were Ray, Tommy and Terry. And of course, Walter. Seventy-seven years to go between us. It's that kind of incidental arithmetic that makes it ridiculous not to think of going over.

Strachey was still there but he didn't count. We just let him get on with it. The rest of the monsters had been locked off upstairs which in some ways was a pity.

The other new members were a real couple of cases: one was Albert Atkin, a double lifer. He'd killed one boy when he was seventeen and another one in the nick inside of his first year.

He'd been a lucky bastard because topping was still in style when he'd done his thing but he'd got himself a reprieve because of his age. Even at this time he was just knocking twenty-one. He was a good-looking boy without his glasses, a bit fey, over six foot. He'd drift around the place looking like the Bad Lord Byron. In fact he was very intelligent. His favourite reading was the Greek tragedies. He was a bit like me, a self-educator. The two of us would have marathon discussions on literature that would irritate the others no end because there was no point of reference for them to use as a jumping-in point. The other thing about him was his conviction that to be any worth he had to be tough and courageous. This was alien to his basic nature but he believed the view of the world he'd absorbed to be true and so he was always in conflict with himself. Apparently it had led him to his second killing: he'd been insulted by his prospective victim and he couldn't stand the idea of himself not being up to the rules and so rather than cop out he'd gone down for another dose of life.

The other newcomer was Jimmy Gearing. We called him Karate, because that's how he'd killed his one. Or so he said in court. Personally I had my doubts. He was an exaggerator. He was one of those guys who are so unsure of themselves, of their acceptability, they just run off at the mouth with stuff about how they've done this and how they've done that and what they're going to do next and the irony is that they become a pain in about one minute flat whereas if they kept their mouths shut for maybe half an hour then at least they wouldn't be left sitting all on their own. Karate would also get extremely excited at any mention of sex or any number of subjects he was allergic to. After a week or so of his presence I began to think the proper nickname for him should have been Lonely.

So being so short-handed, we virtually had the run of the entire wing. We were unlocked at seven in the morning and we didn't have to go away to our cells again till nine in the evening.

All our meals were in association. Within the prescribed limits, we virtually ordered our own lives. There was strictly no ordering about for the sake of it. For instance, Ray and I did the cleaning. Originally this had been done by short-timers. Though there was less work, there only being two of us, Ray and I used to tear into it for about two hours every morning, sweat flowing off us. This way we got more leisure. The screws hated to see it but we now worked unsupervised so they had to lump it.

The rest of them worked in the new wrought-iron shop. That wasn't the only new innovation. There was a new exercise pen, big enough to play football in, and we also got Creasey to organise some tennis gear.

Sometimes in the evenings we'd have lecturers from the local university to give us talks and twice a week the cook gave us cooking classes which was really just an excuse to have a decent meal. The other evening activity was weight-lifting, along with telly-watching, and as we'd got the run of the two TV rooms there was no arguing as to what went on.

Life droned on like this for a little while until I'd decided who to pull as far as making one was concerned. Karate and Atkin were right out. Ray had once been on Walter's firm. At Ray's trial the Filth had offered Ray a trade: although Walter was already inside, they'd told Ray that if he'd give them some more stuff on Walter's operations they'd leave out the bird. Ray had turned it down and he'd got a ten. I'm not saying you deserve anything for not being a grass but even Walter had been moved to offer him a business when he got out. Although at this time Ray wasn't very pally with Walter, I wasn't going to risk pulling in someone who had a present coming from Walter, and apart from Terry whom I couldn't quite suss, that left Tommy. So one day I dropped by his cell.

He was lying on his pit staring up at the ceiling. I sat down on his chair. Neither of us said anything for a while. I took out a couple of snouts and gave one to Tommy and lit us both up and he grunted but that was all. We just stayed as we were, smoking.

'I don't know about you, Tommy,' I said eventually, 'one big happy family it may be at the moment, but I've a feeling the novelty might wear off during the next twenty odd years or so.'

Tommy didn't say anything. The thought flashed across my mind that Walter might have put him in it about the possibility of me approaching him and offered Tommy a little present as well.

'Or is it the time off for good behaviour you're thinking of?' I said.

Tommy smiled.

'Sure, Billy,' he said. 'I don't mind sitting here for fifteen years instead of twenty. There's a big difference, isn't there?'

I smiled and said nothing. After a time Tommy said:

'I'll tell you, Billy. There's only one thing I think about while I'm awake and that's the top of that wall. And when I'm not awake I dream about it.'

I didn't say anything.

'I'm thirty-one, Billy,' Tommy said. 'As far as I'm concerned there's no alternative.'

I didn't want to break the unwritten law by asking him point blank if he'd got any plans; there'd been times when a con had told another con an idea and he'd been beaten to the line. So instead I said: 'Walter's of that frame of mind, too.'

'I thought he might be,' Tommy said. 'Mind you, with him you've got to be a fucking mind-reader.'

'Right,' I said. 'He doesn't put much about.'

Tommy's hamster took a few more turns on its wheel.

So we were both agreed about Walter.

'All I was thinking,' I said, 'was that if either of us were in the running for making one, and it coincided with somebody else, or something like that...'

'I know,' said Tommy. 'You've got to know the form, but there aren't all that many people you can bank on to give you fair odds. So you tend to try and make it sans assistance.'

'That's right,' I said.

There was a silence.

'Course,' he said, 'there are times when you can't do it all on your own.'

I nodded.

'Tell me, Billy,' he said. 'You're a deep thinker. Where would you say you got the most privacy in this wing. Apart from after nine o'clock in the evening, I mean.'

There was only one place in the wing where you could work at making one and that was in the shower room.

The shower room was down on the Ones on the inside corner of the L. There were four stalls on the right hand side as you went in, a tin locker, and a long wooden gymnasium bench and a couple of standard cell issue tables. There was a big window to the left of the door about three foot wide, six foot high and six foot off the ground that faced out into the exercise yard. The window was barred and meshed and wired up to the control room. Apart from this window there was no other ventilation in the shower room and the window would steam up solid and even if the door was open, looking into the shower room from the doorway all you could see were fleshy muzzy blobs walking about. So as far as privacy was concerned the shower room was wide open. But the floor was concrete and the walls were built of three inch stone blocks so they were out too.

But for the sake of the discussion I said: 'Well, obviously, the shower room. But beyond that feature, there's nothing else going for it.'

Tommy sat up and swung his legs over the side of his pit and stood up.

'I want to show you something,' he said, and walked out of the cell.

I hurried after him. We walked down to the shower room in silence.

The shower room was empty except for Strachey. He was sitting on the gymnasium bench reading *Playhour*.

'It's time for "Jackanory", Strachey,' Tommy said.

Strachey wobbled his monstrous head in our direction.

'Out,' said Tommy.

Strachey got to his feet like an over-seventy and dragged himself out of the shower room. When he'd gone Tommy pointed to the corner nearest to the door on the left hand side as you came in. The window to the left of the door was three foot away from the corner. But instead of the wall following on to make a natural corner with the side wall, it cut across the corner forming a diagonal.

'Billy,' Tommy said, 'have a look at this bit of wall here and tell me if you think there's anything unusual about it?'

Tommy liked the dialectical approach to things.

I shrugged.

'Not really,' I said. 'Just a bit of brickwork.'

'Billy,' he said, 'they never do anything in the nick without a reason, no matter how fucking stupid. That corner's been cut off for a reason.'

'Maybe,' I said.

'Bet your fucking life, man. It's either an old chimney or a ventilation shaft that's been bricked off.'

'Could be.'

'It's the same all the way up the Twos and Threes. Must be on the Fours as well. It's got to be. We ought to probe it and see what we get.'

'But Tommy,' I said, 'right here in the middle of the wing it won't get us anywhere.'

'I know, but it might *take* us somewhere. Supposing we could get down into the cellars. Maybe we could find a weakness there. Or maybe we could crawl right up it and come out on the roof. You never know, Billy.'

Tommy looked at me and I looked at the corner.

'What else have we got?' Tommy said.

I nodded my head.

'Sweet fuck all,' Tommy said.

'If we have a crack,' I said, 'just you and me, right? Nobody else.'

'Right.'

'Especially no Wally.'

'Right.'

We both looked at the corner again.

*I lie on my bed, staring at the blackness above me. I can't sleep. I am sick of the remand home. I am sick of being treated like a kid. The whole place is full of kids. My shop breaking offences are rather heady stuff to them. I am the man. Small boys vie with each other to eat my cabbage, which it is forbidden not to finish up. They are just kids and the place is a bore. I must get away. When I'm sentenced I want to go to prison with my mates. I don't want to be the odd one out because of my age. Escaping from the remand home will put me in line for a sentence. I want to take what they take.*

*The next day I escape and make it back to London. I phone my mother and let her think she's persuaded me to give myself up.*

*But when we go for trial, I only get BT. The others have already done their borstal. They get exemplary sentences of five years each. But when I come out again, I'm a bigger man in my field than before.*

*Which is the important thing.*

The next day the wing got an additional member. We could really have very well done without him. A real mad-head called

111

Jerry Chimers. A mug. A half-cocked chancer who'd translated himself into a gangster by pumping off a shotgun in a Saturday night pub just to get even for a well-deserved duffing. He'd got a fifteen and was very proud of it. He expanded quickly in the wing's new permissive atmosphere and on the first day he was walking around in his pressed tie and his sharp grey suit stirring off the screws like a veteran. The next day the suit and tie disappeared. He went off like clockwork about it but it served him fucking well right. The one consolation was that he and Karate were made for each other. That was smashing news for the rest of us.

So Tommy and I gave Chimers a day or two to flex himself before we had a proper go at the diagonal wall.

We timed it so we took our shower after all the others.

We took a small metal peg off the weight-lifting stands and began to chip away at the plaster to find the edge of a brick. Tommy was the chipper, I was the minder. I'd pull the bench out slightly from the diagonal and sit down. This gave me a good view of where the screws congregated on the bottom landing. Tommy would crouch behind me and the bench and I'd warn him if anyone started for the shower room. The diagonal we were working at was at too fine an angle to be seen from outside even if the steam hadn't obscured it. If the screws did want to check on us or deliver a message they would just stick their heads round the door. They didn't want to come into the wet steaming shower room in their bulled-up uniforms. When we finished a chipping stint we just pushed back the bench and that covered up where we'd been working. The screws on their rounds only checked the window and the outside wall. As far as they were concerned nobody in their right mind would try and make one where we were working.

It took us two days to chip the plaster away. Then another five days to get through all the cemented sides of the first brick. The trouble was the diagonal was two bricks thick. It was going to take quite some time. But we had plenty of that and we were on our way. We didn't care how long it took.

*The party is hot and loud and alcohol stinks out the small room. There is no room to jive but people are jiving anyway, clouting into the drinkers. I am standing by the fire-place, holding my glass to my chest, waiting for someone to bump into me. The whisky is pushing sweat out of my face and my stomach is tight with aggression. Across the room I notice two birds talking together, looking at me. I know one of them, Eileen Austen. She's talking into the other one's ear, grinning. The other one has auburn hair and a clever face, a self-rater. Eileen Austen begins to forge her way through the mob, grinning ever wider. The aggressive muscles relax a little and there is a shaft of excitement in my chest because this is the best part, the chatting, the recognition, the reinforcement of my feelings about myself. Later, she'll just be any other bird, a release mechanism; someone I'll resent giving it to, and I'll dislike myself for being weak.*

*Eileen makes the introductions. This is Sheila. Sheila Moss. I've told her all about you, the stupid cow says. But at the same time I'm glad she has. She'll know she's not talking to just anybody. She tries to show she couldn't care less, but I know. Later I walk her home, via Lowther Street and its shell houses. She's good but otherwise she's just like the rest. Afterwards wanting to hold hands, snuggle up, wanting me to ask if I can see her again. Her attitude is totally different to what it was before. Now she's behaving as if I'm somebody.*

Terry used to watch this boating programme on Sunday afternoons and there was this bird who used to cavort all over the place in her shorts and Terry used to drool all over the telly when she was on. One afternoon when we were all in there Ray said to Terry. 'If you fancy her so bleeding strong, why don't you drop her a line?'

'Do leave off,' Terry said.

'No, straight up. She might just write back. Might even send you a photo.'

'You must be joking,' said Terry. 'Do me a favour.'

Walter seized the opportunity to come the old magnanimous bit.

'Listen, my son,' he said to Terry, 'I know a bird you can write to. She's a stripper up West. Candy her name is. A right good girl she is. You write to her and tell her you met her with me and Les one night and she'd write back. With a bit of luck she might even come and see you. On my life, a right good girl.'

'Leave it out, Wally, will you,' Terry said. 'I can do my own snatching.'

This gave Tommy and me the idea to cook one up for Walter. We persuaded Terry to write a letter to this Candy, then we showed it to Walter. Walter almost creamed himself. The benefactor at work. After Walter had read the letter I pretended to go off and post it. About a week later, while we were getting our grub, Tommy and I waited for Walter to come by.

'Here, Wally,' Tommy said, 'that bird of yours wrote back to Terry.'

'She ain't,' said Wally.

'Yeah', I said, 'she sent him a load of nude photos.'

Wally's old eyes lit up.

'He hasn't half had a ruck to get them they're so strong,' Tommy said. 'Only the rat won't bleeding well show us.'

'I saw the PO looking at them in his office, Wally,' I said. 'It was coming out of his eyes.'

Terry timed it just right. He walked past us carrying a big envelope we'd buzzed from the office. He walked along the Twos and into his cell and then he came out again without the envelope and shut the door.

Wally did a real old fashioned double-take. Terry got his grub and we all went into the Twos TV room to eat.

After a while Walter said to Terry:

'Get a letter from Candy, then, did you, my old son?'

Terry didn't look up from his grub.

'That's right,' he said.

'Sent you some pictures, has she?'

Terry nodded and carried on eating.

'Don't we get a look, then?' I said.

'I've already told you,' Terry said. 'No.'

'Nice sort of bleeding chap you are,' Tommy said.

'Tommy,' said Terry, 'do you let me read your letters?'

'Terry,' I said, 'all we want to do is look at the photos.'

'Billy, if your bird sent you some nude photos would you show them to me?'

Then wily old Wally came in again now he thought he could see which way the wind was blowing.

'If Terry don't want to show them to you then that's up to him, isn't it?' he said. 'I mean, it's Terry's privilege.'

'Thanks, Wally,' Terry said.

'I told you she was a good girl,' Walter said. 'She'll visit you if you play your cards right. You keep her sweet, son.'

Terry gave us the pay-off later. Apparently Walter had sidled up to him in the shop later that afternoon when nobody was about and said:

'Terry, I'm right pleased for you about Candy. It's always nice to have someone to write to.'

'You're right there, Wally,' Terry had said. 'I really appreciate what you did.'

'Forget it. Glad to oblige.'

'If there's anything I can do...'

'Well... seeing as I sort of set it up, like... how about letting us have a skerry at the photos?'

Terry had gone all hurt.

'Wally,' he'd said, 'why are you any different from the others?'

'Well, I'm not, but, I mean…'

'I can't let you see them and not the others.'

'Don't be silly, Terry. I shan't let them know.'

Terry had shaken his head.

'Terry, I'm your pal. I told you to write to her in the first place.'

'I know that, Walter, but that wouldn't make it right.'

Walter had gone on at Terry for days like this until he finally twigged it. When he finally twigged it I thought he was going to turn himself inside out. He was speechless for a week. But at least his preoccupation had kept him out of mine and Tommy's business for a while.

*From the yard, I check out the back of the shop. There are no signs of Law, but I know I'm taking a chance. I haven't much choice. The only way to find out how things are is to go in.*

*I cross the yard and try the stockroom door. It's open. The smell of cardboard boxes is released and immediately I think of my father.*

*I close the door behind me and listen. Upstairs there is the muffled sound of the radio. A floorboard creaks. I walk over to the door that opens into the shop and turn the handle. The shop is empty. Dust everywhere. Half stocked. Shabby.*

*I climb the stairs. My mother is in the lounge, half-asleep, sitting by the radio. I walk over to her and tap her on the shoulder. She looks up. For a moment her face is blank. Then she starts to rise from her chair and I help her up.*

*After the tears comes the spiel.*

*'Why, Billy? Why? With only two months left?'*

*I let go of her and move away.*

*'You could have been out in two months. Home.'*

*'I wanted to be out now.'*

*I light a cigarette.*

*'You'll have it to do all over again. And then what will we do,*

me and Linda? We were banking on it, Billy, you coming back. It's too much for us.'

I look down into the street; why the fuck doesn't she shut up. Can't she see I don't want this? If she'd just be quiet, stop asking, maybe I'd help.

'Especially now, the way Linda is. She's always looked to you, Billy, even when your Dad was with us. She needs you here. And so do I.'

The tears start again.

'I am here, aren't I?' I say, because I can't think of anything else.

My mother gives me one of her looks.

'Anyway,' I say, 'what's this about Linda? What's she up to?'

'Billy, I don't dare think. I've heard things, secondhand, but she won't tell me anything herself.'

'What things?'

'I think she might be taking drugs.'

'Drugs?'

'Well, not real drugs. Pills. I don't know what they are. You'll know better than me.'

'Since when?'

'I don't know. All I know is she's changed. Knocking about with all sorts. She never even talks to me.'

'Where is she now?'

'In bed.'

'In bed?'

'She didn't come in till after I'd opened the shop. She's been out since yesterday dinnertime.'

'Go and wake her up. Tell her I want to talk to her.'

'She won't listen.'

'Then why did you keep writing me she needed me? Christ, mother, make up your flaming mind.'

'It won't do any good. I know.'

But nevertheless she goes into Linda's bedroom and rouses

*her. I hear their arguing voices and I face the window and try and fill my mind with the noise of the traffic so that I don't have to listen to them.*

*Eventually my mother comes back into the room.*

*'I can't talk to her. She says she doesn't want to see you.'*

*But even as my mother is speaking Linda walks through the lounge and into the kitchen and begins to make herself a cup of coffee.*

*I walk through into the kitchen.*

*'What's the matter with you, then?' I say to her.*

*She ignores me and concentrates on putting coffee into the coffee cup.*

*'I mean, you haven't seen me for fourteen months. Isn't there anything you want to say?'*

*'Like what?'*

*She doesn't look at me when she speaks.*

*'I thought maybe you'd be pleased to see me.'*

*'Are you pleased to see me?'*

*She takes a sip of coffee and swears as it scalds her lips.*

*'Linda,' I say, 'I'd like a talk.'*

*'Would you?' She begins to walk back to her bedroom. 'Well, I wouldn't. I haven't time. I'm going out.'*

*I stand in front of her, blocking her way.*

*'Linda –'*

*'Will you shift yourself? I'll be late.'*

*I turn to my mother and as I turn Linda goes into her bedroom and slams the door.*

*I shrug my shoulders.*

*'Well, there you are,' I say. 'What's the point. She obviously couldn't care less about what I have to say.'*

Tommy's hamster was very helpful.

We managed about three quarters of an hour a day on the wall. But the longer we went on the bigger the workings got and soon it wasn't enough for us to push back the bench in order to obscure the chiselling. The presence of the hamster came in handy because of the adventure playground Tommy had made for it in his cell. He'd made it out of papier mâché on one of the big three foot by two foot trays that came over from the kitchen. The natural place to keep the papier mâché was in the shower room so that it stayed nice and damp. The bucket had been a permanent fixture in there well before we started on the hole. So when the chiselling began to really show we'd plug the hole with papier mâché. But as we worked round the second brick the dried light grey of the papier mâché began to look a bit sore against the blue of the paintwork. The only thing for us to do was to get hold of some of the same emulsion. And the only way to do this was to approach Ray. In the afternoons, if he got bored, he'd do a bit of painting on permission, re-decorating his cell. I couldn't go to the screws for another load of paint otherwise they'd get suspicious even if they'd no idea of what they were being suspicious of. So there was only Ray. And Ray was no mug. And Walter owed him a business.

I wandered into his cell one afternoon. This particular afternoon he wasn't decorating. He was listening to the football on his headphones. He was a great West Ham supporter and the match he was listening to was West Ham getting beaten at Liverpool. I'd listened to some of it myself earlier. So it wasn't exactly the best moment I could have picked for chatting up Ray. But I couldn't wait for the right moment to arise.

I sat down and waited for Ray to take off his headphones. He sat there on the edge of his pit getting blacker and blacker in the face. Eventually he pulled the headphones off his ears and flung them on his pit.

'Fucking robbers,' he said. 'Bobby'd never bring anybody down in the penalty area.'

'Not unless he had to,' I said. Which was the wrong thing to have said.

'Only if he's provoked,' Ray said. 'Only against a load of fucking heavies like that lot.'

I shrugged. Ray stood up and thrust his hands in his pockets.

'Not decorating today, then?' I said.

'What the fucking hell for?'

I didn't answer. Ray sat down again.

'I was just wondering,' I said, 'whether you had any blue to spare.'

Ray looked at me.

'What for?'

'I thought I'd paint the mirror in my cell.'

There was a silence. Eventually Ray said:

'Billy, don't take me for a fucking mug.'

'How do you mean, Ray?' I said, fishing for my cigarettes.

'You must think I'm bleeding thick.'

'I don't get you.'

Ray stood up again.

'Do you think I haven't noticed all the secret service confabs you and Tommy've been having? Do you think I haven't noticed all the fucking showering? You've blotted me out, you bastard. And you thought I was too fucking thick to rumble. You've got one and it's just you and Tommy, you cunt.'

I lit my cigarette. Ray stood there watching me, waiting for me to speak, protest, say something. But I just lit up my cigarette and threw the match on the floor and took the small jar I'd brought with me out of my pocket and put it on the table.

'I just want some paint, Ray,' I said. 'Just a little bit of blue.'

'What did you think, Billy?' he said. 'That I'd grass?'

'Do I get the paint?' I said.

'What's the story, Billy?'

'No story,' I said. 'I just want a bit of blue to paint up my mirror.'

Ray looked at me for a while.

'All right,' he said. 'Suit your fucking self. All I hope is you come up in the Governor's office.'

'Don't hope too hard,' I said.

Ray gave me the paint and I went to see Tommy and told him about Ray.

'Fuck it,' Tommy said. 'I knew it was going too sweet.'

'All we can do is carry on,' I said.

'Maybe we should have put him in it,' Tommy said. 'Maybe we still can.'

I shook my head.

'If he's going to tell Walter he'll tell him whether we put him in it or not. Ray's been slighted.'

'Do you think he will tell Walter?'

'I don't know. I know Ray's no Walter lover, but then he feels similar about us now he knows he's not been took on.'

But three weeks passed and there was no noise from Walter. In that time Tommy and I had got our first brick out. After that we took a couple more out either side to expose all the sides of a brick in the second line of brick work. And when we got the first back brick out, a faint swish of cool air drifted out of the hole. This was the most exciting moment of the entire operation. Just to smell that fresh air.

What we'd got was a chimney. All sooted up and narrow, but a chimney, and it led somewhere.

Now we concentrated on the back layer of bricks. It was nothing now to get two bricks out in one session and within another week we'd cut back the second layer of bricks well beyond the facing opening, which we wanted to keep as small as possible till the last moment. You could get your arm in now and feel all the soot and rubble at the bottom of the shaft, but even with your arm right in and holding the nine inch home-made chisel, you couldn't feel any solid bottom. We started to scoop the soot out and wash it away down the showers outflow but we needed somewhere to throw the stones and bits of bricks at the bottom of the shaft that were stopping us locating the flow of air. The bricks from the wall itself were piling up and we had no choice but to put them back in the hole which slowed everything taking them out and putting them back every session. The actual opening required only eight bricks. We'd fit them back in and wedge up with socks, then papier mâché over to level with the plaster which we'd then paint with thin emulsion. The end result looked like a piece of wall carrying the sort of fungus that plaster sometimes gets in a damp atmosphere. The screws never gave it a second look. Everything was chugging along just right. Then Walter made his move.

I got it through Tommy. He came into my cell from the shop and said: 'Walter's just asked me if I'd like to make one.'

'And you said?'

'I said: "Dunno, Wally. Where from?" I said.'

'Yeah?'

'And he said "Digging out from the shower". So I said "Leave off, Wally. Where can you dig out from in the shower?" And he said "Through the wall by the window." So I said, "What, through three inches of granite? What are you going to use to get through that?" And he said "We're making a right good tool, Tommy. A right good tool." So anyway, I told him no, leave me out. And I came back here to tell you.'

'That bastard,' I said. 'I knew he'd be in, sooner or later.'

'So what do you think?'

'What about?'

'About him making one in the same place?'

'Talk. Just silly Walter-talk. He's just trying to stir us up a little bit. If he started one there he'd only do it to get us nicked and he daren't do that. He'll try and scotch us, but that bit's just silly Walter-talk.'

But Walter is not silly. The next day Tommy saw Gearing making the tool in the machine shop. Apart from anything else, Tommy was interested to see how Walter intended getting the tool out of the shop past the metal detector. What Walter did was to put the tool in his vacuum flask. While they lined up waiting to be searched, Walter waited until it was almost his turn and handed the flask to Terry while Walter made a performance of getting his cigarettes out and lighting up, dragging out the performance so that Walter was about to be searched while Terry was still innocently holding the flask. But Tommy had been watching Walter's behaviour all morning like his life depended on it and so he said to Terry: 'Don't take it, Terry. Give it back to the cunt.'

Terry took one look at Tommy's face then he looked at the flask then tried to pass it back to Walter but Walter scuttled up to the screw to be searched and so Terry could do nothing. So Tommy discreetly took the flask from Terry and gave it to Gearing. Gearing was dropped on. According to Tommy, Gearing looked as though he was going to hurl the flask and run off screaming but Tommy said to him: 'Take it out as a favour to Billy, eh, mate?'

That had made Gearing swallow it. But he was lucky. He put the flask on the floor while he was searched and that way he beat both the metal detector and the screw.

Back in the wing, Terry did his pieces.

'You cunt, Wally, you nearly fucking did me, you bleeding bastard.'

Walter was unperturbed.

'Don't be ridiculous, Terry,' he said. 'Do you think I'd do a thing like that to you?'

'Yes, you cunt, I fucking know you would.'

'Terry, there's nothing in the poxy flask. Have a look. See?'

Walter showed him the flask which by now, of course, was empty. Terry carried on swearing at Walter but in the end there was nothing he could do but swallow. Unless there's a bible handy you don't stand much chance of winning an argument with Walter.

The next day Tommy came screaming into my cell. He was almost crying with rage and frustration.

'That dirty slag is trying to get us nicked,' he said.

'What's happening?'

'The bastard's only prised a lump out of the shower room wall near where we're working.'

I couldn't speak. My chest felt as if steel hawsers were tightening round it. I just got off my pit and went straight upstairs to Walter's cell, Tommy right behind me.

Walter was lying on his pit facing the door. Gearing was sitting on a chair by the wall.

'Walter,' I said, holding it all back, 'you digging a hole in the showers?'

Walter looked at me for a moment. He assumed an expression of mild interest.

'Yeah,' he said. 'That's right, Billy.'

Tommy couldn't contain himself.

'You know you can't dig out there, Walter,' he said. 'You know you can't. You're not even on the outside wall.'

Walter raised himself up on his elbows.

'Oh yeah,' he said. 'Is that right? Well, just so's you know, we're going to branch left when we get in a little way. And in any case, what are you so excited about? I can dig out without you sticking it in, can't I?'

'Wally,' I said, 'you know we were working in there. Don't take us for a pair of cunts.'

'I don't know nothing about you wankers.'

'Look, just leave it out,' I said. 'After we've had our pop you can have yours. We started first.'

'So why didn't you put us in it? We'd have put you in. I already asked Tommy if he'd like to make one and he said No.' Now Walter was sitting up, waving his arms about all over the place. 'What is it with you people? I'm in here as well, aren't I?'

'That's a load of ballocks, Walter,' I said. 'You're just being fucking crafty. You just leave it out.'

'I'm not leaving it out, son,' he said. 'You can dig your hole and we'll dig ours, won't we, Jackie?'

Gearing didn't look at him. He just stared at the bed, impassive.

'All right, Walter,' I said. 'Let's stop playing. If you don't leave it out I'll break your jaw.'

I gave him the whole bit, right down to the wagging finger. Walter stood up.

'You'd better do it now, then,' he said.

'I'm warning you, Wally.'

'Don't warn me. Do it.'

We were like two kids in a playground. Except we were both acting. I was trying to frighten him and he was trying to blackmail me and I wasn't going behind my door for forty days on account of Walter, not now.

'All right,' I said. 'Down to the TV room. On our own.'

If you pull people on their own they often swallow it, whereas in front of people they're brave because they don't want to lose face. Or in the nick, if there's a screw near by, they rely on it getting broken up before they get hurt.

We walked out of the cell together. A screw on the landing saw what was in the wind, and he watched with interest as we walked into the TV room. Strachey was watching 'Watch with Mother'. He took one look at the pair of us and stood up and left.

I turned to face Walter.

'Walter,' I said, 'I know exactly what you're doing. You're grassing me. You're blackmailing me so's I'll put you in.'

'I'm not grassing you. How am I doing that? I just want to get out of this karsi, just like you. Do you think I want to spend the next twenty stretch listening to those cunts?'

'But you're grassing me, Wally, you're digging a hole that's got to get tumbled, and they'll rip the place apart, and you know it.'

The sound of despair was creeping into my anger.

'Look, Billy, what are we arguing for? This is fucking silly. All I want is a chance, just like you. We can blot that other mug out. Just put me in.'

'Watch with Mother' was still blasting out and Walter's wheedling was getting me dead choked.

'Listen, you cunt, you've had something on the boil for you since God knows when and you'd never put me in that, would you? And that one won't involve digging through walls, will it? Just the best plan your money'll buy you.'

'I don't know what you're on about.'

'No, that's right, Walter.'

'You're out of your skull.'

'I won't let you do it to me, Walter. I've told you, I'll put it on you first.'

'For Christ's sake, do it, then.'

I pushed him with my left forearm. He pushed back at me with his chest. He was strong, even though he was small.

'Go on then. Do it, Billy.'

Walter was pretty sure I wasn't going to hit him, but he wasn't too fond of the tension while he waited to see if he was right or not. I pushed him again and shifted my weight as if I was going to throw one just so as he'd suffer a bit more. Walter was one of those people who defend against fear by going rigid. He made no move to protect himself. The only things about Wally's person that were moving were his nostrils due to his heavy breathing.

Suddenly I got sick of the whole bleeding scene.

'I'm not going to hit you, you ponce,' I said. 'And you fucking know it.'

I opened the door and walked out. The screw was leaning

over the opposite railing, staring avidly at the door. I went straight down on to the Twos and into my cell and sat down on my bed. Fucking Walter. He'd won this one. I should have put it on him. Sod going behind my door. At least I would have got some satisfaction out of it.

A few minutes later Tommy came in.

'What happened?' he said.

'The bastard's got us by the cods. There was nothing I could do.'

'So what happens?'

'We've got no choice but to put him in.'

'Gearing as well?'

'Yes.'

'Fucking bloody hell.'

'Yes, Tommy, but neither of them are going.'

'How do you mean?'

'We'll fuck Walter at his own game.'

'But how?'

'I don't know. But the dirty slag isn't going to ruin this one. We'll think of something.'

*I'm sitting in the Black Boy talking to Harry Fleming about this job we're on in a couple of days' time when Walter Colman and the people who walk behind him sweep in, trying their collective hardest to look like characters out of* New York Confidential. *Everybody in the pub starts the arse-licking bit because Walter and his cousins are the men around town. I carry on talking about the job to Harry but Harry isn't listening. He's sitting there trying to catch Walter's eye so he can give Walter a big friendly smile.*

*When Walter's finally sat down and his minions have arranged the drinks and themselves round him, Harry manages it. Walter, in return, gives him an old-pals-in-the-know nod because it's as important for Walter to have everybody like him* as it is for everybody to be liked by Walter. Everybody, that is, except me.

Walter's eyes flick to me and instead of a nod I get a bit of reflection, a bit of mind-ticking, and a couple of minutes later Walter gets up and wanders over to where we're sitting. Two of the overcoats come with him. Walter sits down but the overcoats remain standing.

'Hello, Billy, Harry,' he says. 'How's things? Keeping ahead, are you?'

'Yeah, fine thanks, Walter,' Harry says. 'And you?'

'Not bad. Not too bad.' Walter offers Harry and me a cigarette. Harry takes one. 'What are you drinking?' asks Walter.

'Vodka tonic, thanks very much, ta,' Harry says.

'Nothing for me,' I say.

'Come on, let me top it up for you.'

'No thanks.'

'Suit yourself.' Walter addresses one of the overcoats. 'Vodka tonic and I'll have a glass of red wine.' Then to me: 'Anyway, why I wanted a word, really, is because I've got this little tickle on, and I think it's something right up your street, Billy.'

'Oh yes.'

'Yeah. Little garage tickle. Four-hander. Only my feller that usually rallies for me's on a three-stretch right now. So I thought, Billy Cracken. The very man. Nice to put a bit of business his way. Nice for me too, knowing how sweet the job'll come off with Billy sorting it.'

I smile and shake my head. Walter all over, this is. He couldn't care less whether or not he put a bit of business my way. And there were a dozen sports he could level at this garage job. And Walter needs the rake-off on six thousand quid like he needs a hole in the head. He just wants to place me, to have me jumping through hoops at the chance of working for Walter Colman. And most important of all he wants to demonstrate to the world at large that Billy Cracken is a Walter-lover, that

*Walter has drawn Billy Cracken into his camp.*

*I shake my head again.*

*'No, not me, Walter,' I say. 'I'm strictly freelance.'*

*Walter masks up.*

*'So's the job,' he says. 'Nothing else. I'm not offering PAYE.'*

*I smile.*

*'Course not, Walter,' I say. 'But thanks, anyway.'*

*Walter stands up. The overcoats are giving me hard glances. At this moment Walter doesn't like anything at all.*

*'Pity, though,' he says. 'I would have thought you'd have fancied the big league for a change.'*

*'I do, Walter,' I say. 'If the big league makes me an offer, I'll accept. Until then, I'll stay freelance.'*

*Walter looks at me for a while, then goes back to his table. He isn't quite frothing at the mouth. The overcoats look at me a little longer, then they too move away.*

The next day I had a word with Ray.

'I suppose you heard about Wally tumbling our business,' I said.

'What business would that be, Billy?'

I grinned.

'Leave it out, Ray,' I said. 'I know what's stirring you up.'

'And so now you're wondering if I put Wally on to it?'

I didn't say anything.

'Listen,' Ray said, 'everybody knows what Wally's promised me because of what I did at the trial. But what I did wasn't because of Wally. It was because of Old Bill. I didn't ask Wally for any fucking favours.'

'I didn't say you did, Ray.'

'Just so long as you don't.'

'I just wondered if you knew when he tumbled?'

'Why?'

I shrugged.

'It was well before you wanted the paint, if that's what you mean.'

'Yes?'

'Wally's no fucking mug, you know. He sniffed it all himself.'

'And he told you he sniffed it?'

'That's right.'

'But you didn't bother to tell Tommy and me.'

'Why the fuck should I?'

'Well now you know why we didn't put you in.'

'If you had have done you'd have known about Wally three weeks ago.'

'All right,' I said. 'So I was wrong. So it's all blown now, what's the difference? Tommy and I were going to pull you eventually, anyway.'

'After you'd made sure I wasn't Walter's man.'

'No,' I said. 'Once we got started. Too many at the beginning was unnecessary. Why take the chance of the screws wondering why there's always a gang of us in the shower. Now we've *got* to take a chance. There's too much stuff to get rid of just on our own.'

'And now you need me.'

'That's right.'

'And who else?'

'Everybody except Karate and Strachey.'

'Walter?'

'That's right.'

'He's really fucked you, hasn't he?'

'That's right. Are you in or not?'

'Of course I'm in. Not because of you. Because I want to get out of this shit-hole.'

'That's all right then. I'll put you in it in the TV room tonight.'

The problem was to dispose of the rubble at the bottom of the hole. That night we scooped up all the loose small stuff and put it in a two gallon tin can that was used to carry anything

liquid from the kitchen to the wing. Then we carried it up to
the TV room and put it in the corner to the right of the door.
The screws seldom came into the TV room, but we kept the
lights off and Tommy worked from the glow of the TV set,
while the rest of us sat there watching the box with one eye
on the landing. Tommy had got a stack of newspapers which
he used to wrap up little parcels of rubble, the idea being to go
to any of the three toilets on the different landings, push the
parcels one at a time past the bend in the pipe and flush them
away. Tommy gave us strict instructions, one flush of the toilet
for each little joey of stones, and only to put one joey down at
a time.

The only risk so far was Karate, who was in the TV room
while Tommy was twisting the newspaper round the rubble.
He knew something was going on but he took his cue from the
silence of everybody else and decided it would be safer for him
not to ask.

Walter was sitting in the chair next to me while Tommy was
doing his stuff with the bundles. At one point he leant over to
me and spoke to me as though the events of the previous day
had never happened.

'Billy,' he said, 'have you fixed anything up for when you get
out?'

I didn't say anything.

'Because I was going to say,' he said, 'I'll see you all right for
dough. I mean, if you like, you can come to South Africa with
me.'

'South Africa, Wally?' I said. 'You've made some plans
yourself, then.'

Walter became all modest.

'Well, you know, a few,' he said.

'Yes I bet you fucking have, Walter. All I wonder is why you
made the bastards. To fit this one or the one you've had cooking
since before I came here?'

131

'I don't know what you're talking about.'

'Of course you don't,' I said.

'Now look...'

I smiled at him.

'Walter,' I said, 'we both know you've had this up your sleeve for yonks. We both know how you got on to this firm. We both know you blackmailed your way in. So don't let's play make-believe and pretend we're pals. Just let's get on with the job in hand and hope that none of us gets our balls broken in the process.'

Walter shut up and I went back to watching the television.

When Tommy had finished he handed us each some parcels. First one to go was Terry. He went down on to the Ones and came back all smiles.

'Went down a treat,' he said.

After a while Tommy took his parcels up to the toilet on the Threes. When he came back it was clear that his had gone down as well as Terry's.

Then it was Walter's turn. He chose the toilet next to the TV room. I could hear the toilet flush even with the box booming out. There was a second flush. A screw walked past the door in the direction of the recess. A third flush. Then I heard the screw say: 'Been flooded out then, Wally?'

Tommy and I looked at each other.

'The cunt,' said Tommy.

Tommy and I shot out on to the landing. The screw had carried on past the recess. Water was flowing out on to the landing, bits of grit and stone awash on the floor. Walter was standing there looking all sheepish. Ray and I kept our cleaning things in the recess so I grabbed some floor cloths and threw them down over the worst bits. Tommy checked that the screw wasn't on his way back and then he got down on the floor with me and we tore into cleaning up the mess. Walter stood over us, hopping about like a pregnant kangaroo.

132

'Christ,' he said, 'that bleeding screw nearly had me.'

'Nearly had *you*!' Tommy said, furious. 'Nearly had the lot of us, you cunt. I must have told you six times to do them one at a time and you go straight out and do the opposite.'

'Well, I'm sorry, Tommy,' he said. 'I knew the screw was around and I thought that if I kept flushing the karsi then he might tumble something was wrong so I tried them all at once.'

'You cunt,' I said, emptying the contents of the cloth down the toilet. 'Why couldn't you have fucking well waited?'

'Well, I suppose I could have, but...'

I stood up and grasped him by the collar.

'Of course you fucking could have,' I said. 'But you didn't bleeding well want to, did you?'

'Come off, Billy, what are you trying to make out?'

I pushed him against the wall.

'If you get us nicked, Wally, you'd better move upstairs with the monsters. Because if you don't you'll wish you never lived.'

Tommy pulled me away from him.

'Leave it, Billy,' he said. 'If you're not careful, *you'll* get us nicked.'

I backed off.

'I don't know what the bleeder's talking about,' Walter said. 'I just thought I was doing the right thing in the circumstances.'

As opposed to the rubble, the bricks were a different problem altogether. We were soaking up a lot of our time getting them out of the hole to get at the bottom and putting them all back when we'd finished. So we racked our brains to think of a way of getting rid of them for good. But the prison authorities themselves gave us the answer; they were installing a new heating system, laying the pipes underground. And the ground where they were laying them was directly beneath our cell windows. There were piles of dirt and rubble out there. All we had to do was to wait until dark and throw our humble offerings out of the window and on to the tips. We couldn't use the two gallon container again because it would have meant the container laying about in one of our cells overnight. It had to be something that could easily be explained away. So we came up with the idea of using Strachey's tea can. Topping up the tea urn was one of the jobs Strachey had commandeered for himself. He kept the empty tea can handy to fetch the water from the tap to the urn. Strachey never used it in the evening because he always went behind his door after the children's television programmes had finished. So at six o'clock I took the can up to the shower room and filled it up with some of the bricks and put the lid back on and got Ray to take it back down to the kitchen and leave it on the table for me to pick up later. The screws were used to cons carrying tea cans back and forth and it was safer to leave the can on the kitchen table than keep it with us in the shower room; no screw was going to lift the lid of a tea can in the hope of sniffing something.

So when I'd finished my work in the shower I went downstairs to the kitchen to collect the can. But when I got in there Strachey was standing by the kitchen table. He was holding the lid of the tea can in his hand and looking at the bricks inside.

I nearly macaronied on the spot.

He must have sensed me standing there. He turned his great head towards me. There were tears in his eyes.

'Billy,' he said to me, 'someone put some bricks in my tea can. Now I can't fill the urn.'

I rushed over and took the lid off him and slammed it back on the can.

'Don't worry, Alan,' I said. 'I'll fill it up for you later. Now you go off to bed.'

'But it's got to be filled up,' he said. 'I always fill it up every day at three o'clock. But the doctor sent for me today so I couldn't do it.' More tears welled out of his eyes. 'And now I haven't got a can because somebody's put bricks in it.'

Fuck the poxy can, I thought. It only needed a screw to walk in now and hear what Strachey was saying.

'Look, Alan,' I said, 'go upstairs. I've told you I'll fill the tea urn. And I'll make sure there's a can for you in future, I promise you. Now off you go.'

'But who put the bricks in there?'

'Never mind about that. Just do as you're told.'

He went but he didn't like it. I went to my cell where Tommy was waiting for me.

'Christ, what's the matter with you?' he said when he saw me.

I told him about Strachey. All Tommy did was to laugh.

'Hell, don't worry about Strachey,' he said. 'He never talks to screws. Christ I wondered what was up when I saw your face. I thought the world was coming to an end.'

'Well, it isn't funny, is it?'

'It was just seeing your boat, that's all.'

When Tommy had finished enjoying himself he minded at my door while I stuffed the bricks out of the window on to the rubble and thought what one great fucking pantomime the whole thing was turning out to be.

We cleared the dust and the really small rubble from the bottom of the hole by filling up plastic bags with water from the shower and emptying it down the hole.

The breeze blew stronger after that.

Tommy did a good nine-tenths of the digging. He really slaved away at it. Walter and Gearing only helped with the little things that had to be done every time we went to work; minding, handling the bricks, giving Tommy the tools he wanted. The hole in front was now wide enough for Tommy to get his head and shoulders right inside so that he could dig two-handed. Soon he'd located the hole where the breeze was coming from. He could push a digger down it and not meet with any obstructions. Whether that meant it was a narrow duct or an opening into a space we couldn't tell.

The opening was to the left and about three foot down running at a forty-five degree angle. So that Tommy could work on it properly we had to remove a lot more of the inside bricks in the shaft which we didn't mind doing because it just made it that little bit wider for when a man actually had to go down there.

But Tommy working head and shoulders in like this had its disadvantages. Though we were still working the lookout system, it would have been impossible for Tommy to get out of the hole before whoever it was came through the door. This used to worry me and I wouldn't let Tommy stay in there too long at a time. I didn't like Wally or Gearing minding, either. They were too careless. So I did as much minding myself as I possibly could.

Even so, one dinner time, it happened.

It was the PO, the one I'd had on the night of the barricades. Kirk his name was.

When I saw him coming I kicked the door to with my foot. I told Tommy to freeze and slammed the bench up against Tommy's legs and the wall, and all the wall bricks stacked in twos beside it. I sat down on the bench, my back smothering the hole. All I had on was my shorts and I was sweating like a pig but it just looked as though I'd had a session with the weights.

The door opened.

'Tommy in here, Billy?' the PO said.

I looked up as though I'd only become aware of him at the sound of his voice. Then I looked round the room, into the steam, as though I'd just been roused out of some personal preoccupation.

'No,' I said, all disinterested. 'No, he isn't here, Mr Kirk.'

Kirk gave me a long look. He didn't care for my answer, or

the way I'd answered. Instead of going out again and yelling for Tommy on the landing, he walked into the steam and looked in all the shower stalls.

I felt the whole thing was falling apart. All over. The whole fucking issue. Because when the PO turned back he was bound to see the hole. There was no alternative. Although my back had masked the hole from someone looking in from the doorway, the hole was visible when looking from the direction of the showers.

I did the only thing I could do, the only thing that had even half a chance of keeping the PO from seeing the hole. I stood up and followed the PO into the steam, leaving Tommy's back and the gaping hole. Tommy must have macaronied his strides seventeen times.

As the PO turned to leave the shower, I was standing a few feet away from him, between the PO and Tommy and the hole. As the PO walked, I walked, keeping myself at a position relative to Tommy and the PO in so far that the PO couldn't see anything even if he'd turned his head because I was close enough to him and positioned well enough to blot out his view. At the same time I kept talking, as if I knew that Tommy was somewhere he shouldn't be elsewhere in the nick and as if I was playing for time.

That made Kirk get a move on.

It was absolutely farcical, the whole scene, me trotting alongside the PO, trying to gauge my position in relation to Tommy. But it worked. The PO reached the door without once even looking to his left. If he had have done and I'd been even slightly out of position, then that would have been it.

The PO walked through the door and I followed him, carrying my towel. I closed the door behind us.

Outside, Walter and Terry had been working at the weights. They must have thought the whole thing was blown sky-high.

'Sir, is it all right if I weigh myself?' I said.

The scales were in the PO's room. The screw was supposed to accompany you in while you got on the scales to prevent you getting anything else besides. I knew Tommy would be out of the hole by now and I had to give him time to sneak out and come to light in the kitchen or the cell to the right of the shower room where the weight-lifting equipment was stored.

The PO said Yes, I could weigh myself, so I walked into his office expecting him to follow. Walter and Terry were still frozen on the landing. The screw didn't follow me. Instead he said to Walter and Terry: 'Seen Dugdale anywhere?'

They shook their heads. Kirk called up to the landings: 'Twos, Threes.'

A couple of screws peered over the landings.

'Dugdale up there?'

'No, sir.'

Kirk stayed where he was, wondering where to look first.

I panicked and went back into the shower. Tommy was standing in the middle of the room like a statue with nowhere to go.

'Jesus,' he said. 'What the fuck do I do now?'

'You can't sneak out, that's for sure. If Kirk doesn't see you, then the others will.'

'Christ.'

I was expecting the all away cry any minute.

'Maybe if I tried to get Kirk away again,' I said.

I wasn't really talking to Tommy. My panic was giving a voice to my thoughts. I went outside and back into the office. Kirk was by the door, shouting to the other screw on the Ones.

'Dugdale, have you seen Dugdale?'

'No, sir.'

'Oh no,' Kirk said. 'No.'

He was in a right state, but not quite as bad as the one I was in. I didn't know what I was doing. I was walking into the office to weigh myself and I'd just supposed to have done that. In any

138

case Kirk hadn't followed me in the first place so why should he follow me now?

Instead he walked back to the shower room and went in.

Walter and Terry hadn't moved. I walked out of the office. They looked at me and I looked at them. This was it. We were nicked. It was all over.

I walked past Walter and Terry and opened the door into the shower room.

There was less steam than before. The hole was an eye-magnet. It must have hit the PO the minute he opened the door. But the PO wasn't standing there looking at it.

He was in the showers, third stall along.

I walked over.

Tommy was jammed up in the corner, a sick discovered look on his face. He was still wearing the overalls he wore to protect his body from the rough edges of the bricks. Standing under a running shower wearing overalls. If that wasn't bad enough there were streaks of soot and dirt all over his face and his overalls.

The PO was between Tommy and me, just standing there, looking at Tommy. For a moment, the urge to chop the PO filled my mind. It wouldn't have done any good, we were finished anyway, but it seemed to be the only thing left for me to do.

Then the PO said: 'You bastard, Tommy. You bloody bastard.'

Tommy stayed where he was, just staring at the PO.

'You bastard,' the PO said again. 'You trying to give me heart failure or something?'

Something began to dawn in the back of my mind.

'I should have realised,' the PO said. 'After the last times.'

The last times. I realised what the PO was saying. A couple of times Tommy had gone missing when there'd been a count. Just to give them a hard time. On each occasion, after turning the nick upside down, the screws had found Tommy sitting in his cell, all innocence, wondering what the bother was about. And now the PO thought the same thing had happened. That Tommy was having one of his games. The PO was so relieved he wasn't even angry. The fact that Tommy was standing under the shower in his overalls didn't seem to register with him.

Tommy cottoned to what the PO meant.

'Fooled you this time, Mr Kirk,' he said, looking all roguish.

'You bastard,' said Kirk.

He turned away and walked past me.

Now he would see the hole.

But he didn't. He just walked out of the shower room, shaking his head from side to side, rubbing his chin as if he was appreciating a very good joke.

The door closed.

Outside, Kirk called to the others.

'It's all right, he was hiding in the showers.'

Tommy and I stared at each other.

The door opened. Walter and Terry came in. Nobody spoke. The shower sizzled on.

Eventually Tommy said: 'Fucking Jesus.'

There was another silence.

'How the fuck did he miss it?' Walter said.

I shook my head.

'Tommy,' Terry said, 'you've still got your overalls on.'

Tommy looked down at himself.

'Fucking hell,' he said. 'I never thought.'

'But he didn't notice,' I said. 'He was so fucking relieved to see you he didn't notice.'

'Jesus,' Tommy said.

'Billy,' said Terry, 'never mind Tommy. Have you seen yourself?'

I looked at him.

'I tried to warn you outside,' he said. 'You've got all black down your neck and back.'

I reached over my shoulder and rubbed my hand on my back. I was covered in soot from when I'd looked in the hole earlier on.

'Christ,' I said.

Tommy sat down on the bench.

'I don't know about anybody else,' he said, 'but after that little miracle, we must get out. God's on our side.'

'For once,' I said.

'He won't be much longer if we don't plug up that hole sharp,' Terry said.

That jerked us back to reality. We got the tools and the spare bricks and plugged up the hole. Then we plastered it up with papier mâché and painted it.

Then, one by one, we left the shower and went back to our cells.

The hole never looked as bad to me as it did that day. It was a monster, eating into my nervous system. I kept having to drift back into the shower room to reassure myself that everything was all right. Every time I saw a screw coming towards me I was certain he was going to tell me that the hole had been discovered.

But it didn't happen. We'd had our luck. It had come at the right time. But we couldn't count on any more.

*We lie together on the rug in front of the electric fire. Sheila's head is resting on my shoulder. She is asleep. I look at the colour of her hair, even more fierce in the glow of the fire. This is the time I hate most. The time she is most content. I hate it because her contentment is due to me. Her happiness makes me resentful. It's as if she's taking something of my character and feeding off it. And yet, recently, my resentment had been lessening. And that is even more worrying because I must be weakening. I must be growing fonder of her than I want to be. I've got to be alone. I can't be the way I want to be with someone else depending on me.*

141

*I move my arm so that her head rolls a little, disturbing her doze.*

*'What is it?' she says. 'Why move?'*

*'Got to,' I say. 'Your folks'll be back soon. They can't find us like this, can they?'*

Now Tommy was really getting at where the hole was coming from.

It wasn't a small passage. It was an opening into the top corner of a cellar underneath the showers.

Tommy had cleared enough space around the air hole to work at enlarging it. Soon it was big enough for us to throw our rubble and spare bricks down through it into the cellar below. Tommy really smashed into it now. For about a week I tore my guts out snatching and jerking the big Olympic barbell up and down on the Ones, making as much noise as I could to cover the sound of Tommy's progress. I'd loosened the weights so that they'd chink and rattle but even though they were right next to my ears they sounded like the dull thuds that were echoing round the wing from inside the hole. Walter and Terry minded Tommy for this period. They used to give me the horrors. When I had a rest, there was always a slight lag between me putting down the weights and them telling Tommy to stop. I kept having goes at them about it but they could never seem to improve their form.

But when Tommy told me that the second hole would soon be big enough for one of us to drop through down into the cellar, I eased Terry and Walter out on to the weights; we didn't want Walter knowing how close we were to making the drop. And the closer we got to the drop the more tension there was between Tommy and myself. The fact that we were under the constant strain of working on our own, just using the others, knowing that there'd come a time when we'd not only have to ditch them but ditch them good and proper, that was bad enough. But there was the other thing: what happened when we got down into the cellar? Supposing there was nowhere else to go? That was the thought that nagged you all the time, and it was a strain just trying to keep it from the front of your brain.

Then one day Tommy came out of the hole and said: 'There it is, then, Billy. We can go through now.'

'What do you mean?' I said.

Tommy looked at me as though I was fucking barmy.

'The hole. Into the cellar. You do know the hole I'm talking about?'

'So why didn't you go down it?'

'You what?'

'Down the hole. Why did you come all the way back and out just to tell me that? Why didn't you drop down yourself?'

'Because you're bigger than me, you stupid cunt. It'll be easier for you to get back up again.'

'Oh yes,' I said. 'I'm bigger than you all right. Supposing I get stuck in the bleeding hole? What happens then?'

'You won't get stuck. I've told you. It's big enough.'

'All right then,' I said. 'But I hope you're bleeding well right otherwise I shall have no choice but to put it down to a touch of the old macaroni in the strides.'

I made to go through the hole. Tommy grabbed me by the arm.

'What you mean, Billy?' he said, all grim faced and full of aggravation.

'What I say, Tommy.' I moved his fingers off my arm. 'And don't come it, old son, eh? You know you haven't got that kind of talent.'

Of course he had to swallow. Then I felt sorry I'd made him.

'Look, Tommy,' I said. 'Forget it. We're both on our nerve ends. Let's strike that bit out, eh?'

'Are you going down the fucking hole or aren't you?'

I left it at that and climbed in the hole. He'd get over it. Then

I crawled along to the second hole and contorted myself round legs first and tried to get through. Tommy had been wrong. I got stuck before I even got near dropping down. It took me nearly a quarter of an hour to get myself free. Which was quarter of an hour too long. All we needed was another session with the PO and without the luck. When I got out again I said to Tommy: 'If you want me to go down into the cellar there's three more days' work for you on that hole.'

'You must be joking,' he said. 'There's plenty of room.'

I wasn't exactly in the mood for a debate.

'Tommy,' I said. 'I'm not asking. I'm telling.'

Tommy thought about it.

'I can't wait that long,' he said. 'I'll take some more stuff out tomorrow and go down myself.'

'That's up to you, Tommy,' I said. 'If you're sure, that is.'

'Don't be a cunt, Billy,' he said. 'Don't start souring it at this stage. It's been nice and sweet so far.'

'Tommy,' I said. 'You take things too seriously.'


Afternoon.

I watched Tommy disappear into the hole. Outside on the landing Walter and Gearing were busy with the weights. For about ten minutes I could hear Tommy taking out some more bricks. Then there was silence. Another ten minutes went by. If there was a check now we'd be finished. He'd never be able to get back in time. The sound of the weights clanked on outside; nobody except Tommy and me knew about the drop. The others just thought it was business as usual.

Another five minutes. Christ, I thought. Any minute now it's going to happen. It must happen. We'd been too lucky up to now. It had to break sometime.

But it didn't.

Tommy crawled out of the hole. He was grinning all over his face.

'Christ, Tommy,' I said. 'Where've you been, Brighton?'

'No, but that's where I'm going.'

'What's the score?'

Tommy began to fill the hole up.

'Tommy, how was it?'

'Wait till I've finished this.'

'What are you playing at?'

'You don't want the PO in here again with the hole gaping in his fucking face, do you?'

I began to help him.

'No,' I said, 'I don't. But just tell me.'

Tommy just grinned. I could have murdered the bastard.

We got the hole plastered and painted. Then Tommy began to take his clothes off.

'Now what are you doing?' I said.

Tommy walked into the showers.

'Just because we're almost there,' Tommy said turning on the water, 'it doesn't mean we stop doing things right. We've got to do things proper. Especially now.'

'All right. But just tell me.'

'Can't hear you, Billy. The shower's making too much of a noise.'

I sat down on the bench and ground my teeth. Eventually he came out.

'Now then…' I said. But Tommy cut straight across me.

'You don't want Wally walking in in the middle of it, do you? Better go to my cell and get out the chess board.'

He was right, of course. But he didn't have to enjoy it quite so much.

We walked out of the shower room. Wally dropped his bar-bell and came over.

'How's it going, then?'

Walter's face was a picture. He knew something was up, but he just couldn't figure out what it was. He certainly couldn't

145

conceive that Tommy and I intended going out without him. It was that kind of knowledge that made the situation all the sweeter.

When we got to Tommy's cell I said: 'All right. Now let's have it, for Christ's sake.'

Tommy lit a cigarette.

'Billy,' he said. 'We've cracked it.'

I waited.

'There's a tunnel from the cellar to the airy in the badminton yard.'

We looked at each other. I couldn't believe it. The badminton yard. It was perfect.

'Tell me about it,' I said.

*Dear Billy,*

*I don't know how I can stand to write this letter to you as I have never felt so terrible in my life before, not since your Dad died, anyway. But I have to force myself as there is nobody else who can help except you. What's happened is that I have heard some terrible things about our Linda, and I know that they are true otherwise I would not be writing. Billy, Linda is going to the bad in the worst way she can. She is set up in a flat with two other girls in Manor Park and the rent is paid by two West Indians. Men go there day and night. Billy, I know this is true. I tried to see her by going round there the other day but she wouldn't see me and sent one of the other girls down to see me. She told me Linda was out but I know she wasn't. What am I going to do? I can't do anything on my own. Please write back now and tell me what you think because I'm at my rope's end.*

*I'll be coming to see you on Saturday,*

    *Love,*

      *Mother*

In the badminton yard, at ground level, there was a wide

ventilation shaft, six foot square. It was surrounded by a seven foot high wall. The shaft was covered by a horizontal grille. Padlocked. Occasionally the shuttlecock would drop down the shaft and we'd have to fish it out with a weighted hook. But when we'd gone fishing nobody ever realised that this shaft connected up with Tommy's tunnel, the one that led from the cellar. The tunnel was four foot high, and you would have to crawl about fifteen feet along it to get to the ventilation shaft in the badminton yard. The entrance from the cellar to the tunnel naturally was barred. Not padlocked. Just barred. And now it didn't matter how many padlocks and bars there were en route. We had a way out. Padlocks and bars were beside the point. So we'd go from the shower to the cellar and along the tunnel and up the air shaft and out into the badminton court.

The badminton yard had a roof.

The roof was high, vaulted. Plastic, fibre-glass type transparent roofing. Far too high to get at from the court. But once on that roof you could drop down and it was just a rope's throw to the top of the outside wall.

The roofing was a tight fit all round the yard. But at one point the inverted peak of the roofing ran across the face of the library window. The library so-called was just a cell with wooden shelving to hold the books and a small barred window the same as in every other cell. But this was the only window on the wing that gave any kind of access to the edge of the plastic roofing in order to make a hole in it. Which was what we planned to do. Rip a hole in the roofing, suspend a sheet rope from the library window down in to the badminton yard, up the rope, through the hole in the roof, across the office roof where it backed on to the wall, swing the hook to the top of the wall.

And over.


'The padlock's no sweat,' I said. 'We can bust that any time. What we need is a hacksaw for the bars in the cellar. The only way is to get one of the others to fetch one out of the shop, sod it.'

'No sweat,' said Tommy. 'I've already got one. I've had it ever since the island. I brought it up hidden in the folds of the box I carried my gear in.'

I could have kissed the bastard.

'So we don't even have to row in Walter for that,' I said.

'No,' said Tommy.

I lit a cigarette.

'Have you noticed how Walter's been sticking close to us the last few days?' I said.

'He's been living up our arseholes.'

'Right. He knows something's on. So he's got to be scotched. And what better way than by bringing him in?'

'How do you mean?'

'What I say. We tell him everything. We tell him about the tunnel, the shaft, exactly what we're going to do. Except we leave out the hacksaw. We go to him and we say, Wally, it's bloody lovely, we'll all soon be over the wall and it'll be fucking not wanking but there's just this one snag, we need a hacksaw. Now as you spend a lot of time in the machine shop we reckon that one's down to you, Wally, all right? And then while Wally's figuring out how to get us the hacksaw, we've already sawn through and whenever we choose to go it won't matter. Wally won't be able to believe it. He'll still be in hospital next Christmas. What do you say to that, Tommy?'

'Fair,' said Tommy. 'Quite fair.'

'Fair?' I said. 'It's bleeding brilliant.'

'So there it is, Wally,' I said. 'Almost there. All we need is the saw.'

Walter pursed his lips and folded his arms and generally got himself comfortable: all set to do the big thinker bit.

'Just the bars you say, Billy,' he said.

'That's right, Walter. The padlock's a doddle. The important part is the bars. Everything rests on getting through them.'

'Mm,' said Walter. 'A hacksaw. Won't be easy.'

'I know, Walter. But that's what we need. That's what you've got to get us.'

'Difficult,' he said.

'I know.'

'Getting one out of the shop. If they tumbled, then we'd never get out.'

'Risky.'

'Might be safer bringing one in.'

'Could be.'

'Gearing's brother might do it.'

'Why not ask Gearing?'

'I might do that. That might be best. I'll have a think about it.'

'Thanks, Walter.'

There was no need for us to go down into the cellar again. The next time we went we wouldn't be coming back up. But we kept the shower hole open to stash the things we'd be taking out with us. Tommy had already cut through the bars to the tunnel and done the padlocks. All they needed was bending back. Everything was perfect. On his travels in the cellar Tommy had even found half a stepladder that would come in handy for when we went up the shaft. I'd knocked up two sheet ropes, one for dangling out of the library window, the other for getting on the wall. I tied this rope to a broom handle which I'd attached to one of the five pounds weights from the weight-lifting gear. It would fix to the top of the wall a treat. But just the same I hadn't forgotten Burnham and with Tommy minding I tried out the pendulum on the brick partition walls in the showers, just to get the feel of it.

Like everything else, it was just perfect.

'How's the hacksaw coming, Wally?' I said.

'Gearing saw his brother on Saturday. He's bringing one in next weekend.'

'Next weekend?' I said. 'Christ, the screws might have tumbled the hole by then.'

'Well, what else can I do?'

'Dunno, Wally. But we can't do anything till we get that hacksaw.'

'What do you want me to do? Bring one out of the shop and get us all bleeding rumbled?'

'Dunno, Wally. The hacksaw's your department. We knew it'd be dicey. That's why we gave the job to you.'

'Well, all right, do you want to try and bring one out of the shop?'

'Better wait for Gearing's brother, Wally. Don't want us all getting nicked at this late stage, do we?'

'For Christ's sake, that's what I've just been telling you!'

'So you did, Walter,' I said. 'And you know what? You were dead right, as usual.'

The library was just another cell with shelves. It was never kept locked. I was always using it so there was nothing suspicious about being in there.

I walked over to the window and looked out. The plastic roofing butted up perfectly to the window's brick surround. I got up to the window and felt the plastic. It was very brittle stuff. The hole had to be made before we went. Breaking through it would make too much noise at night, when the nick was quiet. It had to be done now. This was our biggest risk. Tommy was minding outside the library for me, so that part was covered. The danger was a screw just off-chancing it into the badminton court below.

Feeling the roof I realised that I had to make the hole in one go. Two shots at it and we'd be dead: people hear a strange noise and they wait for it to happen again and when it doesn't they usually dismiss it. But that doesn't apply to a nick. The screws sniff at anything. So I had to make the hole in one then run like fuck. They might discover what had made the noise but they certainly weren't going to discover me standing next to it.

I stuck my arms through the bars and flexed my fingers on the material. I concentrated all my power into my wrists. Then I twisted.

The roofing made a sound like machine-gun fire. The noise racketed round the well of the badminton court and bounced all over the roofing.

I hurtled out of the library. Tommy had already gone.

I found him down in his cell.

'Christ, Billy,' he said. 'I thought Gabriel had farted.'

We waited.

Nothing happened. We'd pulled another one.

*The Wolseley veers right and crashes into the side of the van. In front of us the Standard makes the sandwich. The bang of vehicle on vehicle echoes up the street. The car doors burst open and some of us go to work with the coshes and the handles while two others belt the back doors of the van with hammers. But two of our boys go down and the wages boys pick up their sticks and start laying into us. Two more down and the back doors are still holding. Then beyond the traffic sound comes the noise of the bell. The two at the back of the van drop their hammers and race back for the Wolseley. I shout at them to stay but then the others start to take flight too and there is only me, staving off the blows from the wages boys with a handle. The police car sways into view, in front of the Wolseley. The Wolseley is moving towards the police car. The police car swings round broadside on, leaving no room for the Wolseley to get by. The Wolseley reverses. Policemen pile out of the police car and chase after the reversing Wolseley. The Wolseley clouts the wages van. Doors fly* open and everybody scrambles out again, taking off past me in the opposite direction and as they pass I get a bar over my head and I fall to the ground, spewing all over. Hands grasp my clothes and haul me to my feet and I begin to get a real fitting up but the next moment the hands release me and the punching stops and everybody stands stock still. Somebody has started exercising a shooter. Two shots. One of the coppers is rolling around on the deck, trying to hold his kneecap together, gurgling, part scream, part vomit. The other coppers make for the nearest cover, behind the wages van. Two more shots. Screams up the street, women trying to cram through shop doorways. The boys are away. I smile. Then the next thing is I get the handle over my head again and it's all over.

Tobin keeps coming to see me with the same dialogue.

'I know who they are, Billy. That's not important. I want to know who was carrying the shooter.'

'If you know who they are why not pull them in and ask them. Or are you afraid they might turn out to be on Wally's firm?'

'It's the shooter man I want, Billy.'

'What shooter man?'

Then one time he comes a different tack.

'You know how much you're likely to cop for this time, don't you, Billy. With your form. It's going to be the big one this time.'

'It really should have acted as a deterrent, shouldn't it?'

'Be as funny as you like. It won't change a thing. You're going down heavy. Of course you may not have to. You give me the hero with the shooter and I might be able to fix the court.'

'Oh yes. I can just see it. I give you the name and straight-away wallop the judge knows sod all about the odd few years he's supposed to be knocking off me.'

'Wouldn't be like that, Billy. Not at all like that. We could work it so you gave us the name in court, so we'd both know we're safe.'

'Why only the shooter man? Why not the rest as well?'

'Doesn't matter. The shooter man will give us the others, won't he? He'd want some time off, too.'

'And my time. What would I get off?'

'Half.'

'Half. You're joking.'

'I could get you down to say, eight. Good behaviour, you'd be out in six at the most.'

'And you think I'd do it. You think I'd shop mates just to get myself time off?'

'You're like everybody else, Billy. You're no different. You take your chances but you don't want to do any more than you have to. Why should you? You probably didn't know the stupid bastard was tooled up, anyway. Why do time for him as well?'

'Well you know me. Never did have time for that kind of stuff. Takes all the excitement out of things.'

So I let Tobin think I'm set on the idea. In court, his face is a picture when I keep buttoned up. But then it's too late to reverse the wheels. Everything's fixed and stuck fast. I get my eight years and Tobin gets fuck all. But even so, eight years is eight years. I'm outside again in six months.


I decided that Terry was the only one we could trust. The others we would leave. So when Tommy and Terry and I were together in Tommy's cell I brought the matter up and told him how far we'd got.

'It's perfect, Terry,' I said. 'It can't miss. Just me, you and Tommy. What do you say?'

'I dunno, Billy,' he said. 'I don't reckon it, really.'

'How do you mean? I've told you, it's going to work.'

'Maybe,' he said. 'But I don't think I'll bother.'

I began to think we'd made a mistake. I began to smell Walter.

'Why not, exactly, Terry?' I said.

Terry shrugged.

'Nowhere to go, have I? No firm to go to. No bird. No family. What's the fucking point?'

'Is that right?' I said.

'Don't worry,' he said. 'It isn't Wally. I just don't want to go. There's no point, that's all.'

I didn't say anything. Tommy said: 'I believe him, Billy. I've seen this before.'

'So have I,' I said. 'I was just wondering why he hasn't told us how he felt before.'

'Why should I?' Terry said. 'I've done my bit to help. What I think's my own business.'

'He's right, Billy,' said Tommy.

'All right, so he's right,' I said. 'I'm just bearing Walter in mind. You never know how he's going to pull his strokes.'

'Talking about Walter...' Tommy said.

I looked at him.

'What about Walter?' I said.

'I was thinking,' Tommy said. 'In the light of Terry leaving himself out. It means that now we're going to have to go blind.'

'Now look...'

'No, listen to me, Billy. I'm right. We can do what we like when we get the other side of that wall, we can put the bar over his head in the cellar and leave him down there if you can't wait that long. But we can't go out blind. There's only Ray left and do you trust him? We may as well put Wally in and leave out the suspense.'

'Tommy,' I said, 'I'm more worried about Walter than I am about the fucking screws. You know we can't put him in it. What the Christ have we been fucking about at for the last month? Do me a favour.'

'We can leave him in the cellar, I've told you.'

'Tommy, we can't start fighting this side of the wall, and neither can we afterwards. Listen, he'd try and put it on us before we reached the wall. And on the other side of the wall he'll have help. Look, I've told you, he's had something in the wind since before I got here. Either he'll try and balls it up for us or he'll drop us in it and get away himself. You know his muscle, you know he could arrange it, outside or in. How would you feel if that toe-rag was out and you were still inside, or just inside because of him?'

'I know all that, Billy, but I still think we should take him. It's too dodgy not to. Supposing he sniffs it while we're making it? He'll start yelling and screaming so as to grass us. You know what he's like.'

People were always saying 'You know what he's like' about Walter.

'Look, you know *I* don't want the cunt's help,' Tommy went on, 'but I'm not going to take the chance of him sniffing it out and grassing. Which is what he would do. I'd rather tell him and take our chances that way.'

Walter wasn't going. That was one thing I was certain of, Tommy or not. I upped the stakes.

'Tommy,' I said, 'I'd rather not go than take Walter with us. I'd rather go up there and smash him all round his cell. Then we'd both be out of it. You could go on your own. That's how strong I feel about it.'

There was a silence. In the lull Terry said:

'Tommy, I know it's none of my business, but I think Billy's right. It's wrong to let Wally go. He wouldn't take anybody with him. He's just a stroke-puller and he's pulled too many.'

Tommy sighed.

'I know,' he said. 'I've just got this thing about him grassing us on the night. If we put him in it we could keep an eye on him.'

'Listen, he's still racking his brains over that hacksaw,' I said. 'He's no idea of what's on.'

'Maybe.'

'If you put him in it all you'll have is grief,' Terry said. 'Believe me.'

'I know,' Tommy said. He thought about it for a while. 'All right,' he said. 'Let's keep the bastard blotted out.'

'We've got to,' I said.

After a while Tommy said:

'Although in one way it would have been good to take Walter.'

'How's that?' Terry said.

'It would have really got up their noses. Can you imagine the scream? It would have been worse than Blake.'

*The screw unlocks the door and comes into the cell. I stare up at him from my pit.*

*'Governor, Cracken.'*

*I don't move.*

*'Come on, shift it. He's in his office, waiting.'*

*'What am I supposed to have done this time?'*

*'Move your fucking self and you'll find out.'*

*I stand up very quickly. The screw begins to wonder a bit.*

*'Don't worry,' I say. 'It's too bleeding hot.'*

*The Governor is writing when we march into his office. We wait for him to finish. He looks up.*

*'Leave us, Glover,' he tells the screw.*

*The screw disappears.*

*'Sit down, Cracken,' says the Governor.*

*I sit down. The Governor looks down at his pad for a while, thinking.*

*Then he looks up, in my direction, at a point somewhere above my head.*

*'I am afraid I have to tell you,' he says, 'that last night your sister was found dead.'*

*I look at him. I don't comprehend the words.*

*'I'm afraid it was suicide. An overdose.' The words don't mean anything.*

*'She was taken to hospital. Everything was done that could possibly have been done.'*

'Dead?'

'Naturally your –'

'Dead?'

'– your mother –'

I stand up.

'I've got to see her. I've got to help.'

'Glover!'

Glover and three other screws come into the office. I start to walk through them.

'I've got to see her. I must see her.'

Their hands are gripping me and they begin to pull me to the floor.

'Cracken!'

The Governor's voice fills the room.

Then Glover's voice is soft in my ear as we hit the floor.

'Take it easy, Billy. Take it easy.'

'I must go,' I say. 'I must help. I must help them.'

'Come on, Billy,' says Glover. 'Just take it easy and calm down. You won't help anybody carrying on like this.'

Tommy had to do a bit more work on the hole that led into the cellar, just to make sure I didn't get stuck on the night. This was just the kind of manoeuvre that was bound to set Walter sniffing.

'What's the point of going down there again?' Walter said when we told him.

'Wally,' Tommy said, 'I want Gearing to go down there tomorrow or Wednesday to try it out. I'm not having him getting stuck down there. You know what a clumsy cunt he is. It's bad enough having him with us without him nausing it into the bargain.'

Walter laughed.

'That's all we'd need on the night,' he said. 'One of us stuck in the cellar ceiling and the others waiting to go.'

The afternoon that we widened the hole, the wing got a new arrival. Gil Hardy, a lifer who'd been transferred up from Leicester. I'd never met him but I'd worked with people who'd worked with him and I knew he was sound. He was still on punishment for a try he'd made down there and in practical terms he was still behind his door but I chatted up a sympathetic screw and got him unlocked. Hardy came along to my cell for a chat. We gave each other the heard-about-you glad-to-meet-you jive and he told me how unlucky they'd been at Leicester. He also told me that Dennis Colman had made one down there and I was glad to hear about that because Dennis was in a different class to Walter. Anyway, we were sitting there talking about this and that, and then right out of the blue he popped me off.

'Billy, is there anything on here?' he said. Normally I would have just passed it off. But what with Wally parking half an hour before and the surprise of Hardy asking, my face shopped itself. I tried to compensate for my surprise. I shrugged and said: 'Not really.'

He immediately jumped in and apologised.

'I'm sorry, Billy,' he said, 'I shouldn't have asked. I was out of order.'

This only increased my discomfort.

'No, Gil, it's nothing,' I said. 'You just surprised me, that's all. You're entitled to ask. I'd do the same.'

But we dropped the subject and I knew he'd never bring it up again.

I told Tommy about it that evening.

'He caught me open, Tommy,' I said. 'I couldn't help showing it. But immediately he saw my reaction he backed off. He accepted he couldn't be put in. It makes you sick when you contrast him with that other ponce.'

'Yes,' Tommy said. 'He's a nice fellow, Billy. I knew him down on the Moor. I was going to suggest taking him. But it's up to you.'

'It's not up to me, Tommy. I just didn't want to commit without discussing it first. He's game enough and on my life I don't mind. The way he stoomed up is as good as a reference to me.'

We postponed telling him until the next day: even getting Gil unlocked twice on the trot would have been enough to flare Walter's nostrils, the way he was watching us. In the evening I got Gil unlocked again and gave him the SP.

'Gil,' I said, 'you know yesterday you asked if there was anything on?'

'Yeah, Billy. But...'

'Listen. Tommy and me are together on one. We've got a hole and it's beautiful. It leads all the way out.'

'That's great, Billy...'

'Listen. We're going tomorrow night.'

'Tomorrow night? Jesus.'

'Yes. Tomorrow night. Do you want to make one?'

His face was like Blackpool illuminations.

'Billy, you must be fucking joking. Do I? Jesus. Of course I fucking want to make one.'

We clasped hands and grinned at each other.

'One thing, though,' I said. 'Walter.'

'Walter?'

I gave him the score. When I'd finished he said: 'No sweat to me, Billy. I don't know him but even his cousin thinks he's a cunt.'

'Right. So it's just me and you and Tommy.'

'Sure, but I mean, I'm supposed to be behind my door. How am I going to get out for long enough not to noise it?'

'That won't be any problem. I'll arrange for you to have a shower or go to the library. Don't worry about it.'

Gil shook his head.

'I can't believe it,' he said. 'I mean, over the wall and it's only my third day here.'

'How was your mother?' Sheila asks.

I shake my head.

'The same,' I say. 'She doesn't want to know. She doesn't want to know anything. Still feels that everything's been down to me. You know.'

Sheila puts her arm round me.

'Don't let it worry you,' she says.

'Worry me? It doesn't worry me.'

She rests her head against my chest.

'Anyway I shan't go again. Stuff it. It's too risky. Why should I run the gauntlet just to get that routine?'

Slight pressure from her fingers at the base of my spine.

'Not to mention what would happen to you. Harbouring, you would get three years, easy.' I stroke her hair. 'The whole situation, it's unfair. You're really out on a limb because of me.'

'Do you think I mind?'

'No, but –'

'Well, then.'

There is a silence. The fingers tighten again. She lifts her head and looks into my face.

'And anyway,' she says, 'you wouldn't leave a poor pregnant girl all alone to fend for herself, would you?'


I woke up and stared at the ceiling. The nick was quiet but grey daylight filtered into my cell.

I got up and went to the window and looked out. Light drizzle softly swept across the nick. Instead of doing my exercises straight away, as usual, I lit a cigarette and stared out at the rain. I felt the way I used to feel before a school examination, as if the exam was today, and there was no time for any more work, the feeling that if you hadn't swotted it up now there was no more time so you just had to take your chances on the questions being about the few things you knew. It was a kind of desperate exhilaration, a feeling of excited relief, relief that there was nothing more to be done other than to sit down and do your paper.

During the morning a weight-lifting referee visited the nick and I did a couple of lifts for the inter-prison competition. I weighed exactly 175 lbs and I dead-lifted 520 lbs. It was my best lift to date.

At tea time I got the sheet rope from the laundry basket where I'd kept it hidden and took it up to my cell, and wrapped the sheet round my waist. After that I went down to Gil's cell and briefed him on a few details and told him to get himself unlocked for a shower at about eight o'clock, after he'd eaten. I never had time to tell him very much. He really didn't know what the hell was going on. Then Tommy and I wandered down to the library. Tommy minded by the door while I uncoiled the rope from round my waist. I pushed a table near the wall, got up on it and tied the rope to the bottom of a vertical bar and let out the rest of the rope through the hole in the plastic and down into the badminton yard. It was dark, but if someone went into the yard they would switch on the light. There was no safeguard against that happening. But the chances of a screw going into the badminton yard after dark were slight. When I'd dropped the rope I went down to the weights cell and looked out across the badminton yard. I could only just make out the sheets dangling through the hole. Again, the chances of anyone coming into the weights cell or either of the other two cells that overlooked the yard just to stare out into the dark yard were negligible.

I told Tommy that I thought everything was going to be all right.

Then the cook arrived with the food. Everyone went down except Gil. The cook had fetched the makings of a mixed grill; chops, bacon, sausage, tomatoes, etc. I elected to peel the potatoes while Tommy chipped them. Normally I'd have been policing Walter to stop him staking out the biggest chop or

161

getting at the milk. But tonight I just chipped the potatoes and tried to forget about the rhythm section in my stomach. One time, I thought, on an occasion like this, I'm not going to rise to the action. It's got to happen sometime. And every time I worried that this might be the sometime. But I consoled myself with that very fact: each time I worried that I might fail myself, but so far I'd always come through.

We finished cooking about seven-thirty. The food was shared out and we all went up to the TV room to eat. Tommy took the one we'd pulled out for Gil up to his cell and Gil told him that the PO had been squared about the shower.

Walter and Gearing settled down in the armchairs and watched TV while they ate. I had my meal at the table. I had difficulty in getting it down me. My teeth champed away at the food but I couldn't seem to swallow properly. My muscles hadn't the blood to spare for proper digestion. It was no good forcing it. In the end I just drank some milk.

It was mine and Ray's turn to do the washing up. The kitchens were close to the shower room. I started to collect the trays as soon as everybody had finished eating. Ray stood up as well but I said: 'It's all right, Ray, I'll do it tonight. You have a sit down.'

'Don't be silly,' he said. 'It's my turn as well.'

'Leave it, Ray. I'll do it.'

I must have sounded more abrasive than I'd intended because Walter turned his head and said: 'Didn't you know Billy was in the Scouts, Ray?'

'Yeah,' I said. 'And it's bob-a-job week.'

Ray sat down. Walter turned back to the television.

*I sit in the car and look at my watch. Two minutes to go. Two minutes and the geezer with the four thousand pounds in his satchel will be walking out of the garage office and across the forecourt to his car. Jackie the driver asks me how long and I tell him. I catch sight of my face in the wing mirror. Beads of sweat are decorating my forehead. I never sweat on a job. I'm always dry as a bone, keyed up so that I can appreciate the action as fully as possible. But today it's different. Today the stakes are too high. This is going to be my last job. This one's for Sheila and Timmy. After this one we get out of it. The risks of living the way we've been living are too great. If I get taken again they'll lock the door and throw away the key. They'll slap twenty years on me after the way I fucked them on the last deal. I've taken too many risks and I've been too lucky. Three thousand quid to me on this one and we're out via Ireland.*

*I look at my watch again and then I look towards the forecourt.*

*'All right, Jackie,' I say. 'Slide her over.'*

*Jackie eases the car across the road. The geezer walks out of the office. Jackie stops the car against the kerb and I open the door and get out.*

*The geezer is on the forecourt now. There are two or three cars parked but I know that his is an Austin. I walk up the approach, narrowing the angle, moving between him and the Austin. But instead of making for the car, the geezer swings round and starts running to the other end of the forecourt. I don't get it. He couldn't have cottoned me. He never even looked at me. I was never even in his line of vision.*

*Then I know.*

*All hell breaks out. Uniforms everywhere. And every one of them seems to be shouting my name.*

*I've been grassed.*


Tommy came in while I was washing up.

'Gil squared it with the PO,' he said. 'He'll be coming down to the showers any time now.'

'Good,' I said.

'Thing is,' said Tommy, 'Walter and Gearing have gone up to the Threes to do some soft toys.'

We looked at each other.

The soft toy gear was two floors up in a room on the same corner of the wing as the showers. There was a window in this room that looked out over the plastic roof. The angle was too acute for anybody looking out to see the hole where we'd emerge, but once we were actually on the roof we weren't exactly going to stick by the hole.

'What do you think?' I said to Tommy.

'I don't know,' he said. 'But then you can never tell with Wally.'

'Right. Do you think he caught anything about the washing up?'

'You were a bit sharp, Billy.'

'What else could I do? We didn't want him in here, did we?'

'Well then.'

Tommy shook his head.

'It's just that that old bastard doesn't miss a trick.'

'You don't have to tell me that, Tommy. That is something I know all about.'

We stood there for a minute or two, thinking thoughts of Walter.

'Anyway,' Tommy said, 'I'm going in the shower.'

'I'll follow you when Gil's gone in.'

'Right.'

'And don't worry about it, Tommy,' I said. 'In half an hour you'll be on the other side of the wall.'

# PART TWO

I was tidying up the last of the trays when Ray came into the kitchen.

He looked all round the place before he said anything. I didn't turn round from what I was doing but I knew he'd spotted something.

'You've done them all, then, Billy,' he said.

'That's right,' I said, stacking a load of trays.

'I just came in to see if you needed a hand.'

'Well it's all done, as you can see.'

I dried my hands on the tea towel and looked at Ray.

'Coming up to watch the box?' he said.

'No, I don't fancy that tonight.'

Why the fuck didn't he clear off?

I put the towel down. Ray had never been a prime mover in his life but he'd seen a lot of schemes played and he was sharp enough to realise something was on and he was very reluctant to leave the kitchen.

I took out my cigarettes.

'What's on tonight, anyway?' I said. 'Anything good?'

'Coronation Street.'

I looked at my watch.

'Nearly finished,' I said.

'I'd better go up then,' Ray said.

We looked at each other for a minute or two longer. Then Ray turned and went out of the kitchen.

I waited till he was well out of the way, then I dashed into the shower room. Steam was everywhere. Tommy was already getting the bricks out of the wall and Gil was stacking them behind the bench.

'I think Ray's on to it,' I said.

'Never mind about that,' Tommy said, 'open that door and keep a bleeding look out.'

I began to take my clothes off. In the middle of the room was an exercising bicycle that Ray had left there that afternoon when he'd had a quick sweat up and shower. The bicycle should have been put away in the weights cell with the rest of the equipment. There was something out of place about it sitting there in the middle of the shower room. Especially as Ray had been the last one to use it.

'For Christ's sake, Billy,' Tommy said. 'Get minding.'

'All right, all right,' I said, 'let me get out of my fucking trousers.'

I walked towards the door just wearing shirt and pants. The door opened. We all froze.

It was Ray. He strode into the room, towards the bicycle. But he stopped dead when he saw that the hole had been opened up.

'Ray,' Tommy said, his voice a low shriek. 'What you doing? The bleeding door.'

Ray didn't move. He just stood by the bike and stared at the hole. Then at Gil. Tommy's words hadn't registered at all.

I leant forward and closed the door.

'What's happening?' Ray said.

Tommy bluffed it.

'What do you mean, what's happening?' he said. 'We're stashing some gear, that's what's happening. And you nearly gave us fucking heart failure didn't you, my old son?'

Ray kept looking at Gil. Then in a quiet voice Ray said to me: 'What you told him for?'

The noise of the showers confined Ray's voice to my ears.

'It was Tommy's idea,' I said. 'They used to know each other on the Moor.'

Ray still didn't move.

'Ray come on,' I said, arms beseeching. 'Shift the fucking bike out. If they check the weights cell we're nicked.'

'Either that or give us a hand with the bricks,' Tommy said. 'Don't just stand there like a spare prick.'

Ray thought about it. Then he picked up the bike. He'd had the sense to realise the fact that if he'd offered to help with the bricks, and it was right what he thought, we were making one, then he'd have got a bar over his head. So all he could do was to pick up the bike and leave us alone.

I opened the door and let him out and closed the door behind him.

'Well, that's it,' said Tommy. 'He'll tell Walter.'

'It's too late to worry about that now,' I said, taking my shirt off. I wanted to go down in my underwear to cut out the risk of snagging on the brickwork.

I was the biggest, so it had been agreed that I should go first. I climbed into the hole and eased down head first for the second entrance into the cellars. I wriggled my head and shoulders into the cellar opening but my feet were still sticking out into the shower room through the first hole. It was a tight fit round my shoulders and with my feet outside I couldn't get any purchase to push myself through.

'Tommy,' I said, 'push on the soles of my feet.'

'Right.'

He nearly broke my fucking ankles but the pressure allowed me to force myself through a little farther. And now my feet were in the chimney so I could brace them on the back of the chimney and force myself through that way. When I was half way through I felt in the darkness for the steel girder Tommy had told me about. It ran across the cellar roof and the only way down was to grab hold and swing, unless of course you went through head first on to the cellar floor.

The cellar was pitch black. My fingers found the damp iron. I heaved and swung and then I let go. I hit the cellar floor and overbalanced and jarred my elbow on the floor. I straightened up and lit a match. The bundles of clothes were on the floor. I blew the match and grabbed my clothes and put them on. Then I picked up Tommy's bundle and waited for him to drop through. He was only a couple of seconds behind me. I gave him the bundle and he got changed while Gil made his way down. There wasn't a bundle for Gil. There hadn't been time. He had to take his chances in what he was wearing.

The hooked rope was in Tommy's bundle.

'Got the rope, Tommy?' I said.

'Yes.'

'Christ,' said Gil. 'I can't see a fucking thing.'

I reached out and grabbed hold of Gil and pushed him behind Tommy.

'Hold on to Tommy,' I said. 'He knows the way. I'll hold on to you.'

We moved off. It was slow going. Tommy knew the way through the cellars, knew how many arches there were to the wall where the tunnel was, but he had to feel his way along. I just hoped his arithmetic was up to scratch.

It took us nearly five minutes to feel our way to the tunnel. I kept wondering what was going on upstairs, whether or not Walter had started creating, whether or not the screws had missed us, whether or not they'd found the hole.

'Here we are,' said Tommy. 'And so's the ladder, my lovelies.'

Gil and I stopped. There was a short silence, then Tommy grunted as he pulled back the bar he'd cut through.

'Done it,' he said. 'I'll go through first with the ladder.'

I heard the ladder being pulled through. Then Gil and I felt the bars and found the bent one and crawled through into the tunnel. We had to go bent double like miners in a book of Orwell's I remembered reading, but at least with the tunnel there was only one way to go and that was forward. After a while I saw dim light ahead of me, drifting down the ventilation shaft.

Tommy was already going up the ladder when I straightened up into the ventilation shaft. He took the padlock off and opened the grille and stepped out into the yard without making a sound.

I followed him out, and then Gil. Now we were all out in the open. Naked. No cover.

But the nick was quiet. No commotion. Nothing had gone off inside. Not yet.

I pointed to the dangling rope.

'Gil, up there. And don't make any noise on that plastic. It's murder.'

We ran to the rope and Gil started up. Tommy went next. He was half way up the rope as Gil pushed himself up through the hole.

He made a terrible racket.

You cunt, I thought. Why the fuck did we bring you?

The sound of the plastic rattled and cracked through the yard's silence. Then the racket stopped. Gil must have got to the office roof and pulled himself up.

Tommy went through the hole and didn't make a sound and all the time as I climbed up the rope I was expecting to hear the alarm go off. But it didn't.

I went through the hole without making any noise.

I was in the open air. I could hear the sound of the city.

I looked towards the office roof. We had to cross it to get at the section of wall we wanted. Gil was outlined against the sky, balancing on the edge of the office roof. Tommy and I began to crawl towards him.

Gil waved us back with his hand. Tommy and I stopped

dead. Gil got down on to the plastic and began to crawl back towards us.

'What in Christ's name is he playing at?' Tommy said.

When he got near enough to speak Gil said:

'We're rumbled. There's a screw with a dog looking towards us. He must have heard us on the plastic.'

I felt sick.

'Us!' Tommy said. 'Listen you cunt…'

'Shut up!' I said. 'We'll have to go the other way.'

'What other way?'

'Across the plastic.'

This was the only alternative. Back across the plastic and drop down by the remand wing that butted on to the other side. Then round the end wing to a spot I'd seen when I'd been over the main prison, towards the main gate. I knew we had a good chance of getting over if we could make that spot. In any case, we had no choice. And there was no time left for gut-crawling. We had to leg it.

Gil picked up the rope and wound it round his waist. Tommy went off first, then me, then Gil. The noise was like thunder. As I ran I could see men getting up at their windows in the remand block, silhouetted against their cell lights. Then I heard Wally's voice coming on the wind.

'You bastards,' he screamed. 'You fucking bastards.'

His voice sang in my ears as I ran.

'On the roof,' he screamed. 'Cracken's on the roof.'

We got to the end of the plastic.

Tommy said: 'Hear that cunt?'

'Yes,' I said. 'If we're put back he'll wish he'd let us get away.'

We ran across the roof of the remand wing. Gil unwound the hooked rope as we ran. When we got to the edge of the roof Tommy fixed the rope and we all slithered down to the ground.

The wall was only forty feet away from us but this section

had a continuous line of barbed wire bracketed along its rim. The spot I'd got in mind was where the wall joined a relatively low building near the gate. The nearest part of the building was single-storey, with a flat roof. From this I'd figured we could get up to the rest of the building, then on to the barbed-wire-free wall and down.

Tommy and I ran towards the building. The ground was damp and cold under our feet. Gil was still by the wing, trying to shake the hooked rope free. Tommy reached the building first. He put his foot on a window sill and went up on to the flat roof. I followed him up and waited for Gil. By now he had freed the rope and was running towards us, winding the rope round himself as he went. He was about twenty feet from the building, just past the corner of the wing. I got set to stretch out a hand to help him up.

Then a screw rounded the corner of the wing, coming from the other side. The screw was only a few feet behind Gil but Gil didn't see him or hear him.

'Behind you,' I shouted.

But as I shouted the screw dived. The tackle took Gil entirely by surprise. He hit the ground face first. The screw tried to scramble on top of him but Gil lashed out with his feet and caught the screw in the chest. Gil managed to get to his feet again and made a few more yards to the building. More screws pounded round the corner of the wing. The first screw was up again and charging for Gil.

Gil was at the building now but he was never going to be able to get up on the roof. They'd pluck him off before he got a foot on the sill.

'The rope,' I shouted.

Gil started to unwind the rope but the first screw jumped him again. Gil tried to fight him off but by the time he'd freed himself the other screws had arrived and he was smothered.

'I'm sorry, Gil,' I said.

Gil lay on the ground, fastened there by the screws. He looked gutted, but he nodded to me in reply.

I took off after Tommy. Behind me the whole nick was in uproar.

Tommy was at the far corner of the flat roof looking up at the next part of the building. This was a facing wall, about ten foot high, but about six inches from the top a line of foot long spikes jutted out horizontally. I grabbed Tommy by the waist and pushed him up. He grasped the spikes and heaved himself and swung his legs, wrapping them round the spikes so that he was hanging on the horizontal line. Then he manoeuvred himself so that he was on top of the spikes and then all he had to do was to roll himself over on to the roof.

I took my sweater off and threw it at the spikes until they caught in the wool. I began to pull myself up. But the sweater started to tear. I couldn't trust my weight on it. Tommy was leaning over the edge of the roof, looking down at me.

'Tommy,' I said, 'double the sweater.'

Tommy didn't move. He just kept looking down at me. Every time a whistle blew or a walkie-talkie crackled on Tommy's head would flick in the direction of the sound.

'Double it, Tommy,' I said.

I thought: he's going to leave me.

Then he leant forward and took the sweater off the spikes and twisted it into a rope and lay down and hung the sweater over the edge. I grabbed hold and scrambled up until I could get a hold of the spikes. Tommy straightened up and began to move away. I couldn't seem to lever myself over the spikes the way Tommy had done. I was too heavy. Tommy was out of sight now. In my desperation to get over the spikes one of them cut into my hand and sank into the flesh. Pain flashed up my arm. I almost let go.

'Tommy,' I shouted.

Tommy's voice came from somewhere on the roof-top.

'Come on, Billy.'

'I'm fucked on the spikes.'

There was a silence. Then Tommy appeared back at the edge. I laughed, as though everything was some big joke.

'I've clobbered my hand,' I said.

Tommy leant forward and grabbed my shoulder and pulled me over on to the roof.

'Thanks,' I said.

'For Christ's sake,' he said. 'Let's move.'

We took off on the edge of the roof, along a concrete drainage system that led straight to the section of wall without the barbed wire. Away to our left there was a complex of peaked tile roofing. We got to the wall. From where we'd approached it, the top was only eight feet above us. We scrambled up it like monkeys and looked down over the other side.

We were overlooking a thirty foot drop down on to the road that ran round the nick. Beyond the road was a patch of open common. But there were about twenty screws scattered about at the bottom of the wall.

Even though we drew straight back one of the screws spotted us.

'There's one of them.'

Tommy and I looked at each other.

'What do you reckon?' I said.

'Don't know, Billy.'

Everything was ashes in my mouth. The muscles in Tommy's face were slack and his eyes were full of tears.

'We can't drop from here,' Tommy said.

I looked back at the complex of tiled roofs.

'I'm going that way, Tommy,' I said. 'Coming?'

Tommy didn't move. Screws were rushing about outside the wall.

'Tommy?'

Nothing.

I scrambled across the roofs, away from where the screws were shouting. I reached the edge. I was only twenty feet off the ground. The tiled roof I was overlooking finished up about ten feet above the ground.

Ten feet. All I had to do was to slide down the tiled roof and I was out.

Everything was very quiet. Light from curtained windows fell softly on the back gardens. The faraway sound of the city rustled in the night air. I stayed where I was for a while, taking stock.

To my left, the cobbled street disappeared, cut out of sight by the buildings that supported the roof complex. But although I couldn't see, I knew that that way the road must lead back towards the nick, to the main gate. To my right, where the last garden was, the road made a right-angled turn beside the garden and then disappeared out of sight beyond the last house.

That was the way I had to go.

I lay there for a little while longer, listening. The nick could have been a thousand miles away: behind me all was silence. I decided to move.

I pulled myself up and straddled the roof. Then I froze. Footsteps. Coming from the direction of the nick, clattering up into the night air from the cobbled road. I looked down. Screws. About fifteen of them. All bunched up, running towards the end of the gardens where the road turned sharp left.

I stayed where I was. A perfect silhouette against the night sky. But not one of them looked up. They rounded the corner and disappeared behind the end house. This was the time to make my descent, in the shadow of their noise, to cover any racket I might make. I swung my other leg over the roof, gripped the ridging and let my body pendulum down against the tiles. Then I let go. I slid the rest of the way down the roof. Then there was empty space. For a second, I was in free fall, touching nothing. Then the ground, soft earth jarring through my whole body. I toppled and rolled the fall and then I was still, my face sideways in the damp tickling grass. I moved my fingers and felt the earth and the wetness of the grass. I breathed in and the clean moist smell of outside filled my brain.

Then I pressed my hands against the earth and stood up and walked to the edge of the cobbled road. The sound of the screws had gone now. I looked to my left, back towards the end of the nick. Nothing. I turned to my right and took the same route as the screws. When I got to the last house, I turned left, still going the same way as the screws had gone. But over on the right there was a T-junction. I turned into this, never looking to either side of me, just straight ahead.

I was really hitting it now. The road was recent. Ahead of me, it ran over a humpback bridge. Beyond the bridge, a well-lit street, intersecting the road I was on.

To my left, a blank wall.

To my right, a police station.

The illuminated sign jutted out from the wall. POLICE. They were all in there, typing their reports. No idea that Billy Cracken was standing outside in the dark a few yards away. Now I knew I'd made it. I began to run towards the bridge.

I crossed the bridge. Behind me it was still dead. I slowed. In front of me were the bright lights of the intersection. A single-decker bus slowed down to cross the road I was on before it turned up towards a shopping centre that I could now see to my left. If I'd had any money I'd have hopped on it. But the bus crossed the road and picked up speed and ground its way up towards the shopping centre. A cold wind stirred the puddles and shredded the sound of the bus's grinding gears. Then the intersection was quiet again.

I ran across the intersection and made for the pavement and took off the way the bus had come. About twenty yards ahead of me was another road, turning off left, which would put me back on the same direction as the one I'd taken from the nick.

But between me and this turning, a young man wearing a blazer was standing by the edge of the pavement. He'd been watching me since I'd crossed the intersection, as if he knew something was up. I kept running towards him. He moved to step in front of me. I thought for a moment that he was going to make a grab for me. I could have punched holes in him but that wasn't the point: so far I'd got away sweet and I wanted it kept that way. I kept going, my eyes on his eyes all the way. When I reached him he stepped to one side, one foot in the gutter. I turned my head as I passed him so that I could still keep eyeball contact with him. Neither of us said anything. There was just the sound of my footsteps and the billowing of the night wind.

Then I reached the side road and turned left. Now I was completely out of sight of the intersection.

This new road climbed narrowly upwards, shop-fronted on both sides. And there were people in it. But I guessed from the gloom at the far end of the road that it was leading me away from the town centre. So I kept on running, past the betting shop and the Boots and the Co-op and the pub and past the staring faces of the people until there were no more people and no more lights, to where the shops fell away into the darkness. And to my right, even darker than the road, a common. I cut into its erasing shadow and slowed to a walk.

I was on a dirt path that led diagonally across the common. Ahead the night-black silhouette of a church with a sprawling graveyard. To my right, the beginning of a line of trees that joined the path farther ahead of me. It was nice not to have to run, to feel secure. But best of all was the openness, the freeness, the limitless sky and the shuddering wind.

I looked back to the road. A car was pulling up at the edge of the common. Coming from the direction I'd come from. The car stopped. Nothing happened. Then the doors opened. Men got out wearing dark blue uniforms. They stood by the car, looking into the darkness of the common.

I ran. Straight for the sanctuary of the trees. The surging power of my run soothed away the alarm. This was what fitness was all about. Not competing for medals or prizes but for your life. As I ran I felt unbeatable. I flew along on the wind. Nobody was going to take me back now.

I reached the trees. Their dark protection closed around me. I smiled to myself as I pushed forward in the blackness.

Then, suddenly, I was treading air. Mug, I thought. You fucking mug. Then I hit ground again and I started to roll, over and over, flattening saplings and bushes until I crashed into a big tree and slithered to a stop.

I lay there in the backness, cursing.

I didn't feel any pain. I knew I'd injured my wrist from the way I'd fallen, but when you break something in the course of being shocked by something else, the pain sometimes waits a little while before coming. I moved my body slightly. Nothing. If there had have been, the movement would have let in the pain. I moved my legs, Again, nothing. I sighed relief.

Then I realised I'd lost a shoe. I began cursing again. I rolled over on to my knees and swept the ground all around me. It was useless. I couldn't even see a hand in front of my face. Fuck it, fuck it. I'd rather have broken my wrist.

I slowly became aware of the sound of water behind me. I stood up. Water lapping on mud. The river. I walked to the edge of the water and forced my eyes to accustom themselves to the darkness.

The river was about twenty-five yards wide at this point. On the other side of the river the bank was dark and treelined, just like the side I was on, but beyond the trees were the lights of houses winking a hundred yards back from the bank. No sounds of search parties. But behind me, on my side, foliage shifted and branches crackled.

I kicked off my other shoe and slowly walked into the water, making no sound. Then I chested forward and launched myself in a silent breast stroke. The middle of the river felt very open and exposed but I made the other bank without any scream going up. I crawled about ten yards up the bank and into the trees and sat and listened. Everything was quiet again.

Now the whole balance had changed. Wet clothes and no shoes meant I had no chance of passing in the street. God alone knew when I'd be able to make the phone call. For the next few hours all I could do was keep out of the way.

After a couple of minutes I heard the occasional shouts and barks and the flashing torches of the search party as it splashed about on the other side of the river. Now and then a duck would go up and that was all the luck they were going to get. I went up the rest of the bank and set about finding my hidey-hole.

Beyond the trees was a complex of gardens criss-crossed with paths, like allotments, only neater, more floral, stretching up as far as the row of window-lit houses. The houses were all terraced, no gaps, so I found myself a nice bush to crawl under and lay there massaging my clothes with the palms of my hands to try and get rid of some of the damp.

Rain began to fall again, heavy and determined, slapping down the leaves of the bush I was under. At irregular intervals I could hear groups of young people arriving at the houses, singing, shouting, slamming doors, switching lights on and off and generally creating a racket. I lay there for a good hour, listening to the goings on, hating all the noisemakers for being what they were, free and young and full of future. But gradually the noise died as the arrivals got fewer and fewer and soon I was able to hear different sounds, the sounds of searchers going through the gardens. I crawled from under the bush and made for the houses. Most of the lights were out now. I picked a back yard with less illumination than the rest and slipped through the back yard gate and closed it behind me. The yard was small, about fifteen feet long by twenty feet wide. I got into a corner and pressed myself against the wall so that the outhouse guttering would give me some protection from the rain. Upstairs in the house some students were moving about getting ready for bed. The light from their upstairs window fell in a bright square in the yard, but where I was my dark clothes sank into the shadows. Another hour must have gone by. Then the downstairs light came on and the back door opened. An old boy came out and went over to a dustbin which was only six foot away from me. He lifted the lid and slid some rubbish into the bin. If I'd moved there'd have been no chance. He was facing directly towards me. And of course the shivers were never more eager to dance through my muscles than at that particular moment. The old boy put the lid back but it slipped down between the dustbin and the fencing. The old boy bent forward and fumbled about down the side of the bin. Finally he got a proper grip on the lid and fished it up and clanged it down on top of the bin. Then he went back inside the house and closed the door. I decided to move. All I needed was the alarm to go up and all the search parties would be concentrated together round the river bank and I'd have no chance. So I went through the yard gate and back into the gardens and found another bush and laid down again until by my reckoning it was about eleven o'clock, near the graveyard hour.

It had stopped raining. Now the moon was up.

I picked my way back down to the river and walked along the bank in the direction I'd been following before I'd had my swim. On both sides of the river was beautiful landscape with trees casting long shadows over the rolling lawns. I must have gone for almost a mile when the scenery abruptly changed. Ahead of me was a riverside industrial estate, all wire netting and sodium lighting. One way round it was to move inland and make it back into the streets. Which in my present state was suicide. I stood at the river's edge and looked at the water. The current was running the way I wanted to go. Depending on my fitness, there was a chance I could swim most of the way out. And there's nothing like testing the limits of your fitness, I told myself.

I waded back into the water. This time the cold was much worse. It hit me like the coldness of a swift-running tap. I went farther in and lunged forward into a swim. My skin felt as though I was sliding over iced razor blades. I kept telling myself that soon I'd get used to it, but my body wasn't listening.

I swam past a half-submerged pipe. A long tailed rat was sitting on the end, its fur spiked by the wet. The rat watched me as I swam by, curious but unafraid.

The cold got worse. It was blanketing my strength. No use. I had to give it up. Any farther and I'd be good for sod all. I veered right and crawled out of the water.

I'd got out by a piece of derelict ground, the remains of a demolished warehouse. The chasms of former cellars pitted the wasteland. This wasteland was bounded on three sides by the backs of Victorian warehouses. The fourth boundary was the water. There was no way out except back the way I'd come.

I sat down on the ground and stripped off my clothes and wrung them out. Then I picked up handfuls of dirt and rubbed the dirt all over my body, trying to soak up the damp and the cold. Across the river I could see the red neon of a cinema clock rising above the skyline. It was a quarter to twelve.

I walked up and down at the water's edge, trying to warm my body so that my brain would unfreeze. One thing was for sure. I wasn't going back in the river again. And I wasn't going trotting around the town at this time of night either. When the streets were empty the law had eyes the bigger to see you with. And in any case I had to have some daylight to see if there was any way out of the wasteland.

I put my clothes on and clambered down into one of the cellars. I found a brick alcove and sat down, my back to the wall. The only thing I could do was to wait for the morning.

The night was endless. Sleep was out because of the cold. To pass the time I counted out every quarter of an hour in seconds and then when I thought a quarter of an hour had passed I'd get up at the cellar's edge and look across at the cinema clock to see how far out I was. This kept me going for a couple of hours. For the rest of the time I roamed about in the cellar pit, trying to walk off the aches that the cold had put in my muscles.

Then the first deep blue of daylight began to colour the sky. When the blue had turned to grey I got out of my hole and did a reccy round the backs of the warehouses to see if there was a way out.

At one point there was a fifteen foot break between the warehouses: a fifteen foot wall, no more than ten feet high. I swung myself up and found myself looking into a cluttered builders yard. There was a small office and inside the office there must have been a telephone. It would have been simple to break in and use it. But I couldn't start moving again till the next evening so that would have been madness. And the office was new, not a rotten old shed. You never could tell what would be wired and what wouldn't these days.

But beyond the office there was a double iron gate that opened on to the road. That was all I needed to know.

I dropped down again and went back to my foxhole and watched the dawn break. Sounds of the city's awakening drifted across the river. In the road beyond the builders yard traffic began to pass by more frequently. Milk carts whirred and buses rattled. At seven o'clock the gates to the yard clanged open. Then after a while bright sunlight penetrated the haze and began to warm the earth and colour the city. A light breeze sidled off the river. I settled down to wait for the night to come again.

Seven o'clock. Evening. I straddled the wall and checked the yard. Nothing – I dropped down and walked to the side gate, soundless in my stockinged feet. I listened for any sounds in the street outside and then when I was certain everything was fine I climbed over the gate and landed on the cobble-stones beyond.

The street was empty. There were no pavements. Eyeless warehouses butted right up to the cobblestones. Brighter lights winked at the end of the street. I began to walk towards them.

I came out into a well-lit motorway feeder. To my right, a roundabout.

I crossed the road and made for a group of old Victorian office buildings that promised darker back streets. The beginning of the first street I reached was bridged by one of the roundabout feeder roads, and as I walked underneath I could see a bowling alley on the bank above me, its entrance crowded with boys and girls spilling out over the pavement in a twittering flux, unaware how rich they were.

I carried on down the back street. If I saw anyone approaching me I'd cross over to the opposite side of the road so that they'd have less chance of noticing my stockinged feet.

After about a mile the buildings began to thin out. I was reaching the edge of the city. Straggling pockets of suburbia twinkled all around me. Then even the semis became fewer and I was in open fields.

Rain began to drizzle down. Away to my left I heard a train go by, a mile or so away. I decided to make for the track. It would be perfect. A straight road without traffic or pedestrians. I climbed over a gate and began to trot across the fields, avoiding roads and farms as much as possible.

Then I came up against the poxy river again.

I stood on the bank and swore. It was narrower here but it was still the poxy river. There was no way round it. If I wanted to make the railway I had to cross the river.

This time I took my clothes off and wrapped them up into a bundle and walked into the water holding my clothes aloft and began to swim. The river was much swifter here. It might as well have been twice as wide the time it took me.

In the middle I was tipped by the current. The bundle nearly went under but I trod water and managed to keep the bundle above my head but I was swept quite a way down the river by the swiftness of the current. It took me over twenty minutes before I finally made the other side.

I climbed up the bank and tore some leaves off the bushes and rubbed myself all over. When I was as dry as I could get I unwrapped the bundle and began to get dressed. Then I realised that I'd lost my socks in the river. It had to be the river. I'd been careful to roll the socks up on the other side. They must have dropped out of the bundle when the current had jolted me. Just the same I ferreted about on my hands and knees in case they'd fallen out on to the ground. But even as I looked I knew I wasn't going to find them. I punched the ground with my fist and swore at the sky. I didn't deserve to be out. First the shoe and now the fucking socks. They'd never have let me in the scouts. I stood up. Another train went by on the distant track. I looked towards the sound. I was only wasting time.

It must have been nine o'clock when I reached the track. I climbed the bank and began to run at a comfortable pace, making sure I kept to the sleepers. But the pace was the only comfortable thing about that run: the track had been laid on a base of flint, like shingles. A lot of the stones had flowed on to the sleepers. With almost every step a flint cut into the soles of my feet. It was too dark for me to be selective and there was no alternative to running so I had to bear the pain or give up. A typical Cracken situation. The only way I could cover it was to blank the pain out of my mind by thinking of what was waiting for me once I'd made the phone call. I thought of Sheila and the kid and my mates and all that freedom they'd got laid on for me back in the Smoke. I thought of Sheila and Ronnie as they would be right now, wide awake, by the phone just waiting for the call. And the kid, fast asleep in his cot, not knowing he was going to see his Daddy. I kept running and I kept thinking and the pain kept ripping into my feet.

After four hours or so, I had to stop. My feet couldn't take any more. What had made things worse for me was having to scramble off the track and down the bank every time a train came along: the relief it gave my feet only increased the pain every time I got back on the track and started to run again.

I came to a railway arch and sheltered there until dawn. It was no use trying to sleep: the drizzling rain had soaked me just as completely as the river had done.

I waited for the dawn.

But, surprisingly, I did sleep. It might only have been for a few minutes, but I slept. I awoke out of a dream that was full of screws dancing round a rope and on the end of the rope was me, trying to drag myself up, to the top of a limitless wall, but my muscles weren't operating properly, they were stiff and cramped and my body was heavy, waterlogged, and all the screws were laughing because the fall was inevitable, and before falling I looked into each of their faces and each of their faces was Walter's face. The laughter grew louder and I let go of the rope and I awoke.

Daylight. Still raining. A train was coming down the track. I ran out of the archway and sprinted along the track, looking for cover. On either side of me were, at the bottom of the banks, hedgeless fields. No cover at all. All I needed was for a car to pass over the arch and for the driver to see this fleeing shoeless madman on the track below him. The train was getting nearer. Was it close enough for the driver to spot me? I veered sharp right and skidded down the bank and kept on running. Ahead of me was a small solitary bush, sprouting crazily next to the never-ending fencing. Pain told me that the sprint had opened the wounds in my feet. Wind rushed in my ears and there was the taste of blood in my throat.

I reached the bush and dived underneath. There was hardly enough of it to cover me. Then the train roared past and the bush shook and the noise grew fainter and then there was silence.

I peered out of the bush. I was only about eighty yards from the road. As yet there didn't seem to be much traffic but if I left the bush only one driver had to spot me and that would be enough. Likewise with the trains. There was nothing I could do but wait for the darkness again.

The drizzle turned to heavy rain. I was soaking again. My resistance was getting lower and I was feeling the cold now. My feet were swelling and I felt sick with hunger. But all I could do was stay put. I wasn't going to screw it up just for the sake of a day.

I'd been there about two hours when a man I guessed to be a young farmer drove a small horse box along a dirt track, stopped, and led a horse into the adjoining field. At first he urged the animal to canter round and round the field, calling to it, whistling at it, generally enjoying the exercise even more than the horse was doing. Then he called the horse to him and gave it some sugar and when he'd done that he took his gear from the horse box and bridled and saddled the horse and rode the horse round the field for the best part of half an hour. The man and the horse made me feel better. I felt some kind of contact with them, as though they were players and I was an audience and the show was entirely for my benefit. There was a security in watching them, a feeling of rightness about their movement.

But I felt even emptier when the man loaded the animal back into the horse box and started the engine and drove away.

The rain kept raining. The bush gave me hardly any protection. Raindrops were causing me even more discomfort than the cold. When I'd been moving the rain wasn't too bad, but just lying there the raindrops gradually began to feel like ice-cold needles jabbing at my skin. I kept thinking that the rain had to stop soon, but it didn't. Sometimes it would come down even harder, perpendicular, spiteful, but these bursts only lasted a minute or so at a time.

A tremendous instinctive inertia forced me to stay put, no matter how uncomfortable it was becoming. A thousand times I must have said to myself, fuck it, take a chance, move, but each time I forced myself to stay put. It was like being paralysed: each moment I thought my body would break into flight, but each moment nothing happened.

But by the afternoon I was too cold. I couldn't stay there any longer. Although night was a long way away, the rain was causing a false dusk, gloomy enough for me to risk it. Once I'd decided, acted, I was glad. Sod the risk. It was worth it to be moving again.

I ran under the arch and along the track for about half a mile. Then I came to a gangers' hut. I couldn't believe my luck. Somewhere I could get dry. Somewhere out of the piercing bloody rain.

I opened the door. Vandals had smashed everything worth smashing and tarred their initials on the walls. But there was a bench that was still intact so I closed the door behind me and sat down and began to strip off my soaking clothes. I happened to glance up at the door. Hanging from a nail was an old greatcoat. I stood up and slowly walked over to the door. I couldn't believe it. A coat. I reached out and touched it. It was dirty and mouldy and tatty but was a coat. I took it down from the nail and held it in my hands. It was the warmest thing I'd ever felt in my life.

I went back to the bench and draped the coat over it and took off the rest of my clothes and wrung them out and then I lay down on the coat and watched the steam rise off my chest. If I'd had something to eat or drink I'd have been the happiest man in the country.

When night came again I set off again down the track. But before I left the hut I'd torn up my winter vest and wrapped the pieces tightly round my feet and ankles. This gave my feet more protection than if I'd just been wearing socks. I took off down the line as fast as I could go.

After about half an hour I saw that I was running into a small town. A few minutes later I came to a small housing estate which lay to my left; on one of those quiet street corners there would be a telephone kiosk. I left the track and climbed a slatted fence and walked across a patch of wasteground that joined a straggling, going nowhere road that led out of the estate.

The streets were deserted. Light from curtained windows fell warm and cosy on the neat front gardens. Now and again as I passed a house I could hear the muffled telly sounds beyond the curtains. Upstairs lights were on up and down the street; bedtime for the kiddies.

I turned a corner and straight in front of me, opposite a bus shelter, was a telephone booth. There was no one about. I walked up to the booth and opened the door and went in and dialled the operator. This was it.

'Number please?'

'I'd like a transfer charge call, please.' I gave the number and the false name.

'One moment, sir.'

The operator went off the line. Wind droned round the phone booth. In a house across the road a light went off.

The operator came back on.

'Go ahead please.'

'Yes?'

Sheila's voice.

'It's me.'

She began to say my name, but I had to cut her off in case the operator was still plugged in.

'Tell Ronnie I'll see him in the morning.'

I gave her the phone number, the street and the name of the town. I told her to tell Ronnie to bring the clothes and the money and to pick me up at the phone booth at eight o'clock the next morning. There was no time to tell her anything else. She began to say how she thought I wasn't going to make it but I had to cut her off again.

But not before I'd heard, in the background, Timmy's cry.

I opened the door of the kiosk. Rain was falling again. The street was still empty. I walked back towards the railway. I didn't see a soul. I climbed over the slatted fence and squatted down, my back leaning against the planking. The rain began to come down harder. I thought about Sheila and Timmy and what it would be like tomorrow when I saw them. I stayed like that for about an hour. And got thoroughly soaked. I couldn't stay there all night. There had to be some shelter somewhere. I followed the line of the fence but there was no cosy railwaymen's hut along this stretch and I didn't want to get too far away from where I was going to get picked up: the less open ground I had to cover in daylight the less chance of somebody seeing me and arriving at a brilliant deduction.

I climbed over the fence and went back into the estate. Still lifeless. Rain raced down the dead streets. I walked to the edge of the estate, but keeping within a good distance of the phone box. Here there was an older street, pre-war suburban, more respectable than the estate it flanked. The very best sort of council estate with dainty little front gardens contained behind neat privet. Some of the houses had garages built on to the side walls. I stopped outside a house that had a double garage. There was a light on in the hall but the bowed front window was black with night. I opened the front gate and walked up the path and round the side of the garage. There was a trellis gate and beyond that the back garden with the dining room light twinkling on the wet grass. I pressed the latch on the gate. The trellis-work shuddered. Beads of rain cascaded down on to the concrete path. I pushed against the gate. Wood scraped on concrete. I stopped pushing. In the next house a toilet flushed and a landing light went on and off. I waited a few minutes and pushed the gate again. It shuddered open enough for me to squeeze through. I went round the back of the garage. There was a small door that led into the garage, right next to the kitchen door. The kitchen was in darkness. I could hear the television beyond the dining room curtains. I tried the garage door. It was unlocked. I opened it and went in.

A small square window in the garage's front door let in the light from the street lamp. There was a Hillman Minx and two children's bikes. There was also a door that led into the house. There were panes of frosted glass in this door. Beyond the panes, darkness.

I hunted round the garage for a tap. But there was no tap, only a box full of empty bottles stacked by the back door. I took each bottle from the box very carefully, to see if there were any dregs. There were lager bottles and beer bottles and spirit bottles but they were all empty. But at last I came across a lemonade bottle. There was an inch or so of flat liquid in the bottom. I unscrewed the cap and sniffed it, in case it was paraffin or something like that. But it wasn't. It actually was lemonade. I put the bottle to my lips and drank. It was beautiful. The nearest I'd ever get to the Elixir of Life. I kept the lemonade in my mouth for as long as I could, just so the taste could keep working on my palate. Finally I swallowed the stuff but the taste stayed with me.

I put the bottles back in the box. Then I went over to the Hillman and tried the doors. All except the nearside rear door were locked. I opened the rear door and got in and lay down on the back seat. It was real penthouse stuff to me, feeling the softness of the upholstery against my body. But even so, I couldn't sleep. I was too full of excitement at the prospect of the next morning. I just lay there in the warmth of the car, imagining what it would be like in a moving car, belting down the motorway towards the Smoke.

When daylight came I stayed in the car for another hour. I reckoned that whoever lived in the house wouldn't be a shift-worker, and that the earliest they'd be up and about would be around half-past-six. I didn't want to move before I had to, so I lay there in the car trying to pace out the time to around six o'clock. But after about an hour I began to panic. Lack of sleep and food was making me light-headed. I began to want to doze off. One time I actually closed my eyes and almost fell asleep. I jerked myself upright in panic. It was no good. I couldn't chance it any longer. I had to take my chances in the street. But at least I was warm and dry and in an hour or so I'd be travelling at seventy miles an hour.

I opened the car door and held it open to let some of the stale air out. Then I noticed some mud on the upholstery so I leant back into the car and wiped the seat. After I'd done that I closed the car door very quietly and went over to the garage door, the one I'd come in by. My fingers closed over the door handle. I took one look over my shoulder just to check that I hadn't left anything out of place.

Then a shaft of light spurted through the frosted glass panels of the door that led into the house. Inside, somebody called goodbye. Then footsteps, coming towards the door with the frosted glass panels. The footsteps stopped. A bolt was drawn. Then a key turned.

I opened the garage door and pulled it to behind me but without closing it properly. I heard the other door open and close and then footsteps going over to the Hillman. I looked to my left. The kitchen light was on. I could be seen from the window. I went round to the side of the garage. The neighbouring house was in darkness. I leant against the side of the garage and waited. I heard sounds of more bolts being drawn. Then one of the garage doors was opened. I looked towards the end of the garage. I heard the other door being opened. It swung into view, overlapping the end of the garage wall. I could see the man's fingers gripping the woodwork and his feet beneath the door. And the door was the one with the window. When the door was completely open he walked back into the garage. I saw his head as he passed the window. Middle-aged, glasses. A trilby. All he would have had to do was turn his head.

The Hillman started up. It idled for a minute or two, then it crept out of the garage. The car stopped, a door opened. Footsteps back to the garage. The fingers appeared again round the edge of the door. The door was dragged shut. Now I could see the Hillman. The man walked past the car to the gate that opened on to the road. He lifted the latch and swung back the gate. Then he got back in the car and drove the Hillman out into the road. I pressed myself against the garage wall as he walked back from the car to close the gate. All he had to do was to look as he fastened the latch. But he didn't. He walked back to the Hillman and slammed the door and drove off.

I waited a few minutes before I made a move. I listened for noises in the street and round the houses. When I was as satisfied as I could be I walked away from the garage to the gate. I felt naked. I lifted the catch but I was shaking so much that I let it drop back again and before I'd realised what I'd done I'd tugged at the gate, making a row that rang up and down the empty street. Whoever was left inside the house must have heard it. I'd made the whole of the fencing rattle. I got the gate open and without bothering to close it I took off down the street. But I stopped running when I saw a milk float whirring round the corner. I couldn't change direction because that would have looked great, a running man, changing direction, with rags on his feet, haring off the minute a milk float appeared. I kept on walking towards the milk float, playing up the shuffling tramp bit, hands in greatcoat pockets, shoulders hunched. The milkman gave me a quick look but it didn't interfere with his whistling. He opened a garden gate and rattled his crate down on a doorstep and pressed the doorbell. Settling-up time. I was tempted to shamble over to the float and lift myself a pint, but at this stage in the game blowing the whole thing with only an hour or so to go would have been suicidal.

I carried on until I came to the phone box. I went in and rang the operator and asked her what I should dial for the time and she said such and such a number but she could give me the time herself, should she do that? Well it was just coming up to twenty-five to eight. I thanked her and put the receiver down. Twenty-five to eight. Twenty-five minutes.

They'd be here in twenty-five minutes.

I opened the door and went outside and sat down on the low wall next to the box. About two hundred yards away to my left was the main road. Dual-carriageway. Traffic already zooming up and down it, the morning sunlight flashing on the racing paintwork. That was the way they'd be coming. A right turn, a U-turn, the door would open, and there I'd be, sinking in warm upholstery, a steady seventy under the morning sun.

The street was still empty. The man with the Hillman must have been the only early starter. It would be after eight o'clock before they all started making it for wherever they spent their eight hours a day. But still I was taking a risk by sitting there. My euphoria was making me careless. The milkman hadn't sorted me but it was the kind of street that wouldn't be keen on a tramp taking up residence outside the telephone box. A nose between the lace curtains and a quick phone call to the local nick would be enough to put the damper on things. So I got back in the phone box and watched for the Rover.

I calculated the time to be five or ten minutes past eight. People had started to leave their houses, walking or driving, on their way to work. One or two kids were amongst them, uniforms buttoned, satchels swinging, eager for the new day.

It must be quarter past eight now, I thought.

A big car turned into the street off the main road. My heart leapt. The car was white. The right colour. I peered through the dirty panes. Yes. The right colour. But the wrong car. A Triumph. It purred past the kiosk and disappeared down the street.

Never mind. What's quarter of an hour? Jesus, if they're here before half past eight I should think myself lucky. Anything could happen. Traffic bottlenecks. Slow service at petrol stations. Anything.

More time passed. Clouds drifted across the face of the sun. The street became grey again. Gone half-past now, I thought. Must be gone half-past.

Another car came in off the dual-carriageway. It was white. I could see that much. And the right size. But this time I waited. The car got closer. A Rover. Yes, it was. A bloody beautiful Rover. I pushed open the kiosk door and ran to the edge of the kerb. The Rover was fifty yards away. It began to slow down. They'd seen me. This was it.

But the Rover didn't keep on coming. Instead the car turned left into one of the side streets. All that was left in the street was the echo of the Rover's engine. Then nothing.

I felt sick. This time I'd been sure. I stood there on the edge of the pavement staring at the spot where the Rover had turned off. Then I heard footsteps approaching along the pavement. I turned my head in the direction of the sound. A schoolgirl. About twelve years old. Staring hard at me, almost faltering in her step, wondering whether or not it was safe to pass by. Her parents had done their job well. I turned away again. The footsteps quickened and then she passed me. I watched her as she walked away. She didn't look back.

I went back into the kiosk. More and more children appeared. I watched them go by, trying to keep the panic from rising too far up my chest. After a time there were no more children. The street was empty again. Nine o'clock. It must be nine o'clock, I thought. An hour. Where were they?

Then the phone rang. The sound screamed up and down my nervous system and I whirled round and scrabbled the receiver off its hook.

'It's me.'

Sheila's voice, crackly and distant.

'What's happened?'

My own voice sounded high and twisted.

'They won't be there.'

I stared into the reflection of my eyes in the kiosk mirror.

'They won't be here?'

'The car broke down. Miles from anywhere, on the way up. Ronnie had to phone a mate to fetch them back.'

'Why didn't he come up with him?' I said, already knowing the answer, just letting the panic operate my mouth.

'How could they? The other feller wasn't in it.'

'Why didn't you come up on the train with clothes and money?'

'Billy, don't be a damn fool, you know...'

'All right, all right. So what's happening. What the Christ is Ronnie doing?'

'He's fixing somebody else. He has to be careful. He can't risk it again himself so he's got to spot someone safe.'

'So what about me? I've got to be bleeding careful too, haven't I? I've...'

'Billy, listen. I'm seeing Ronnie at one o'clock. He'll have fixed it by then. I'll have to phone you after that.'

'Just like that. Listen. I wouldn't be risking hanging round this box if I hadn't...'

'Billy, be careful. Don't blow it now. Not now. Phone me back. That's all you *can* do.'

I couldn't say anything else. I put the phone down in the middle of something Sheila was saying. I closed my eyes and

195

leant against the door. I felt terrible. I'd geared myself up to being collected at eight o'clock, to getting in the car, to eating, to changing. Now I had to wait till two o'clock to find out what was going to happen. I might not even have someone come for me for a couple of days. Christ. And now I had to start the discipline all over again. I had to keep myself together till two o'clock. And then till God knew how long after that. I'd sustained myself for the last twelve hours on the thought of that lifeboat travelling up from London. Now I had to start all over again and it was an adjustment I couldn't take. The thought of it utterly demoralised me. I felt beaten, and I began to treat my depression with the balm of self-pity. For the first time I began to think I might fail.

The kiosk door opened a little against my weight. I pushed the door the rest of the way open and walked out. For a moment or two, I just stood there, staring down the empty road towards the dual-carriageway. Then across the road a front door opened and a woman appeared. She was carrying a shopping bag. Her actions were quite normal until she reached her front gate and noticed me. Then she slowed down and gave me a long look. She took her time opening and closing the gate. Her eyes were on me all the time. Even as she walked away she kept looking back over her shoulder at me.

I had to pull myself together. I'd allowed myself to take too many risks because the thought of the Rover speeding up to get me had made any thoughts of danger seem trivial. But now I was down to earth. I was a million miles from home and I had to be careful. Again.

I hurried down the road and turned right, back towards the edge of the estate, towards the railway. I had to find somewhere to lie low until two o'clock. On the wasteland to my right there was a row of three hoardings. Nothing behind them except more wasteland and beyond that fields and a few houses. I crossed over and made for the hoardings. One of them was advertising Skol Lager. A picture of a great big glass full of translucent yellow liquid and the glass dripping with ice-cold perspiration. I remembered the swig of lemonade I'd had in the garage.

I rounded the hoarding and squatted down in the damp grass. At first I closed my eyes and tried to get sleep to blot out my depression but sleep wouldn't come. The thought that I might fail kept dragging across my brain.

For the first time I began to feel really thirsty. No hunger, just thirst. I kept thinking about that big yellow glass of lager on the other side of the hoarding. I wanted to get up and walk round and have a look at it, as if just staring at it would make me feel better. The thirst was so bad I was beginning to feel light-headed like a man in the desert with his mirage of a palm-shaded waterhole.

Then, a long way away, I heard a clock strike. Ten o'clock. Four more hours. But at least I'd know when to move for Sheila's call. That made me feel a little better. But not much. My skin had begun to obsess me. I felt like an alcoholic with withdrawal symptoms: every inch of my skin was crawling and I couldn't stop scratching. I'd scratch in one place and get blessed relief only to have to move on to the next area in a never-ending process.

Then the rain started again. This time a fine drizzle, as depressing as the view across the dead wasteland. The whole world seemed damp and dead and motionless.

The faraway clock struck a quarter-to-two. I stood up and peered round the edge of the hoarding. There was no one about so I walked over to the road and made for the phone box. As I got close to it I tried to fight the uncontrollable hope that was welling up inside me. I had to keep that down in case Sheila's news was bad. My system couldn't have taken another bashing.

I got in the phone box and waited. Half an hour went by.

Maybe I'd got the time wrong. Maybe she'd phoned just before I'd got to the box. But if that was so, she'd keep ringing wouldn't she? I picked up the phone and got the operator to dial Sheila's number. No reply. Maybe she was still with Ronnie. Ronnie could be having trouble fixing things up and that's why she wasn't back. Or she could have been picked up. The Filth could have sussed out the new flat. They'd never be able to hold her, but they just might play awkward to make things difficult for any arrangements we were making. Anything could have happened.

I leant on the metal directory holders and looked out at the drizzle. The box was warm from my body heat. I began to feel drowsy. I wanted to sleep. Maybe when I woke up I'd find it was all a bad dream, and in fact I was lying next to Sheila between clean sheets.

There was a rat-a-tat on one of the glass panels. I jerked upright. A woman, waiting to use the phone. I pushed the door open and stumbled out, saying something about being sorry, waiting for a call, and the woman glared at me and frowned as the warm smell from the kiosk hit her. But I was too numb either to react to her or to worry about any consequences there might be. I just sat on the wall and stared at the houses opposite and waited for her to come out again.

She didn't take long. The door swung open and she bustled out, pulling on her gloves and giving me all the contempt she could muster. I avoided her gaze and stood up and went back into the box. Now there was a faint female smell mixed in with my own, a pleasant furry glovey silky smell that made me feel nostalgic for a past experience I couldn't quite define.

And still there was no phone call. After about an hour I phoned again. No answer. I began to sink into a maudlin apathy. The whole thing was becoming too much of an effort. I had a pain in my chest and my breathing was becoming shallow and rasping. The warmth of the kiosk was hatching out all kinds of wishful thinking in my passive brain. One idea that kept drifting in and out of my mind was to get myself committed to hospital. At one point this really became a very attractive proposition. A nice crisp clean bed and something to drink. Some hot soup, say. Tomato soup. That would be fantastic. Hot tomato soup. I rationalised it by telling myself that they wouldn't check me out, but really it wasn't a rationalisation at all, just an example of the weakness that had crept into my brain.

Children began to pass the kiosk on their way home from school. The chest pain was getting worse. Breathing was very difficult now. Purely psychological, I thought. A way out of the impasse. A way of excusing myself if I failed. I could say that I couldn't go on, my chest was too bad, I had to give in, how could I go on? If I hadn't gone to the hospital, well...

More time passed and the decision to risk the hospital got stronger and stronger. A couple more people arrived to use the phone and each time I left the box I almost kept on walking, but out in the cold drizzle my thoughts would take a reverse. The phone box was my life line, my oxygen mask. Outside the box, all I wanted to do was to get back into the warm, near to the phone.

When the street lights came on I tried to get Sheila again.

This time she was there.

'Where were you?' I said.

'Ronnie's had problems.'

'I've been here all the time, waiting...'

'I phoned twice. The line was engaged. Listen...'

'I just...'

'Listen. They'll be there at eight. Eight o'clock. They've got everything you need.'

Outside on the pavement there was a young fellow waiting to use the box, looking in at me.

'They're on their way?'

'Yes. They're in a red Morris Oxford. One of them will be wearing a sheepskin jacket. Are you listening, Billy?'

The young fellow on the pavement kept looking at me.

'I'm listening.'

'They'll stop by the box and the one in the sheepskin will get out and go into the box. They'll do this every quarter of an hour until nine. Right? Then they'll go. They'll have to go at nine. So you've got to be there.'

I don't care what main-liners say about the heroin racing through their bloodstream or what women say about having a baby, this news was the complete ecstatic experience. They were on their way. The weight of the last few hours fell away from me. I was alive again. The transfusion was working.

'I'll be there,' I said.

'They can't wait after nine.'

'I know,' I said. 'Don't worry. I'll be there.'

I put the receiver back on its cradle. This time the face in the mirror was smiling.

I pushed open the door. The man who'd been waiting had gone. I didn't look to see where to. All I could think of was the phone call. This time I knew I'd be all right. It had that feel to it. Adrenalin pumped my elated thoughts through my brain as I strode back towards my hoarding. Just a couple of hours. Nothing. A couple of hours meant nothing. Not now. I was breathing properly now and I could smile at the pathetic defeatism of the hospital idea. I knew that even if the car never showed I would be able to adapt accordingly. The spell was broken. My strength and self-reliance had returned and I was determined not to rely on anything but my own abilities again.

I began to cross the road to the turning that led to the hoarding. Three men stepped out of the darkness of the turning. One of them was the guy from outside the phone box. There was no mistaking who they were. The Filth. The elation I'd got from the phone call had furred up my other faculties. I should have tagged the rozzer outside the kiosk as soon as I'd seen him, no trouble. But I knew I had no worries. They were as surprised to see me as I was to see them. They'd probably been called out on a routine check because somebody had phoned in to say they'd seen a tramp hanging round the phone box obviously up to no good. And so the Filth had come out, just in case, but not really expecting to come up with Billy Cracken, so they'd only sent them three-handed. And when the young rozzer had copped for who the tramp actually was, they'd got no choice but to come at me before I cleared off, while the uniform in the car radioed in and upset half the dinners in the town.

I stopped walking. They stopped as well. There was about twelve feet between us. The soft drizzle was still falling. Behind me, at the far end of the road, the traffic swished by on the dual-carriageway.

The young rozzer was the one to speak.

'Can we have a word with you, sir?'

You really had to hand it to them. Faced with Billy Cracken, a twenty-five year man, they still kept themselves covered. They still gave you the 'sir'.

One of the other rozzers had been staring at me particularly closely. Eventually he gave the nod and said: 'That's him.'

They began to walk forward again. They moved with a controlled casualness, as if they weren't really closing in on Billy Cracken, as if there wasn't going to be any trouble at all.

There wasn't.

I let them get to within six feet of me. Then I took off. Straight down the road towards the dual-carriageway, the wind roaring in my ears, the rain flicking in my face, coat flying, my face grinning a wild grin that described my feeling, my knowledge, that nobody was going to take Billy Cracken.

Fighting with the wind in my ears was the voices of the rozzers, calling for me to stop, and I thought, silly bastards, of course I'll stop, I never realised that you wanted me to stop, or else I wouldn't have taken off in the first place.

As I neared the dual-carriageway I checked the traffic as I ran and I gauged that if I kept running straight on, straight across the opposing flows of traffic I'd get over without being run over. Which I did. Cars braked and swerved but I made it. I glanced behind me and saw two of the rozzers hesitating while the traffic dispersed. The other rozzer must have been beating back to the squad car. On my side of the dual-carriageway was a low slatted fence, the perimeter of one of those multi-purpose school playing fields with a dozen football pitches crammed end to end and side by side. I clambered over the fence and took off into the flat darkness. Eventually I reached a concrete playground and beyond the playground there was a bicycle shed and behind the shed another fence. I went over this fence and I was in allotments again, but this time they were the real thing with sheds and neatly dug vegetable patches and the rusty paraphernalia of the suburban gardener. I paused for a moment. I couldn't see the rozzers against the lights from the dual-carriageway but that didn't mean to say that they weren't there, beating across the field after me. I took off again. Over another fence into a street of small flat-fronted terraced houses. I kept going. This street would be alive any minute now. Patrol cars would be screaming on their way. I turned right as soon as I could, into another street with the same kind of houses. Then I turned off left and then right until I was a good three or four streets away from the allotments. But I couldn't just keep on running. I'd be picked up in no time. I had to find somewhere to hide. But whatever I found was bound to be chancy, especially if they did a house to house. But there was no choice. I was finished if I stayed on the streets.

The street I was in was terraced just like all the others. Every now and again there'd be a passage, tunnel-like, leading to the back gardens. I turned into one of the passages and at the end of it were two latched gates, one right, one left. I took the left one; there were no lights shining from the house on to the back garden. Everything was quiet. I closed the gate behind me and walked to the end of the narrow garden. At the bottom of the garden was a lumber shed about as big as a small outside toilet. The door was split in two, half way up, like a barn door. I opened the top section and looked inside. It was too dark to see anything so I leant over the bottom half of the door and felt about in the dark. My fingers touched something solid but loose and dusty at the same time. Coal. What did you expect, I thought. A four-poster? I climbed over the bottom half of the door and pulled the top half to and lay down on the coal and tried to make myself comfortable. Then I waited and I listened.

It didn't take them long. I guessed there were seven or eight squad cars screeching into the area, building up over a period of about a quarter of an hour. Then there was silence for a while. What were they going to do? Hang around and do the house to house or assume that if they couldn't spot me straight away I was making it farther away and spread themselves accordingly? Even if they did that, they'd leave somebody on tap, just in case I was still around.

I lay there in the dark, trying to find some foolproof way of gauging when to move. I only had a couple of hours to play with before the car showed up at the box.

After a while I heard a different kind of vehicle sounding off a few streets away: the door-bell tones of an ice-cream van. An ice-cream van, at this time of the year. But of course they'd have drinks on sticks and probably orange juice and Coca-Cola. The thought of something like that within easy reach began to stir the coalhouse dust in my throat and my nostrils.

If this whole scene had been down south, the phone box would be alive by now. If it had been the Yard that was involved they'd have already gone over the box from top to bottom and then got it staked out so that in no way would I have got back to it without being picked up. If you've got to have the rozzers after you, I thought, the farther north you are the better. I had to take my chances, but at least I wasn't up against the Yard. And the chances had to be taken.

I waited for what I guessed to be an hour. No klaxons, no fresh screeching of tyres. I climbed out of the coalhouse and made my way up the garden to the passage. Then along the passage. I stopped half way along and listened. Nothing. I moved towards the arch of light. Very slowly I poked my head out. The street was empty. Now all I had to do was walk out into the street. That was all. Once out, there was no cover, nothing. A patrol car could pass the end of the street and I'd have no chance. But there was nothing else for it.

I stepped out. At least my footsteps were silent. Which was as well because I'd decided to run: no use trying to play the dawdling tramp any more, not now they were wise to me.

I darted to the end of the street and pressed myself against the wall of the end house and peered round the corner. Again, nothing. Crazily, the old joke passed through my mind about the fellow falling off a skyscraper and as he passes each floor he says, 'so far so good, so far so good.'

I took off again and filtered through a few back streets stopping and starting like this. Finally I came to the last row of terraced houses and when I stuck my head round this last corner I could see the allotments and playing fields straight in front of me.

I could also see a patrol car.

The car was parked almost exactly where I'd come out of the allotments. There was only one of them in the car. That probably meant that at least one other rozzer was wandering about doing a bit of casing. And there was no way of telling where the casing was being done. whether in the allotments or in the streets around me. But that didn't matter as much as the problem I had of getting across the road. The only thing in my favour was that the car was facing away from me so that if I moved the only way the driver could see me crossing was in his driving mirror. But it was still too risky. The slightest movement on an empty road would be enough to make him flick his eyes up to the mirror. The other alternative would be for me to backtrack into the streets and finally come out at the far end of the road, far enough away from the car to chance making the crossing. But this meant travelling through streets I hadn't travelled through before, and there was no way of knowing what I'd find in them. For all I knew there could be a patrol car in every one of them.

I leant against the wall and swore. Then I heard the bells of the ice-cream van again. I chanced another look round the corner. The van was coming down the road where the police car was, travelling slowly along in the same direction that the police car was facing. Only the van wasn't an ice-cream van. It was a fish and chip van. A fish and chip van with an ice-cream sound. It swished slowly past the end of my road and the smell drifted across to me in the van's slipstream and my stomach turned over. The smell of the fish and chips was stronger than my thoughts on how to get over the road. The sickness of my hunger churned around in my stomach.

Then I heard the van begin to slow down. It was stopping. I chanced another look round the corner. The van was stopping. Pulling in behind the police car. Pulling in between me and the rozzer.

It must have been one of the van's regular pitches. I heard the doors being opened and then I saw women drifting over to where the van was standing. But I waited a while because now more than at any other time the rozzer would be looking in his mirror and I'd no way of telling how much his view had been obscured by the chippie.

Then the door of the police car opened. The rozzer slowly got out and dawdled over to the van and stood by the group of women clustered round the serving window. As the women were served they hurried back to their houses with the warm newspapers pressed to their bosoms. And then they'd all gone and there was just the rozzer. He stepped up to the window and gave his order and stood back with his hands on his hips and looked up into the night sky. Then the chippie handed the parcel through the window and the rozzer sorted out his money and gave it to the chippie and took the parcel and turned away and strolled back to his car, unwrapping the parcel as he went.

It was then that I crossed the road. As I reached the kerb on the other side I heard the clunk of the police car door as the rozzer closed it behind him. Now there was no way that he could see me in his mirror. The chip van was completely obscuring his view. The van's engine started up and I straddled the allotment fence and dropped down the other side.

I moved carefully away from the fence, into the darkness of the allotments. After I'd gone a little way in, I looked back to the row of terrace houses, unearthly bright under the sodium street lights. The rozzer was still in his car, feeding. There was no sign of anyone else.

This time I avoided the school and hit the playing fields at a different spot. I began to walk across to the lights of the dual-carriageway.

Then, outlined against the bright lights, I saw six or seven rozzers walking towards me, all strung out on a sweep operation. They had no lights; at least if they had they weren't using them yet. They'd use the lights when they got to the school and the allotments. No point in using them on the playing field. Cracken wouldn't be hiding out in the middle of a playing field.

They hadn't seen me yet. I wasn't silhouetted the way they were. But if I moved, if I tried to get back to the allotments, they'd be on to me. And the same if I tried any other direction.

My heart felt like concrete. Tears welled up in my eyes. After everything, this. I'd been too cocky. I'd been too sure.

The rozzers got closer. Still no one spotted me. Then I realized something. They'd just come out of the bright sodium of the dual-carriageway; I'd been flitting about in darkness for the last couple of days. My eyes were adjusted to the blackness: theirs weren't. There was a chance.

Very slowly, I let myself sink to the ground. I didn't make a sound, but I moved in ultra-slow motion. Then, when I was on the ground, I curled myself up into a ball and pressed myself into the wet earth. Then I waited.

I could hear their footsteps now. Then the rustle of their clothes, the sound of their breathing. I lay there wound up like a spring, waiting for a boot to stumble into my back and burst me open.

But they passed. There was no boot, no sudden cry of surprise. The rozzers passed me by.

I didn't move until I heard them hit the allotment fence. Then I chanced turning my head to see what they were up to. I saw the lights go on and the legs swing over. Now I could move. But I didn't get up. I crawled until I got close to the dual-carriageway, but not so close that if I stood up I'd be picked out by the sodium. Which was what I had to do. I had to get to my feet so that I could see over the perimeter fence and suss out what the Filth had fixed up on the other side.

There was a van and a couple of cars. Complete with drivers. Three of them, standing together, having a natter.

I dropped down again. I could do nothing but go parallel with the perimeter until I got far enough away to go over the fence without being seen.

But this time I didn't crawl. I ran, bent double, like Quasimodo. I covered about two hundred yards like this but I had to keep stopping for a rest: doubling myself up had brought back the pain in my chest.

I reached the end of the playing field. The perimeter fence

made a right-angled turn in front of me. Beyond this there was no sodium lighting. Just suburban houses that faced on to the dual-carriageway. But the houses formed a curve, not a straight line. So in front of them the dual-carriageway must follow the same curve. Enough of a curve to make my crossing invisible from the crowd of rozzers way down below me.

I climbed the fence and dropped down into the back garden of the first house. There were no lights on in the house. I walked round to the front garden. Cars flashed by but there were no pedestrians. I went through the garden gate and began to walk along the pavement until there was a long gap in the traffic. Then I took off across the road and into the nearest side street. When I came to the first house without any lights showing I got off the road and worked my way back to the telephone box via a route of back gardens. This way I only had two streets to cross. Finally I came out into a front garden about twenty yards away from the kiosk. I dropped down and made my way to the privet hedge and pushed myself into the leaves and looked over the low brick wall towards the kiosk on the other side of the road.

The street was empty. All the chopping and changing I'd been doing made me lose track of the time. It could have been eight or it could have been nine. I'd no idea. As far as I knew the Morris could be just half a mile away, on its way back to the Smoke. It might even have passed me on the dual-carriageway. No, I thought, it couldn't have done that. They'd have spotted me for sure. Surely they would. The feeling of desperation began to creep back into me again, like the awareness of my physical condition now that I was stationary again. The pain in my chest, the damp, the hunger. All spreading through me...

The sound of a car. A car had turned into the street. Slowing down as it approached the phone box. Then it stopped, but the engine didn't cut out. A door opened. I pushed my face through the leaves and looked towards the phone box. It was a police car. A rozzer got out and walked over to the box. He glanced round as if he didn't really expect to cop for anything. I just stayed how I was, staring through the leaves at the rozzer and the car and the phone box. I daren't move in case the leaves rustled and I was spotted for. But in my gut there was enough movement for me to be going on with. All that I needed now was for the Morris to show while the rozzer was still glancing round.

But eventually the rozzer got back in the car and the car pulled away and then the street was silent again. So that's what they call a stake-out up here, I thought. A periodic visit to the phone box. If I'd have been in any other condition I'd have had to smile. That and the fact that their visit might coincide with the Morris's visit.

Then about three minutes after the police car had taken off there was the sound of another car engine approaching the box. I peered through the leaves again. A Morris Oxford. And it was stopping. My heart jumped but then it began to fall on a sickening downward curve. The Morris wasn't maroon. It was black. Sheila wouldn't have made a mistake: telling me the wrong colour could have had me back inside, no trouble. She'd said maroon and that was what she'd meant.

The Morris pulled up next to the box. No one got out. I couldn't see into the car because a strip of sodium was reflecting off the windscreen.

Then the offside door opened. A man got out and walked towards the telephone box. The man was about twenty-five years old. He had close-cropped fair hair. And he was wearing a sheepskin coat. Sheila had told me to look out for a man in a sheepskin coat.

The man in the sheepskin coat looked around the area where the box was in much the same way that the rozzer had done. In my mind I was trying to decide which was wrong, the car or the coat. Suppose Sheila had been told the wrong colour, and this was their last circuit? The man began to walk back to the car. He shook his head once as he went. I stood up and swung my leg over the wall. The man carried on walking but whoever else was in the car must have said something because the man stopped and turned and looked straight at me.

'Billy?' he said.

I nodded my head.

'Billy?'

'Yeah,' I said. 'Billy.'

I began to move towards the car, slowly at first, then my movements got quicker and quicker until I was almost falling headlong over the bonnet. The man in the sheepskin coat was holding open the rear door. Everybody was talking at once.

'Christ, what took you so long?' said the sheepskin.

'We've been here waiting for nearly five minutes,' the driver said. 'We've already been here once before.'

'The car. It should have been maroon,' I said.

'It is maroon,' said Sheepskin.

'Maybe it looks black in this light,' said the driver. 'Sodium does that.'

'That's what it must have been,' I said. 'The sodium.'

The car U-turned and made for the dual-carriageway.

'You hungry?' said Sheepskin. 'You must be. How does fish and chips grab you? Got 'em from a van in between circuits.'

I smiled, a weak, silly smile. Fish and chips. From the van I'd seen earlier. Me and the rozzer. The same fish and chips.

'Yeah,' I said. 'Great.'

Sheepskin twisted round in the passenger seat and handed me the warm parcel.

'What about a drink? Scotch, beer or tea?'

'Tea,' I said. 'With a drop in it.' A thought struck me. 'You don't have any lemonade, do you?'

'Lemonade?'

'Doesn't matter. Tea'll do nicely.'

Sheepskin began unscrewing a flask. The driver said:

'There's fresh clothes under the back seat. You'll have to lift it. I should change once we get out of this place.'

'Thanks.'

'There weren't any road blocks on the way up,' Sheepskin said, handing me the flask cup.

'They still think I'm in the area,' I said.

'Shouldn't have any trouble then.'

I took the tea and drank. The car turned on to the dual-carriageway and began to pick up speed. On my right were the playing fields.

'Plenty of Filth about at any rate,' Sheepskin said, twisting round in his seat and looking through the rear window at the police cars and van still parked by the playing fields.

The tea spread through my body and I began to feel a wonderful weak helplessness. No more decisions, no more risks. They were being taken from me. I felt like a child again. Protected and cared for. The town disappeared behind us and we were in the limbo of the night motorway, unrelated to the real world. I emptied the cup and sank back in the warm unholstery.

Sheepskin turned round again.

'Want some more?' he said.

I shook my head.

'How are you feeling now?'

'Fine,' I said. 'Fine.'

'Wait till you see the papers,' he said. 'You'll feel even better. Christ, you're the biggest thing since Hiroshima. I mean…'

The driver cut in on Sheepskin.

'Later,' he said. 'Leave it till later. All he wants to do now is to sleep. Don't you, Billy?'

# PART THREE

I awoke.

The first thing was the perfume. That was the first thing I noticed. The soft sweet smell of Sheila's body drifting into my senses.

I opened my eyes and turned my head. Sheila was in a deep sleep. Dark auburn hair tumbled over the pillow and over her bare shoulders. Her breath was soft and slow. I could feel the light warmth of it on my neck. I looked at her a long time before I turned away. Then I just lay there and enjoyed the luxury of the traffic sounds in the high street beyond the bedroom window. Rumbling lorries and swishing cars and blaring motor horns. It was music.

After a while I slipped from the bed and walked quickly over to the door of the adjoining bedroom and opened it without making a sound. Timmy was still asleep in his cot. I moved across the room and knelt down and looked through the bars. Timmy was lying on his back, his arms stretched out above his head, palms turned upwards, his face blank with innocence.

I knelt there, waiting for him to wake up.

After a time, I felt a shadow behind me. I turned my head. Sheila was standing in the doorway. I saw from her face that she'd been watching me for some time. She didn't say anything. She didn't even look a certain way. But almost as soon as I saw her I got up and walked towards the door. Then she moved too, away from the door, back towards the bed in our room. As she lay down and I lay on top of her she whispered in my ear:

'You can wake Timmy up later. Only otherwise we'd have to have waited till tonight again, wouldn't we?'

Breakfast. The transistor's tiny burble. The all-embracing smell of fried bacon. Timmy chattering in his high chair. Sheila talking as she prodded along the breakfast in the frying pan.

'... so there was no bother. He never thought anything of it. Just accepted that you were on nights and that was it. In any case, you don't actually have to go through the shop to get in and out. Well, you probably saw last night. You go down the stairs and along the passage and out through the other door. It's perfect.'

'Did you tell your Ma?'

She shook her head.

'She knows I'm with you. But she doesn't know where.'

'And?'

'What do you think?'

'Yeah.'

I poured another cup of tea.

'And nobody else knows where we are.'

'Only Ronnie.'

I drank some tea.

'It doesn't matter, does it?' Sheila said. 'Only I thought...'

'No, it doesn't matter,' I said. 'Ronnie's all right.'

'I mean I played it safe. I only came here the once, to take the place. And I came in the wig and all...'

'It's all right, love. Don't worry about it. You've done fine.'

I mopped my plate with a piece of bread and crumpled up the bread and ate it. Sheila poured me another cup of tea. I drained the cup and leant back in my chair and gave Sheila a cigarette and lit us both up.

As Sheila blew out the smoke she said:

'Do you feel like talking yet?'

I grinned at her.

'Do me a favour,' I said. 'You didn't exactly give me much chance last night. Or this morning.'

'You know what I mean Billy and don't be so bleeding saucy. I mean about the future.'

'Yeah, all right,' I said. 'I don't mind talking about the future.'

She put her elbows on the table and looked into my face.

'Well,' I said, 'this is how I see it: we're all right for money. We've no immediate worries on that score. In fact if we were going to stay put we'd be all right for well over eighteen months. It was lucky for me that Ronnie was on the job with me. Some of them wouldn't have handed over if they didn't have to.'

'He let me have it the day after you went down.'

I nodded.

'But anyway. We'd be all right if we were going to stay put. But we can't stay put, can we?'

Sheila looked down at the table.

'If we want a future it's got to be bought. Somewhere other than in this country. And that'll take care of most of the money, the way we'd have to go.'

I stubbed my cigarette out in the ashtray.

'But it's a vicious circle. We can't move yet. Not for six months. Maybe not for even a year. And by that time we'll be well into our money and there wouldn't be enough left in the kitty to pay for the kind of passage we'll need. So where does that get us?'

She waited for me to tell her.

'For a start,' I said, 'you don't have to worry about me. Whatever happens, I'm not going out on any more jobs. That's out. I'm here now and I'm not going back. I wouldn't have gone on the last one if it hadn't been because of that commitment to Ronnie.'

She didn't say anything and I knew what she was thinking from the way she wasn't saying it.

'Anyway, there's no point going into all that. It's what I do from now on that matters. And I'm doing no more jobs. So where does that leave us? Maybe a year lying low and at the end of it not enough readies to get us out.'

She looked up at me again. I leant across the table and took hold of her hand.

'There's only one person I can trust to do me a favour and that's Ronnie. We know that. Ronnie and I are real mates. Now the only way I'm ever going to get the kind of readies we need is to get Ronnie to place some of the money for me. To buy it. There's The Stable Club and there's Little Egypt and he could maybe even fix something up in the Chesterfield. He'd do that for me, I know. I mean, if he'd gone down with me then he wouldn't be in those places either. So in his position all he has to do is every now and again stake a tame punter on a good red number, nothing greedy, say twenty back at a time, give his punter a percentage, take his own percentage, funnel the rest back to me. In a year or so I can double what we have now.'

For a while Sheila didn't say anything. Then eventually she said:

'Only this, Billy. Maybe Ronnie will do it for you. On the other hand he might reckon on having done it all already. But the main thing is who he works for now. I mean, those clubs are Walter's.'

I smiled.

'Sure they're Walter's. That's one of the lovely things about the idea. Wally's boiling his nuts up in the nick while I'm sitting down here in the bosom of my family playing the stock market on his tables.'

There was another silence. Then she said:

'Don't do anything that'll send you back, Billy.'

I looked at her.

'Like what?' I said.

I sank back in the bath. The third bath in twelve hours. It was the quickest way of getting rid of the stiffness. But that apart, the novelty of the locked bathroom door and the smell of Sheila's toiletries mixing in with the steam, and the flowered wallpaper and the pink bath, they were all equally necessary.

I stretched an arm out and swivelled the dial round on the transistor. I stopped when I got to the news. The newsreader was talking about Billy Cracken. About how the search had moved to London. About how the Yard had moved in on the scene.

I listened until the item finished then I switched off the radio.

Then I leant forward and ran some more hot water into the bath.

I pulled the polythene wrapper off the shirt and held the shirt out in front of me. It was soft and woolly with a button down collar, one of those casual sportshirts with just the three buttons at the neck. Two more shirts of the same kind in different colours lay on the bed.

Sheila said: 'I like the brown best. Brown suits you.'

The one I was holding was red. Bright red.

'Oh, I don't know,' I said. 'I think I like this one best.'

I took all the newspapers that Sheila had saved and spread them out over the dining table and read each of the reports about the escape. The only fact that was consistent throughout was the description of Tommy's capture. And that was only because he'd never got down off the roof. They couldn't very well get that wrong.

Most of the papers carried pictures of the outside of the prison, pictures littered with speculative arrows describing my progress over the wall. Only one of the papers came near to the truth, and then for the wrong reasons.

I even rated an editorial in one of them. One of those civic-minded, hands-up-in-horror ones bleating on about the safety of citizens in their beds while Public Enemies found it easy to get out of maximum security. Tightening of restrictions, tougher conditions, all that kind of cobblers.

Only one of the photographs made me look at all human. A picture she'd taken of me herself, at Brighton, on our honeymoon. The rest were police stuff, in some cases specially retouched under the eyes and round the cheekbones.

Just so nobody got the wrong idea, like.

'Now then,' I said, 'this one's all about Peter Rabbit. See Peter Rabbit? And that's his Mummy and all his brothers and sisters. Now Peter's a very naughty bunny rabbit. Because he's always getting into trouble. Never out of it. See, here he's in the vegetable garden and he shouldn't be there, should he. No, he shouldn't. Because his Daddy was once in the vegetable garden and Mr McGregor shot him with his shotgun, didn't he? And he put him in a rabbit pie and ate him all up, didn't he? Yes he did. So Peter ought never to be in that old vegetable patch, ought he. He ought to keep well out of it if he doesn't want to finish up in a pie, shouldn't he?'

I lowered Timmy down into the cot and slid him under the sheets but he wasn't having any of it. Immediately he pushed the sheets back and squirmed round and sat up and stretched his arms out to me. I picked him up again and held him tight to me. His arms went round my neck and small fingers gripped the hair at the back of my head. We stood like that in the semi-darkness for a while. Then I dislodged his arms and put him down again. This time there was no squirming, no sitting up. This time he was content to lie there, just looking up into my face. Slowly the eyelids began to droop, but I stayed where I was, looking down, because every now and again his eyes would snap open, as if to reassure him that I was still standing there. Each time that happened he would smile and his eyes would flicker and close, and the smile would gradually drift away until the next time his eyes opened. After a while, when he was finally asleep, I left the bedroom and went back to Sheila.

'Look,' I said, 'Ronnie's all right. You don't have to worry.'

'I know he is. But it just worries me. I mean, even me Mam doesn't know we're here.'

'You're only talking about the bloke that had me fetched from Aston.'

'I know. But I didn't know he was working for Walter. I just didn't cotton on about the clubs.'

'He's been there for ages. Besides, Ronnie isn't Walter's man. He's got his own operations. He just uses Walter. Screws him to pay the rent. Ronnie's my mate.'

'And Walter knows that.'

'All right, what's Walter going to do? Get Ronnie to grass me? You don't know Ronnie.'

'But I know Walter.'

'And I know Ronnie. Ronnie'd never let Walter get a lock on him.'

Sheila showed Ronnie into the living room. He was as sharp as ever. Beige mohair, black shoes, dark shiny tie, his black hair cut immaculately. He smiled his wide smile.

'Well now,' he said. 'What do we call you now? Blondie? Or is it Danny La Rue?'

I smoothed a hand over my hair.

'What do you think?' I said, smiling back.

'Great. Bobby Moore'll want to know the name of the salon.'

'That's one address nobody's having.'

'Right.'

We shook hands.

'Thanks for the lift,' I said. 'I appreciate what you did.'

Ronnie sat down.

'Forget it.'

'Sheila,' I said. 'Do the drinks for us. What is it these days, Ronnie? Still Rum and Black?'

'Vodka tonic. Lemon if you've got it.'

'That the In Drink now, Ronnie?' Sheila said.

'With me it is. You stay fresh as a daisy next morning.'

'I'll have a Scotch, Sheila.'

Sheila began to make the drinks. Ronnie lit a cigarette.

'No, I mean it,' I said to Ronnie. 'Well, anyway I don't have to say it. You know what I mean.'

'Sure.'

Sheila gave us the drinks. I raised my glass.

'Absent friends,' I said. 'Even Walter.'

'Absent friends.'

We drained our glasses and Sheila filled them up for us. We drank again, but this time not all the way down. I looked at my glass.

'You might not believe this,' I said, 'but this is the first one. Well, the second. It is, isn't it, Sheil?'

'That's right.'

'First one. I waited until you came.'

Ronnie drank a little more and said cheers. Then Sheila got up and took her coat off the hook and began putting it on. Ronnie said:

'You off, Sheil?'

'Going round to see my mother.'

Ronnie tried not to show anything but he couldn't help it. I grinned and said: 'Forget it, Ronnie. Sheila'll never get copped for. She's too sharp for them.'

'Won't they be covering her Ma's place?' Ronnie said, but he didn't say it like a question.

'Sure,' I said. 'Only she isn't going to her Ma's place. Her Ma's meeting her in the Barley Mow off Upper Street. Her brother and her sister-in-law are going as well. Sheil wants to let them know things are fine.'

'What about her Ma? Won't they have someone on her?'

I shook my head.

'Her Ma went shopping up West this morning. She's been dodging about all day.'

Sheila leant down and kissed me on the forehead.

'Don't tie too big a one on, Billy,' she said. 'Remember, you can't run round the Green tomorrow to get rid of it.'

'No, all right,' I said. 'I'll take it easy.'

Sheila said goodbye to Ronnie and went out.

Ronnie emptied his glass and I stood up and took it from him and refilled it.

'Don't worry about Sheila,' I said. 'She's been with me long enough to know the form.'

I gave Ronnie his glass and poured another for myself.

'Anyway,' I said as I sat down, 'how's business?'

'Quite rosy at the minute,' Ronnie said. 'Lots of prospects.'

'What, with Walter?'

'No, I'm not with his firm.'

'What about the clubs?'

'Just bunce. It suits me to let Walter think I'm one of the family.'

'So who are you with?'

'I'm with myself. Freelance. Sort of an agent. A promoter'.

'Promoting what?'

'Anything likely. Mainly van work. Done two in the last three months. I get a bit of intelligence, pull a few trusties together, do the job, back to the dress suit in the evening, Bob's your uncle. Don't see any of the fellers till the next time. Just supposing they're the same fellers, that is.'

'Sounds as though you're doing well,' I said.

'Never mind, Billy. Old Bill can't make up his mind. Whether it's me or whether I've really settled down like what it looks like. I mean, I'm on a sweet number with Walter. Why should I chance anything?'

'Clever,' I said. 'So you're rolling in greengage.'

'Can't complain. Mind you, we go out tooled up, so that makes the odds better.'

'Heavy?'

'Why not. Doesn't matter whether it's a pea-shooter or a sten gun. You get done just the same way whatever you happen to be holding.'

'You're chancing getting what I got.'

'You got yours for different reasons, Billy. Everybody knows that.'

'Maybe.'

'So anyway,' Ronnie said, after a pause, 'what've you got scheduled?'

'Nothing,' I said. 'Not for a year at least.'

Ronnie didn't say anything.

'I've got to lie low, haven't I? And after that I've got to get out of it. Right out. There's no future for me on this island. Sure, I might last a long time. Three years, five years, maybe more. But one day they'd have me. And next time they'd throw away the key. I'd have no chance.'

Ronnie lit another cigarette.

'I suppose you haven't any choice.'

'Too right. I've got a life to live.'

'Where would you go?'

'Ireland, first. Then I'd fix things for South Africa.'

Ronnie nodded.

'It'll cost you,' he said.

'I know.'

'Can you manage it?'

'Right now, yes. In a year's time, I'm not sure. I've got to promote some bread in the meantime, that's for sure.'

'You can always come in on one of my tickles.'

I shook my head.

'Sheila wouldn't wear it.'

Ronnie grinned.

'Come on Billy,' he said. 'Do me a favour. Sheila wouldn't wear it? Since when has a bird decided things for you?'

'Listen,' I said. 'I got out for Sheila. And for Timmy. If it wasn't for them I wouldn't be sitting here now. I'd have been to Liverpool and off.'

'All right, Billy,' Ronnie said. 'All right.'

'Just so as you know.'

There was a short silence.

'So what *are* you going to do for bread?' Ronnie said.

'I was wondering if you could give me a hand. And don't get me wrong, I don't mean a loan.'

'And don't get me wrong either, Billy: I don't mind lending to you. If I've got it, I'll lend it, depending on who it is.'

'I know,' I said. 'But no thanks. I already owe you.'

Ronnie shrugged.

'Then how?'

'At your tables.'

Ronnie thought about it. Eventually he said:

'How exactly?'

'I give you some bread. You give the bread to a punter who's into you for something or other and your operator lets him win a couple. You knock ten per cent off the punter's account and take a few off the top for yourself and give the rest to me. Do it half a dozen times and I'd have the capital I'm looking for.'

Ronnie's tongue clicked against the back of his teeth.

'Don't get me wrong, Billy,' he said. 'But there'd be problems.'

'It's done all the time,' I said.

'Yeah, I know. But not at one of Walter's places. Not unless Walter says so.'

'You run them, don't you?'

'Yeah, I run them. And there's plenty of other geezers as'd like to as well. All working for Walter. There wouldn't exactly be a shortage of grasses if I started pulling strokes like that. I'd rather give you the money. It's not me, you understand. It's not me I'm looking out for. It's Doreen and the kids. You know what Wally's like. He'd put his heavies straight on to them. They like that sort of thing.'

I didn't say anything.

'You know what I mean, don't you?' Ronnie said.

I took a drink.

'Well, don't you?'

I nodded.

'I'd do it if it wasn't Walter. I really would.'

I nodded again.

'I can lend you some. Let me lend it to you.'

'No,' I said. 'I can't take your money. Besides...'

'Besides?'

'You couldn't lend me enough. I'd need at least a grand on top of what I've got. Maybe two.'

'Jesus. I thought you meant half a grand tops.'

'When I go I want to go right. And that's expensive.'

Ronnie didn't say anything.

'Well, as I said, I can help you out a bit. Just let me know if you change your mind. And of course, if you change your mind about going on a tickle. You'd certainly raise it that way.'

'Yeah,' I said. 'I know.'

I took Ronnie's glass again and filled us both up.

'Anyway,' I said, 'I've only been out five minutes. Plenty of time to fix something up.'

'Sure there is.'

'Didn't bring you here just to pull you for that. This is meant to be a celebration. Born Free and all that.'

'Yeah. Let's sink some.'

'We'll do that.'

Three o'clock on a warm Sunday afternoon.

I looked out of the window and down into the street. Bright sunlight lightened the shop windows and leftover drunks from the lunch time sessions stood in the shop doorways. Kids with nowhere to go slouched along the pavement. I turned away from the window and sat down in an armchair and picked a newspaper up off the floor. It was no use waiting by the window to watch for Sheila and Timmy coming back from the park. It was like standing by a stove waiting for a kettle to boil. Besides, they'd only been gone an hour. And the afternoon was warm and bright. Why should they hurry back?

I found an item in the paper I hadn't already read but after the first couple of paragraphs I lost interest. I got up out of my chair and turned on the television. The station was showing an old movie with Greer Garson and Ronald Colman. I stood five minutes of it and then I switched over to the other side. Football. That was better. I settled down to enjoy it but the commentator began saying there were only a few minutes to go, they were in the dying seconds of the game and all that crap. Then the whistle went and the adverts came on. I stood up again and switched the set off.

In any case, watching television on a Sunday afternoon had reminded me of the nick. That dead period between dinner and tea, the time when the thoughts of the outside were hard to keep out of your mind.

I went over to the window again. A bus rolled by, almost empty on top. One of the passengers was a blank faced man in his fifties with a check scarf round his neck and the collar of his mac turned up. We stared into each other's eyes as the bus jolted by. He probably wouldn't have changed his expression if he'd known who he was looking at.

But at least he was going somewhere. I wondered where someone like him was going on a warm Sunday at three o'clock in the afternoon.

Ronnie phoned up one Wednesday evening and asked if he could come round and discuss something with me.

He got there about half an hour after he'd phoned.

'I've been hearings things I think you ought to know about,' he said.

I got him a drink and sat him down.

'What things?' I said.

'To do with Walter.'

'Oh yes?'

'He's after getting you sent back.'

I smiled.

'What else would he be doing? You know Walter.'

'Sure, but he's really coming it strong. He's got Tobin working on it.'

'Tobin!' Sheila said. 'Jesus.'

'Tobin's still on the force then,' I said.

'He was lucky. It worked out perfect for him, Walter going down when he did. Now Tobin gets his cake and eats it. He's still on the payroll and the geezer that foots the bill is inside on a thirty stretch.'

'And now he's being paid to turn me over.'

'Right,' Ronnie said. 'He's appearing nightly. He's been through every grass south of the Shell building. He's even put pressure on a couple of geezers who are paying in a century apiece into West End Central so you can tell how dedicated he is.'

'Who were the geezers?'

'Maurice and Alec.'

'How did they react?'

'They gave him the elbow and reminded him about a couple of deals they could drop him in over, no trouble. But that's beside the point. He's working at it. I thought you should know in the light of any movements you or Sheila might be thinking of making.'

'Has he been to see you?' I said.

'Yeah, he's had a word with me.'

'Has he any idea of what you laid on for me?'

'If he had I wouldn't be here now. And Walter wouldn't care, either. He'd trample me to death to get at you. But nobody knows anything. I arranged everything by remote control.'

After Ronnie had gone Sheila said:

'What do you think? Move on now or sit it out?'

'Sit it out. Tobin won't get anywhere because nobody but Ronnie knows anything. If we move we give him the kind of chance he's looking for.'

Sheila came and sat on the floor by my chair and leant against my legs.

'So now it's both of us,' she said. 'I'll have to do my shopping next door, once a week.'

'I expected this would happen,' I said, just to make her feel better. 'I'm only surprised it didn't happen sooner.'

The next day I awoke at half-past-five. My eyes snapped open and my brain was working straight away, as if I'd been awake for hours.

I lay in bed, listening. I was listening even before I was fully aware of what I was doing. A reflex. Ronnie's message must have really stirred me up.

I could hear nothing out of the ordinary. The fridge was humming away in the kitchen. A bus rattled by outside. The ticking of the alarm. Next to me, Sheila's breathing. Nothing out of the ordinary.

I got out of bed and went into the living room and over to the window that looked out on to the street. I parted the curtains ever so slightly.

The street was empty.

No big removal van was parked twenty-five yards down the road. That was the way they always did it. They always came in a big removal van, or something like it. They'd sit inside and talk into their handsets until it was time to move and then they'd pile out and surround their objectives. And they always made their move before eight o'clock. Nobody had ever been picked up after eight in the morning. If you got past eight o'clock you could fairly bank on being safe for at least the rest of the day.

I went into the kitchen and lit the gas and filled the kettle and put it on the stove to boil. I stood by the stove and looked at my reflection. I saw the kitchen door swing open. Sheila was standing there. I turned to face her.

'Just making a cup of tea.'

She nodded and pushed a strand of hair from her eyes. Then she sat down at the kitchen table and lit a cigarette. The kettle boiled and I poured the hot water into the tea pot. When the tea had mashed I poured us two cups and took them over to the table and sat down. I lit one of Sheila's cigarettes and looked at the clock on the cooker. It was five past six. I wondered if Tobin was at home, tucked up in his bed. And if he was, I wondered what he was dreaming about.

'It's no good,' I said. 'I've got to get out.'

'Billy, you mustn't. Not yet. Not with Tobin on the lookout.'

'That was a month ago. In any case, he can't be everywhere at once.'

'But knowing our luck…'

'Our luck,' I said. 'Listen, living this way I may as well be back in Aston.'

'Up there you'd have me and Timmy, would you?'

'Look, Sheil, you know what I mean. I'm going out of my skull. It's been two months. Over two months. I just have to go out. Even if it's only for an hour.'

Sheila sat down and lit a cigarette.

'Where do you want to go?' she said.

'I don't know. Anywhere.'

'Round here?'

'Well you don't think I'd hop on a bus and make straight for the Skinners Arms do you?'

'I don't know what you'd do.'

I knelt down next to her.

'Look, all I want to do is go out for an hour. Just walk around a bit. I'd be careful. You know that.'

She didn't say anything.

'I mean, you've been out.'

'Yes I've been out but if I'm nicked it's not exactly the same is it? I'd be out in six months. I mean, you do see the difference, don't you?'

'There's no need for that...'

'Yes there is. There is if you're thinking of going out. Risking it all just for an hour outside.'

'Sheila you don't know what it's like...'

'I do, Billy. I do. I know how you must feel. But you've got to stick it out. Just for another month or so. Then when Tobin's eased off, well, maybe then. But not now. You know I'm right.'

I stood up and went over to the window. She was right. I knew that. It would be madness to go out.

I looked down into the street and watched the people move in their enviably aimless directions.


'I shan't be long,' Sheila said. 'But I'm going to the launderette so if I'm held up a bit, don't worry.'

'I won't,' I said. 'You could bring me some paperbacks if you've time.'

'Anything in particular?'

'James Hadley Chase, something like that.'

'I'll find something.'

Sheila took Timmy's hand and manoeuvred the fold-up pushchair and the laundry bag out of the door.

'Say Bye-Bye Daddy, Timmy,' Sheila said.

Timmy beamed up at me.

'Bye-Bye Daddy,' he said.

He began waving his arm.

'Bye-Bye Timmy,' I said. 'See you later.'

'Seelater,' he said.

Sheila pushed Timmy out on to the landing.

'And some lemonade,' I said. 'Get us some lemonade.'

'You and your bleeding lemonade,' Sheila said, closing the door behind her.

I listened to the pushchair being bumped downstairs. Then I walked over to the window and waited to see Sheila and Timmy emerge on to the pavement below. I watched Sheila unfold the pushchair and negotiate Timmy into it. Then she balanced the laundry bag on the back of the pushchair and started walking towards the zebra crossing twenty yards down the road. I watched as she waited for the traffic to thin out, looking right and left, just another mother with her kid on her way to the launderette. Then she moved forward on to the crossing. A minute later and I couldn't see her any more.

I walked away from the window and into the bedroom and took my overcoat out of the wardrobe. I stood in front of the mirror on the wardrobe door and put the coat on. It was the first time I'd worn it in three years. The coat felt strange and heavy. I went over to the chest of drawers and took out a dark blue scarf and wound it round my neck. Then I took my black leather gloves from the same drawer and slipped them on. I turned and looked in the mirror again. I felt like a tailor's dummy, unreal, with the bleached hair and the waxy complexion and the stiff overcoat and the shiny gloves.

I bent my arms and flexed my shoulders and tried to shrug some life into my reflection but it didn't seem to make any difference. The only answer was to turn away from the mirror and ignore the reflection.

I walked into the lounge and opened the door into the passage but before I closed it I checked that I'd got the spare key. Then I closed the door behind me. The Yale lock clicked shut.

I walked the few feet to the top of the stairs and looked down. Daylight from the street doorway flooded the grubby hallway below and illuminated the shiny green paintwork. I lowered a foot on to the top step. A part of my mind kept telling me how crazy I was but the light at the bottom of the stairs drew me downwards. Halfway down I became aware of the draught from the street. The traffic noises got louder and then I could hear the sound of the voices in the street. And then I was at the bottom of the stairs, looking straight ahead of me into the light.

People and traffic hurried past the doorway. I moved forward. A woman glanced in as she went by, glanced away again before she was even out of sight. Now the dusty outside air was on my face, and I was standing in the doorway itself. There was nothing else between me and outside. I stepped out on to the pavement. I felt much lighter, almost as if I needed some kind of anchor. I looked into the faces of the passing crowd. Nobody was taking any notice of me. I hesitated for a moment, then I turned left in the opposite direction to the one Sheila had taken and began to walk. The pavement felt hard beneath my feet. I imagined that my footsteps were louder than everybody else's. I imagined that my walk was different, and my clothes. But nobody took any notice.

I got off the main road as soon as I could and weaved my way through back streets of warehouses and 'Buildings' and scrapyards and run-down offices and small shops. There was hardly anyone about. As I walked I'd sometimes look up beyond the skylines of the buildings, just to watch the clouds drift across the sky.

I walked for over twenty minutes. Turning into a new street I saw that at the end of it there was another main road. I stopped and looked around. Behind me there was a street narrower than the others. Half way down this street was a pub. I looked at my watch. It was quarter past eleven. The idea of having a drink in a pub appealed to me. After all, it'd been over two years. And I was in an area where no one knew me. If the landlord had an arrangement with the law he'd only be on to the local villains. Again the warning voices filled my head but I began to move towards the pub. I'd just have one, I told myself. Just one drink, at a bar.

I pushed open the door.

There were no customers in the pub. Once it had been split in two or three bars, but the brewery had done it up and now the pub was all one bar, circular, with a pink laminated plastic top and plastic wrought iron work making pointless divisions.

A woman was standing behind the bar. The till had No Sale rung up on it and she was looking thoughtfully into the cash drawer. On the counter a freshly lit cigarette was burning away on the edge of an ashtray. The woman didn't turn her head until I reached the bar. Then she turned abruptly, released from her thoughts by my presence.

'Yes, dear,' she said. 'What would you like?'

I cleared my throat.

'I'd like a lemonade shandy,' I said.

'Half or a pint, dear?'

'A pint, please. I'll have a pint.'

'Pint of lemonade shandy,' she said, already holding the pint mug underneath the beer-tap.

The woman was getting on for fifty, but she'd taken care of herself. Her platinum hair and Ruth Roman lips were immaculate.

'There we are, dear. Seventeen p.'

I took a handful of silver out of my pocket and gave her two two-bob bits.

'Ta, dear.'

She rang up the till and came back to the bar.

'Three p change, dear.'

'Thanks.'

The woman turned back to the till and began writing something on a pad.

I took a drink and sat down on one of the bar stools. There was a folded copy of the *Express* on the bar. I picked it up and opened it out and pretended to read it. But instead of reading I just sat there savouring the atmosphere of the pub.

A few minutes later the woman finished what she was doing at the till and came and leant on the bar near where I was sitting. I turned a couple of pages of the paper.

'Nothing worth reading in there,' she said.

I looked at her.

'I say there's nothing in the paper today.'

I shook my head.

'Never is these days. Only gloom and despondency.'

'That's right,' I said.

The conversation lapsed. I carried on pretending to read the paper. But inside I felt human again. I'd talked to another human being and that was what I'd needed: outside contact, to prove I was real.

I drained my drink and left the pub.

I got back five minutes before Sheila. I was sitting in the chair reading when she and Timmy came through the door. Timmy ran towards me and threw his arms round me.

'Timmy back, Daddy. Timmy back.'

I kissed him and picked him up and whirled him round at arms' length above my head.

'So I see,' I said. 'And has Timmy been a good little boy for his Ma?'

'Yes, Daddy.'

'He's been a little sod,' Sheila said, kicking off her shoes.

'Kept trying to open the dryer door.'

'Have you been trying to open the dryer door, then?'

'Come on, it's time for your sleep,' Sheila said, taking Timmy from me. 'It's a wonder you're not worn out.'

Sheila put Timmy to bed and came back into the lounge and flopped down in an armchair.

'Mind you,' she said, 'I'm almost dead on my feet, trying to get round in no seconds flat.'

'Fancy a cup of tea?' I said.

'You must be joking.'

'I'll put the kettle on,' I said. 'Or…'

'Or what?'

I knelt down on the floor by Sheila's chair.

'Or shall I make it after?'

'After what?' Then she cottoned. 'Here, now hang about…'

'Timmy's in bed, isn't he?'

'Yeah, I know, but…'

'But what?'

'It's the middle of the day.'

'Since when did that worry us?'

I pulled her down on the floor.

'I still got me coat on,' Sheila said.

'Quiet,' I said. 'It won't get in the way.'

A few days after I'd gone out Ronnie phoned to say he was coming over. He said he'd got a proposition.

After I'd put the phone down Sheila said:

'What did Ronnie want?'

'He's coming over. Said he's got a proposition for me.'

'And what sort of proposition would that be?'

'I don't know till he gets here, do I?'

'Well if it's a job…'

'It won't be a job. Ronnie knows I wouldn't go on a job. So he won't offer one, will he?'

'I don't know. But if…'

'Sheil, leave off, will you? Just wait till he gets here, eh?'

Ronnie arrived half an hour later. After we'd exchanged the usuals, Ronnie said:

'It's like this: there's this little firm I've got an interest in, not an active one, you understand. But an interest. Now they're doing not too badly at the moment, and things are going to get even better over the next two or three months. They've got several things lined up…'

Sheila cut in on him.

'Ronnie, I thought Billy told you all that was out.'

Ronnie kept on looking at me.

'Leave it out Sheila, will you? Ronnie's trying to do me a favour. He doesn't have to come here.'

'He'll do you the kind of favour that'll get you straight back into the nick.'

'Sheila, I'm telling you…'

'It's all right, Billy,' Ronnie said, showing all over his face that it wasn't all right. 'I don't mind.' He looked at Sheila. 'Sheila, I'm not asking Billy out on a job. Honest. I wouldn't. I know how he feels.'

'Then what are you asking?'

'Why don't you shut your fucking trap and listen,' I said, standing up.

'You going to belt me, Billy?' she said.

I managed to stop myself. But only just.

'Are you?'

I sat down again.

'You can piss off, the pair of you,' Sheila said and with that she slammed off into the kitchen.

Ronnie was looking at me.

'I'm sorry about that, Ronnie,' I said. 'But you know how it is. She's just scared…'

'Sure she is.'

'I mean, she feels the same as me about what you've done. Straight up.'

'I'm with you, Billy. It's all right, I'm telling you.'

'Anyway. Carry on. She'll be taking it out on the kitchen for a while.'

Ronnie lit a cigarette.

'Well, it's like this. They're pretty well tooled up. A shooter for every occasion. But of course they've all got form and if they're done in possession, well, I don't have to tell you, do I?'

'Go on.'

'So they're looking for a minder who's not likely to get turned over himself. And it occurred to me that you'd be the very man. Because you're not going to get turned over, are you? Not unless you're very unlucky. And I'd make sure it was worth your while, because, as I said, I've got an interest in the firm and I know the firm can afford it. So what do you say?'

I took a sip of my drink. It sounded good all right. It didn't matter whether I was in possession or not if I was turned over again. No difference at all.

'Who'd know?' I said.

'Only me,' Ronnie said. 'I'd be middleman. The stuff would have to be brought here by a couple of the boys but you and Sheila could stay in the bedroom when they came. You could lend me the key and we'd let ourselves in, dump the stuff and leave. After that it would only be a matter of me coming here and collecting what was actually needed. What do you say?'

'It sounds good, Ronnie,' I said. 'Thanks for putting me in it.'

'So you're on, then?'

I nodded and stood up.

'I'd just like to tell Sheila before you go. So you'll see that it was just worry that made her act that way.'

'Look, Billy, you don't...'

'You stay there. I won't be a minute.'

I went into the kitchen. Sheila had got the ironing board out. She didn't look up from what she was doing.

I leant against the kitchen door.

'Ronnie wants to put me in a bit of minding.'

She stopped ironing for about ten seconds, then carried on again.

'So he didn't come here to pull me on a job,' I said.

She didn't answer.

'He came here to help me. To help us. It'll be good money and Ronnie wanted to put it our way.'

She still didn't answer.

I walked over to her and put my arm round her shoulders.

'Look, love,' I said, 'I know you were only thinking about us. I know that. But Ronnie's done a lot for us and it looks as if you don't appreciate it. And that makes me look bad. So why don't you make us all a cup of coffee and bring it through and let Ronnie know you're pleased the way he's looked out for us.'

Sheila put the iron down and leant against me.

'I was just so frightened that you'd want to go if he had a job lined up,' she said. 'I mean, what with being cooped up the way you are. I know you. I just thought you'd go.'

I turned her round so that I was looking into her face.

'Listen, love,' I said. 'All I care about is us. Me, you and Timmy. Our future. If we can sit this one out and we have the breaks then we'll be all right. Do you think I'm going to put chances on that not happening?'

She shook her head.

'Well, then,' I said. 'So you make us that cup of coffee and bring it through in a minute when I've arranged things with Ronnie. All right?'

I heard the key turn in the lock. Sheila and Timmy were sitting on the bed behind me. Timmy was asleep in Sheila's arms.

I bent down and looked through the keyhole. Ronnie came

in first, pushing the door wide open. Then he stood back and two young tearaways carried a packing case into the room.

'Anywhere,' Ronnie said. 'Just dump it anywhere.'

The tearaways placed the packing case in the centre of the living room floor. Then they had a good look at their surroundings.

'Nice gaff,' one of them said.

'Yes, it is,' Ronnie said. 'And now you've been here forget how nice it is. And the nice neighbourhood.'

Ronnie ushered them out. Before he went he placed the key on the dining table. Then he closed the door behind him.

I opened the bedroom door and went over to the packing case. The top was open and there were some objects wrapped in newspaper packed in the straw. I unwrapped one of the objects. A cut spirit glass. I smiled. Ronnie must have noticed we weren't very well off for glasses. I took all the glasses out of the packing case. There were a dozen altogether.

Sheila came into the lounge. She'd laid Timmy down on our bed.

'Ronnie brought us a present,' I said.

Sheila looked at the unwrapped glass but she didn't say anything.

I rummaged under the straw until my fingers touched something very cold. Much colder than the glass. My fingers closed round the object and I lifted. I pulled out a sawn-off shotgun. It was a beauty. Almost brand new. Sheila watched me, her arms folded, while I broke the gun and snapped it shut again and held it the way it was meant to be held.

The snap of the shotgun must have woken Timmy up. He came through the door, running towards me.

'Dat, Daddy?' he said. 'Dat, Daddy?'

I looked at Sheila. She turned and went into the kitchen.

'This?' I said. 'Nothing. Nothing for little boys.'

Sheila and Timmy were out. Rain streamed down the windows, muffling the noises from the street outside. The air in the flat felt hot and sticky. I tried to read but I couldn't concentrate. I got up and went into the bathroom and turned the bath taps on. While I was waiting for the bath to fill I looked at my face in the cabinet mirror. My complexion was the colour of old newspapers.

I went into the bedroom to get a bath towel from the airing cupboard. But instead of doing that I went over to the wardrobe and got my hat and coat and put them on. Then I went back into the bathroom and turned off the taps.

This time there were people in the pub. Quite a crowd, considering where the pub was situated. And this time the woman wasn't alone behind the bar. Two young barmen, Kilburn Irish, were scurrying up and down doing the drinks while the woman occasionally dished out shepherd's pie. I ordered a shandy and went and sat down at a table by the window. The pub felt stale. The smell of cigarettes and damp macintoshes filled what air there was. None of the customers could be called locals. Just lunchtime trade from the offices. And there were too many of them for my liking. I wasn't used to so many people squeezed together in one spot. They all seemed to be pressing in on me. I'd wanted company, a change of scene, but I hadn't expected it to be like this, and this was too much to take.

I finished my drink and got up and left the pub. The street was almost deserted. I pulled my hat down against the driving rain and began to walk back towards the flat. I turned into the street that led back to the High Street. Half way down I was aware of a car turning in off the main road, coming towards me.

By the time I realised that it was a police car there was nothing I could do about it.

I couldn't turn and run. There was nowhere I could shelter myself before the car got to me. I could do nothing.

Except keep walking.

I froze all thoughts about my own stupidity that had come flooding into my mind. Those could wait. I tried to blank my mind of any thoughts at all, as if by doing that it would be easier for me and the police to pass each other without me being recognised. Make myself an ostrich and everything would be all right.

The car was nearly up to me now. The street was narrow, a one-way, and the car was sitting on the crown of the road. Four feet, five feet away from me at the most as it passed.

Somehow my legs kept working and I kept going forward. The car kept moving at the same speed. No slowing down prompted by recognition. I sensed rather than saw that there were three rozzers in the car. Two uniforms in the front, plainclothes in the back. All eyes would be on me, however briefly: there was nothing else in the street for them to look at. I couldn't turn my face away. That would really do it. I just kept walking into the rain as the car swished past me.

The head of the plainclothes man turned in my direction.

Then the car was past me.

It didn't stop. When I reached the end of the street I turned right and I ran.

I lay in the bath, staring up at the ceiling. Sweat poured off my head: it hadn't stopped since I'd seen the police car. I felt weak, both physically and mentally. I'd nearly blown everything. Just for the sake of going to that fucking pub.

I heard the front door open and the sounds of Sheila and Timmy coming in the lounge. Then Sheila's footsteps as she hurried from room to room, looking for me. I called out to her.

'I'm in here.'

The bathroom door banged against the side of the bath.

Sheila burst in and stood by the bath, looking down at me to make sure there wasn't just bathwater in the bath.

Then she went limp and leant against the edge of the door.

'Jesus, Billy,' she said. 'Jesus.'

'Thought they'd been and gone with me, did you?' I said.

'Don't joke,' she said. 'I really did.'

There was a silence. I said:

'Why don't you go and make a cup of tea?'

Sheila looked at the glass of brandy at the end of the bath.

'What, you as well?'

'Makes me sweat,' I said. 'So does tea. I've got to keep myself in trim somehow.'

I looked at my watch. The luminous face told me it was quarter-to-five. The faint blue of dawn was beginning to lighten the oblong shape of the bedroom window. I hadn't slept all night. My mind had been too full of the turning head in the police car. I'd seen that head turn a thousand times since I'd got into bed at eleven-thirty. The minute Sheila had switched off the light, the face had been there. But it was a face without features, as impressionistic as when I'd actually seen it. And however hard I tried I couldn't imagine what I hadn't seen: the expression. Had it been curious, blank, full of recognition, what?

I couldn't have been recognised. The car would have stopped, wouldn't it? But if the recognition had been late in coming, and by the time it had dawned on them I'd made it round the corner, then that would be different. They'd have thrown in everything they'd got. They'd check out the occupants of every house, flat and room in the area. And sooner or later they'd check who was living over that tobacconist in the High Street, and for how long, and then in no time at all they'd have it sorted. The removal van would be out and I'd be answering the door sometime shortly before eight in the morning.

I got out of bed, pulled on my dressing gown and went

into the lounge. I turned on the gas fire and lit it and lit up a cigarette at the same time. I sat for a while crouched over the fire watching the whistling gas-jets.

When I'd finished the cigarette I got up and went into the bathroom and opened the door to the airing cupboard. I carefully took a pile of washing from one of the shelves and put the washing down on the bathroom floor. Then I slid forward the cardboard box that had been hidden behind the washing and opened the lid. I took out one of the snub-nosed revolvers and a box of ammunition and loaded the chamber. Then I put everything back the way it had been before. After I'd done that I unscrewed the top of the lavatory cistern and took some bandage tape from the bathroom cabinet and taped the gun to the underside of the cistern lid. After I'd done all that I went into Timmy's bedroom and sat by his cot until he woke up.

Sheila came into the kitchen at a quarter-to-eight. I'd already given Tommy his cornflakes and I was mashing up his boiled egg for him as Sheila came through the door. I could tell from her face that she knew I was worried but I also knew that she wouldn't say anything until we were well into a safer part of the day. Sheila didn't believe in tempting fate.

'One thing about old Tim,' I said as Sheila poured herself a cup of tea, 'he doesn't half like his eggs. Don't you, me old son?'

Timmy grinned and a globule of yellow ran down his chin.

'Funny,' I said, 'because when I was a kid I couldn't stand them. Probably something to do with not having them during the war: by the time you could get them again I'd probably got set in my likes and dislikes. You know how kids are.'

I shot a glance at the clock as Sheila drank some tea. Ten to eight.

'Timmy's always liked his eggs,' Sheila said.

Timmy dropped his spoon and I picked it up for him.

'What are you going to have?' Sheila said.

'Nothing,' I said. 'I had some toast.'

'Shall I do you some bacon?'

'No thanks,' I said. 'I'll have another cup of tea, though.'

'It's stewed. I'll make some more.'

Sheila filled the kettle and lit the gas and emptied the tea pot. Timmy finished his egg and squirmed off his chair. He ran out of the kitchen and into the lounge, got one of his comics and ran back into the kitchen again.

'Daddy read,' he said. 'Daddy read.'

I hoisted him up on to my knee and spread the comic out on the table in front of us.

The clock said five to eight.

Instead of reading to Timmy I pointed to things in the comic and asked him what they were. Sheila made the tea and put my cup down on the edge of Timmy's comic. A moment later Timmy violently turned over one of the pages and upset the cup of tea. I jolted the chair back but some of the tea went on Timmy's legs and he began to scream.

'You stupid bloody bitch,' I shouted. 'Have you no fucking sense?'

Sheila took Timmy from me and sat him on the edge of the table and sponged the tea from his legs with the dishcloth.

'It's all right, darling, never mind, you were frightened weren't you? Wasn't very hot, was it? You were just frightened, that's all.'

'Bloody stupid thing to do.' I said.

'If you're so bloody clever why didn't you see it coming and do something about it?'

'I'd no time, had I?'

'No, course not.'

'Now look, don't go trying to blame it on to me.'

'There now, lovey, that's better. Feeling better now? There's a brave little soldier. Let's give you a biscuit for being so brave. All right? There we are.'

Timmy sniffed a bit and munched on the biscuit. I poured myself another cup of tea and sat down again. Sheila turned to the sink and began to slam dishes about in the bowl.

I looked at the clock again. It was five-past-eight.

I got up and carried my tea into the lounge and pulled the door to behind me and walked over to the window. I parted the curtains slightly and looked down into the street.

The Avengers blurred across the TV screen, out of focus in my mind. The sound seemed to come from a long way away. Sheila was sitting opposite me, knitting a cardigan for Timmy. I was thinking of the night ahead. Would I be able to sleep now that a day and a half had gone by or would it be worse now that the odds had shortened? I wanted to talk to Sheila about what had happened, but of course I couldn't, not without admitting what I'd done.

As if she'd been reading my mind, Sheila said:

'What made you think it was going to happen this morning?'

I looked across at her. She still had her head bent over her knitting.

'Nothing really,' I said. 'Just one of those feelings. You know the sort.'

'Yes,' she said. 'But I just wondered… maybe you'd heard from Ronnie. Maybe he'd said something to worry you.'

'If I'd heard from Ronnie I'd have told you.'

'You might not. Not if you didn't want me to worry.' She let her knitting fall on her lap. 'I'd rather know if there was anything, Billy.'

'There isn't, love. Honest. I just had one of those feelings. I couldn't sleep last night. It sometimes happens.'

Sheila went back to her knitting. The Avengers finished and the commercials came on. In a minute it would be News at Ten so I got up to get myself a beer while the commercials were on.

The cool of the kitchen cleared my head a little. I opened

the fridge door and took a can of Bass out and poured it into a glass. I drank some of the beer and topped the glass up.

The door bell rang.

I just stood there. I couldn't move, I couldn't think, nothing. I was vaguely aware of Sheila's panicked movements in the lounge. Then the kitchen door opened. I turned round and I was looking at Sheila's staring eyes. We stayed like that until the door bell rang again. Then I rushed out of the kitchen and into the bathroom and began to unscrew the cistern lid. Sheila followed me.

'Christ, Billy, who is it? Who is it, Billy?'

'I don't know.'

I lifted the lid and ripped the shooter off it.

'Billy, what are you doing? What…?'

'Don't be bloody silly.'

I put the shooter in my pocket.

'Billy, don't…'

I took hold of her by the shoulders.

'Listen, we don't know who it is. So we go back into the lounge. Whoever it is knows we're in because of the telly. So we answer the door. If it's the Filth we're snookered. There's no way we can get out now, not without the shooter. So we answer the door and if it's the law I cop for the first one and put the shooter on him. That's the only chance I've got.'

'But you said you'd never…'

'I know what I said. This is now.'

The door bell rang again.

'In any case,' I said, 'it could be anybody.'

Sheila looked at me. I looked away and walked past her. She followed me into the lounge.

'Just open the door,' I said, pressing myself against the wall.

Sheila didn't move. I saw that she was crying.

'Sheila…'

There was nothing I could say to help. It wasn't a time

246

for saying things This could be the last time ever we would be together; but to act as if it was would make things even worse.

Sheila dried her eyes and slid back the bolts and turned the lock. I braced myself.

There was no great rush into the room. Sheila just opened the door and looked at whoever was standing there.

A voice said: 'Can I come in, Mrs Cracken?'

I knew the voice but for a moment I couldn't place it. Then it fell into place with the features of the face in the police car. Pettit. Detective Sergeant Pettit. And at that moment I knew I wasn't going to be done. Not because I knew Pettit particularly well, but because of the whole atmosphere of the scene.

'Who are you?' Sheila said.

'A mate of Billy's,' Pettit said. 'Or at least I will be.'

Sheila wanted to look at me to see what she should do, but she daren't, still thinking that I wanted to stay hidden against the wall. Then Pettit walked into the room and Sheila stood back and I said: 'Come in and make yourself at home.'

Pettit turned his head briefly in my direction but he didn't stop moving.

'What are you going to do? Chop your way through a dozen uniforms?'

Pettit drifted round the room, like a bored tourist in a museum.

'There would have been that many, would there?' I said.

'For Billy Cracken?' he said, pursing his lips. 'All of that, I would have thought.'

'But there aren't any, are there?'

'No,' said Pettit. 'That's right, Billy. There aren't.'

Pettit stopped moving and looked at me properly for the first time.

'Close the door, Sheila,' I said.

'Mind if I sit down?' Pettit said.

I gave a tired smile. Pettit sat down. Sheila stayed where she was, by the door. Pettit looked at her, then at me.

'Mr Pettit wants to talk to me alone, Sheila,' I said.

'Billy...'

'Don't worry, love. It's all right. Everything'll be all right. Just go into the kitchen.'

Sheila looked at me for a while. Then she turned away and went into the kitchen.

I sat down opposite Pettit.

'I didn't know you were bent,' I said.

Pettit smiled.

'You're sure about that, are you?'

'Do me a favour,' I said.

There was a silence. Pettit said:

'I almost did for you yesterday.'

'I wonder what made you change your mind?' I said.

Pettit carried on as if he hadn't heard.

'In the car, when I saw you, I nearly called out your name, I was so surprised. In fact the driver went so far as to ask if I'd seen a face and did he want me to stop? I just said I thought I had, I'd been mistaken.'

I didn't say anything.

'Thought you'd been lucky, did you?' Pettit said.

'I had, hadn't I?' I said, looking him straight in the eye.

He smiled again.

'I could really do myself a lot of good by taking you in,' he said.

'So you could,' I said.

He looked at me for a long while, as though he was deciding what he was going to do.

'Know why I'm not going to?' he said at length.

'Yes,' I said.

'Yes, but the reason.'

I shrugged.

'All I want to know is what you think it's going to cost me. That's all I want to know.'

'The reason I'm not going to take you in,' Pettit said, 'and I want you to know this, because, in a way, you ought to know, the reason I'm not turning you over is because I'm sick of it all.'

I watched and waited.

'Just sick of it all. Sick at the thought of sixteen straight years doing my job, and getting fuck all out of it while those others…'

'Don't give me that crap,' I said. 'Or else *I'll* be sick. And I haven't paid for the carpet.'

Eventually Pettit smiled.

'All right, Billy,' he said. 'I heard you were a direct sort of a person. I'll tell you what it's worth to me. It's worth a grand. In fact it's worth a lot more, but I'm realistic. And I shan't keep coming back for more. In the circumstances I think that's very reasonable of me.'

I gave the matter some thought.

'As I see it,' I said, 'there are three things I could do. First, I could tell you to piss off. If I told you to piss off, you could either piss off or try and take me in single-handed. And you're not going to do that. Or I could take you apart and throw you down the stairs and before you came to I'd be somewhere other than sitting in front of this fire. Or I could tell you I haven't got that kind of money and there wouldn't be any alternative for you but to piss off or, as I said, try and take me in. Now, where, among the alternatives, is a course of action which gives you an advantage over me?'

'Billy,' said Pettit, 'in a way, you're under-estimating yourself. You don't think I'd come to Billy Cracken wide open, do you? If I'm not out of here and back with my driver in…' he looked at his watch '… in fifteen minutes from now, then my driver'll radio through to send them up here mob-handed.'

I smiled.

'And for why?' I said. 'Why should they? That'd mean you'd have had to let on, and you daren't do that.'

It was his turn to smile.

'Don't be naïve, Billy. All I've let on to my driver is I might be on to something big. That's all. Given him the impression I'm glory-seeking. What could be more natural than wanting to case Billy Cracken's place on my own. I mean, all I was doing was making sure before I called the hounds in. Just unlucky, being clobbered. But it happens to us all.'

After a while I said: 'I don't believe you. You're on your own in this one.'

Pettit shrugged.

'Believe what you like,' he said. 'But if you're wrong then there's no way other than that you go back inside. And you'll have the next twenty-five years to work out how much a grand is actually worth.'

I rubbed my temple with my little finger.

'What's to stop you coming back at me once I've paid you off?' I said. 'After all, that's been known before as well.'

'True,' he said. 'But you won't be here an hour after I've gone. So I'd have to start looking all over again.'

'Not if you went back to your driver and said Billy Cracken's up there, he's moving, let's get the lads down to give him a hand.'

Pettit laughed.

'Billy,' he said, 'you should learn to trust people.'

There was a silence. I thought about things.

'I could only manage eight,' I said.

Pettit looked at me, lips pursed again.

'Is it here?'

'Yes.'

Pettit leant back in his chair.

'All right,' he said.

I stood up.

'I'll go and get it,' I said.

I walked towards the kitchen door. As I passed the chair Pettit was sitting in, I said:

'Oh, by the way...'

Pettit leant forward in his chair so that he could turn and look at me. As he was twisting round in his seat I took the shooter from my pocket and hit him just to the right of his ear, at the base of his skull.

He rolled off the chair without making a sound.

I ran to the kitchen door but before I could get to it Sheila had burst into the room.

'Billy, what's happened? What have you done?'

She tried to get past me to examine Pettit but I grabbed hold of her.

'Listen,' I said. 'He's all right...'

'But...'

'Listen. We've got to get out. He said he wasn't on his own. I think he was lying but we can't chance it. We've got to get out anyway now. But don't panic. If you panic we're sunk. Are you listening to me?'

She nodded.

'Start packing. Two suitcases. Anything you can't get in, leave. They'll do the flat for prints so that doesn't matter. While you're doing that I'll call Ronnie. But don't wake Timmy yet. Do the packing first.'

Sheila ran into the bedroom. I picked up the phone and dialled Ronnie's number.

Ronnie's wife answered the phone.

'Doreen?'

'Speaking.'

'It's Billy.'

'Billy. I was...'

'Where's Ronnie at tonight?'

'Tonight? He's at the Stable. But...'

'Doreen love, I can't talk. I'll be seeing you.'

I killed the line and dialled again. Eventually a woman's voice said:

'Stable Club.'

'Ronnie, please.'

'Who's calling?'

'A friend of Walter's.'

The woman went off the line and there was some clicking at the other end of the line. Then Ronnie came on.

'Yeah?'

'It's Billy. Can I talk?'

'Hang on.'

Silence. Then Ronnie came back on.

'What's up?'

'I've had a visit. Everything's all right but I've got to move on. I need somewhere for us tonight. And I need fetching from here.'

'Jesus.'

'Ronnie?'

'Yeah, yeah. Listen. Tobin's got a man here tonight. And he's covering the flat pretty regular. I've got to be careful.'

'I need moving fast, Ronnie. I might only have ten minutes.'

'I couldn't be there inside of ten minutes anyway. Listen, Billy, can you meet me somewhere?'

'Where, for Christ's sake?'

'I don't know. Can't you walk somewhere, and wait?'

'Hang on.' I called through to Sheila. 'Sheila, is that park open at night?'

'What?'

'The park where you take Timmy. Is it open?'

'I don't know.'

I cursed and said to Ronnie:

'Look, there's this park near us, five minutes' walk away, on the road we're on. We'll meet you there. At the gate.'

'I'll get there as soon as I can.'

I put the phone down and ran into the bathroom and pulled the cardboard box from the airing cupboard and carried it into the bedroom. Then I got Timmy's carry-cot and set it on its wheel base and lifted the carry-cot mattress and stacked the unassembled guns in the bottom of the cot. Then I got a blanket and folded it up and wadded it over the guns and put the mattress on top.

Sheila finished packing the suitcases and opened the wardrobe and took out my jacket and my coat and handed them to me. While I was putting them on she went into Timmy's room and I heard her disturb him. I followed her in case I could help. Sheila was lifting Timmy out of the cot, bedclothes and all. She hurried back into our bedroom again, and again uselessly, I followed her. Sheila made a cocoon of Timmy's bedclothes and eased him down into the cot. He moaned a bit, but he didn't open his eyes. Then Sheila tucked her mac over the top of the bundle and adjusted the hood of the cot. I went back into Timmy's bedroom and stuffed his Teddy and his Matchbox combine harvester into my coat pocket.

'Billy!'

I hurried back into the bedroom and picked up the suitcases. Sheila was already by the open door. She pushed the carry-cot out on to the landing. I followed her with the suitcases. I put the cases down and closed the door behind me and together Sheila and I manhandled the carry-cot to the bottom of the stairs. Then I ran back up the stairs to get the cases.

The park gates were locked. We couldn't stay on the main road so we kept going until we came to a left turning which ran alongside the park. Half way down this turning there was a smaller park gate.

'You stay here,' I said to Sheila. 'I'll walk back to the corner and wait for Ronnie.'

'Billy, they'll see you.'

'What else can I do?'

'You stay here, I'll go.'

'Supposing the Filth think you're a brass? The park and all.'

'It's still safer.'

Sheila walked back to the corner. I looked at my watch. It had been nearly twenty minutes since I'd phoned Ronnie.

Timmy stirred in his cot. I leant over him and peered into his face. His eyes were still closed. I tucked the blankets more snugly round his head. Then I straightened up again and looked back towards the corner. Sheila wasn't standing there any more. Then a black Dormobile rounded the corner. Christ, no. I turned and looked at the carry-cot. I couldn't run. I could do nothing. The van slowed down. I sagged at the knees. The van stopped. Sheila got out one side and Ronnie got out the other.

Tears of relief sprang to my eyes.

'Christ, I thought it was the Filth,' I said.

Ronnie was round the back opening the van doors.

'No chance,' Ronnie said. 'In ten minutes time, maybe.'

Sheila and I loaded the carry-cot in the back and Sheila got in after it. I followed her and Ronnie handed me the suitcases. Sheila and I sat down on the floor and leant against the bench seats. Ronnie slammed the doors and ran round to the front and got in the driver's seat and we took off.

'Thanks again,' I said to Ronnie.

'What happened?' he said.

I told him.

'Jesus Christ,' he said. 'Pettit. That bastard would have sold you right back inside again. He's a real twisted little bastard. You can't trust him no way.'

'That's what I thought.'

'Anyway, the point is, what about accommodation? My place is right out. Too dicey for all of us.'

'I know. And we daren't risk the night in a flea-trap.'

'There is one answer,' Ronnie said.

'What's that?'

'This,' Ronnie said.

'What?'

'The Dormobile I was thinking when I came up: I garage this very private, know what I mean? Secluded in Kentish Town. Nobody goes there except me. Once the garage doors were locked behind you you could kip down in this, no trouble. I could come round tomorrow and we could sort something out from there. What do you reckon?'

Ronnie and I stood by the garage door.

'I'll take a cab over to the Doll's House,' he said 'Then if anybody asks they can't prove nothing. I was just travelling between one club and another. Anyway it won't come to that.'

'Thanks again, Ronnie.'

'Forget it,' he said. 'I'll be round as soon as I can with some nosh and tea and stuff.'

'Look out for yourself,' I said.

'Don't worry about me.'

Ronnie stepped through the inset door and was gone. I bolted the door behind him and went back to the Dormobile.

Sheila had made pillows out of a couple of my sweaters and laid out two blankets apiece: she'd been bright enough to pack one entire suitcase with bedding. At least we weren't going to freeze to death.

We both lay down on our respective bench seats. In the darkness I stretched my arm across the aisle and found Sheila's hand and squeezed it in my own hand. Neither of us said anything. I could hear Timmy's breathing coming from the carry-cot in the aisle between us.

He'd never woken up once.

Ronnie didn't show the next day.

I started getting worried about midday. Timmy was crying for his dinner. Sheila had stuffed some chocolate in her pocket the night before and Timmy had thought this was great, chocolate for breakfast, but by one o'clock he was beginning to get upset with hunger. As to the rest of it, he'd thought it was the best thing yet, waking up in the Dormobile.

'Billy,' Sheila said. 'We've got to do something if Ronnie doesn't come soon. I've got to see to Timmy.'

'He said he'd get here early,' I said. 'I wouldn't mind if he wasn't so bleeding reliable.'

'Supposing he…'

'Yeah,' I said. 'I know.'

I wandered round the garage and tried to think of reasons why Ronnie hadn't shown up other than the one that was charging about in the front of my brain. But no reasons I came up with could supplant my real convictions.

I sat down on an oil drum and looked round the garage.

In the van Sheila was trying to get Timmy to go down in his carry-cot. I got up off the drum and walked over to the van and got in the driver's seat and twisted round so that I could see her.

'It's no use, Billy,' she said. 'He's got to have something. I mean if Ronnie's been… well, we just don't know, do we? We don't know when he'll be back.'

'No,' I said.

'I'll have to go and get something. We could be still waiting this time tomorrow.'

I thought for a while.

'All right,' I said. 'I suppose you've got to go. So as long as you've got to, you could call Ronnie's flat, see if anything's happened. Then at least we'd know what to do next.'

After the half hour I started to get the twinges. I started to wonder whether I should have let Sheila go. I mean, we could

256

have sat it out. Ronnie might show up any time. Anything could have happened. Needn't necessarily have been the law. He might just be playing it safe.

I looked down into the carry-cot. Timmy was asleep now. I'd soothed him down within ten minutes of Sheila's leaving.

I shouldn't have let her go. The past six months cooped in the flat had eroded into my sense of reality. I'd got like some of them get in the nick: unable to sort my thoughts and make the right decisions.

I shouldn't have let her go.

An hour passed. All she'd had to do was to go to the nearest shops and then to a phone box. Where was she?

Timmy woke up. He began to cry immediately. I picked him up and tried to comfort him but he wasn't having any. I looked at my watch. Another quarter of an hour had gone by.

Then the inset door opened. It was Sheila.

'Billy, we've got to get out,' she cried, running towards me.

Still carrying Timmy I scrambled out of the Dormobile and met her half way.

'What's happened?'

'Ronnie. They've fixed Ronnie.'

'Who fixed him? The law?'

'No, Walter. Walter's boys.'

Walter.

'Fixed him? How?'

'Billy, we've got to move.'

'Tell me.'

'Listen. I phoned Ronnie's flat. First couple of times there was no answer, right? Then Doreen came on. She was in a hell of a state. They came for Ronnie in the night and took him away. They found out he'd been helping you and they knew about Pettit and they wanted to know where Ronnie'd taken you. So they took him away. They brought him home half an hour ago. They did him something awful. Fingers, everything. Doreen's...!'

'Did he tell them?'

'He must have done. You know yourself.'

We looked at each other.

'Christ,' I said. 'Ronnie. That cunt Walter. I…'

'Billy, we've got to move.'

'Yeah,' I said. 'Right. You're right. We'll take the van. You drive.'

I put Timmy down in his cot and hurried over to the garage door and slid the bolts back on the main doors. Sheila was already backing up the Dormobile. I was about to swing back the doors but something stopped me. The sound of a car drawing up in the street outside.

I looked at Sheila. She was twisted round in her seat, wondering what was stopping me. A car door opened. Footsteps. Whoever it was stopped on the other side of the garage door. Listening to the Dormobile's engine. I pressed myself against the door. Then the latch lifted on the inset door. The door swung open. Sheila screamed at whoever she could see. The barrel of a sawn-off shotgun appeared round the door.

'They're here,' a voice called. 'At least the bint is.'

Another car door opened.

I moved.

I stepped forward and took hold of the barrel of the shotgun and pulled with all my force. A figure fell through the inset and I lashed out with my foot before the geezer hit the floor, catching him low in the gut. He hit the floor face first and I put the other boot in the side of his head and grabbed the shotgun.

I looked through the inset.

Half way between me and the car the other heavy stood frozen in the road. There were three more heavies in the car, a driver and two others about to get out. All staring at me and the wrong end of the gun.

'Right, cunt,' I said. 'Don't move a fucking eyeball.'

He didn't.

I pulled back the garage door. The heavies, in the car were still motionless.

'Can you get through, Sheil?' I shouted.

Sheila let the handbrake off and the van began to back out. I walked out of the garage and stood between the car and the van. I was close enough to the heavy to smell his aftershave.

Inside the car there was a movement. It was only a slight movement, but it was enough.

I fired one barrel into the windscreen. The other I fired into the nearside front tyre. The heavy in front of me screamed and dropped to his knees, covering his head with his hands. I walloped the visible part of his head with the barrel of the shotgun and threw the gun to the ground. The heavy reached the ground first.

Behind me Sheila was grinding the Dormobile's gears, almost hysterical with panic. I jumped in her side and pulled her over on to the passenger seat. Timmy was screaming in the back, Sheila was saying something about I should never have used the shooter but all her words were running into one another, one senseless shriek. I swung the Dormobile round and jammed down on the accelerator and took off down the street. In the driving mirror I could see the car doors open and the heavies fall out and take off on foot in the opposite direction before the street filled up with sightseers.

I went up through Finsbury Park and Manor Park, making for the A11 and the forest. If the law was going to be on this one the Dormobile would be suicide in London. The quicker we were out of it the better.

Sheila was calmer by the time we reached Epping, but not calm enough. I was still having to go over what had happened, to try and make her see that I'd had no choice in doing what I'd done.

'What could I do?' I said. 'What could I bleeding well do? Just stand there and say "Yeah, well, I know I took a dead

259

liberty in leaving Wally behind, I'll come along and take what's coming?" Sure. I mean, they might even have been after taking me to Tobin. That would have been great, wouldn't it…'

'It was the gun, Billy,' she said. 'You shouldn't have used the gun.'

'Then what should I have used? Timmy's pea-shooter?'

'There'll be real law in on it now and everything. And when the papers find out you were involved the law'll really pull its finger out.'

'Love, there was nothing else I could do. Tell me, what else could I do?'

'I don't know. But…'

'Right. You don't know.'

She fell silent for a while. Eventually she said:

'So now what do we do?'

'Spend tonight in the forest. Tomorrow we dump this and get back into London and get a new place.'

'Just like that?'

'Well, what else can we do?'

'We can't risk going back without a place to go to, Billy.'

'So what do we do? Stay in the forest forever?'

'I'll have to phone Mum. She'll have to fix something up.'

'And how long's that going to take?'

'I don't know. No longer than it'd take us to fix something up. And a damn sight safer.'

I didn't answer. But she was right. Her mother could sort a place for us, then Sheila could go into town on her own and fix it up for us. There was nothing else we could do. But the forest was only safe for a couple of nights at the most. And staying in a hotel was out.

I saw a telephone kiosk a hundred yards ahead of us.

'You better phone her now, then,' I said. 'Get her on it straight away.'

It was getting dark when we finally parked the Dormobile. We were as deep in the forest as we could get. Sheila unpacked what she'd bought at the shop earlier: bread, butter, cheese, corned beef, tinned ham, biscuits, milk, tinned beans and a tin opener. She opened one of the tins of beans and we had them cold, then she made bread and cheese. After that she gave Timmy some chocolate and a drink of milk and he went down without any bother. We both felt exhausted after the day we'd had. Too exhausted to think or to worry or to consider the future. It was enough just to lie down on the bench seats and close our eyes and black out everything with sleep.

At eight next morning I drove the Dormobile as close to the edge of the forest as I could without the van being visible from the road. Then I left Sheila and Timmy and the van and took some money from my money belt and left the forest and walked back into Epping. Sheila had kicked up about me going instead of her but I told her I had to take the chance: she might be even more suspicious – a bird buying a used car, cash. I stopped at a newsagents and bought the *Express*. The shooting incident was written up as a second lead on the front page. There was a photograph of the street and the car and the police had pulled in the two heavies I'd laid out but there was no mention of me. Which meant either that Walter had intended for his boys to finish me off, or that Tobin had been involved and it wouldn't have looked good for him that Walter's heavies had been bringing me in on his behalf. I skimmed the rest of the paper. There was also no mention of anything connected with Pettit. I hadn't really expected there to be: that would have meant a mention of myself. Pettit must have decided that discretion was the better part of valour. But none of all this meant that I was clear. The whole of West End Central could know where I'd been yesterday and have kept it out of the news for their own reasons, surprise value being perhaps one of them.

I folded the paper and carried on walking until I came to the garage I'd sorted as we'd driven through the day before. There were about fifteen cars for sale parked out on the forecourt, set out in two neat rows. I walked along the front row until I came to a clapped out '66 Mini marked up at a hundred and ninety-five pounds. It was the cheapest car on the lot and its anonymity was just what I needed. I tried the doors and looked inside and waited for someone to appear. A minute or two later one of the lads came out of the service kiosk and strolled over to me.

'Yes, sir,' he said. 'Can I help you?'

'Just looking at the Mini,' I said. 'That its real mileage?'

'Course.'

'You must be joking. Nineteen-sixty-six?'

'Maybe you'd like to try her out? Then you'd know how well she's been looked after.'

'Looked after? I look after my old lady better than that.'

I walked away from the Mini and looked at the next car, a Cresta marked up at three five five.

'Make me an offer, then,' he said.

'You really must be wanting it off the lot.'

'Just interested to see what you think.'

I turned and looked at the Mini and pretended to think about it.

'A hundred and thirty,' I said. 'That's what I think.'

He smiled and shook his head.

'And I think you've got a sense of humour.'

We went on like this for a couple more minutes until I told him I'd got cash. A hundred and fifty quids' worth. Five minutes later I was driving the car off the lot.

I parked the car near the first phone box I saw and rang Sheila's mother. She'd managed to fix up a flat in Beckenham. A basement. One room. Use of toilet and bathroom. Eight quid a week. She'd told the landlord we'd been up in Scotland and I'd changed my job fast and needed her to fix something for us while we travelled down. The landlord had swallowed and she'd paid a month in advance plus a bit over the top. We could pick up the keys from the landlord's office any time during the day. After she'd told me all that I came in for the usual earful but in the light of her getting us fixed up I let her go on for more than usual. I finally got off the phone by pointing out that Sheila was waiting for me and the longer I was away the riskier it was for her.

I drove back to the Dormobile. The phone call had made me feel better. We'd got a place to go to again. Four walls.

'Can I speak to Ronnie, please?'

'Who's calling?'

'Billy.'

There was a silence.

'You want something, do you?'

'No, I don't want something, Doreen,' I said. 'I just want a word with Ronnie.'

'Last time you had a word…'

'I know what happened last time,' I said. 'I'm sorry.'

'You know what they did to him, don't you?'

'I can imagine.'

'And you're sorry?'

There was no way of replying to that.

'Is he there?' I said.

Doreen went off the line. I could hear voices in the background. Then the phone rattled at the other end and Ronnie said:

'Hello, me old son.'

'Ronnie,' I said. 'I was just phoning to see how you were getting on.'

'Not too bad,' he said. 'Can't complain. I'll be back in action in a fortnight or so.' There was a pause. 'About what happened…'

'Don't worry about it. I know what Walter's boys are like.'

'If I hadn't told them...'

'How'd they get on to you?'

'Somebody grassed.'

'Who? I mean nobody knew anything about me and you. Except the two boys that fetched me down.'

'It wasn't either of them, Billy. You know that. No, somebody's been watching me closer than I thought. They couldn't know anything, but they could guess.'

'Yeah. Maybe Pettit filtered something to Tobin.'

'Maybe.'

'Look, Ronnie,' I said. 'I wouldn't have put you in it if I'd known Walter was going to turn it on.'

'You couldn't know that, Billy, so stop worrying.'

'Yeah. I know, but...'

'Forget it. Water under the bridge. I'll get my compensation when I find out who the grass is.'

'I'd like to be there.'

'Listen, Billy, about the shooters. There's a job on day after tomorrow. I'd better have your new address so I'll be able to pick them up.'

'When do you want to come?'

'I shan't be able to come myself. I'll have to send somebody.'

'Look, Ronnie,' I said. 'I know you wouldn't send anybody you couldn't trust, but I'd rather you came yourself.'

'I can't, can I, Billy? I'll still be on my back. Otherwise I would, wouldn't I?'

There was nothing I could do about it, the way I owed Ronnie. He'd given me to Walter, but that didn't change anything. That couldn't be helped. I still owed him.

'Yeah, all right,' I said. 'When?'

'Wednesday morning. Half nine.'

'Billy, I don't like it,' Sheila said. 'I don't like anyone knowing where you are. Not even a mate of Ronnie's.'

'So what's the alternative? I've got to let Ronnie have his shooters.'

'I don't know. You'll have to hide.'

'Where, in the bathroom?'

'Where else is there?'

'Oh, Christ,' I said. 'I'm sick of this. I'm not fucking about hiding in bathrooms any more. If I'm going to be out of the way I'm going outside.'

'Out of the house?'

'Yes, out of the fucking house. I walked about in Epping without being collared. So why shouldn't I walk about round here?'

'Billy, that was different. This is London.'

I took hold of her shoulders.

'Look, love, there's a little cut a couple of houses down over the road. Leads to some waste ground at the back where the kids play. I could go there. It'll only be for half an hour. And I could take Timmy. I've never taken Timmy out to play in my life. It'd be great. The only risk would be in getting from here to the cut. I'd have to be bloody unlucky to be picked up between here and there.'

'You've been unlucky all your life, Billy.'

'Not this time I won't be,' I said. 'Not with little Timmy with me.'

I looked at my watch and put my jacket on. Sheila zipped up Timmy's anorak.

'Going out, Mummy,' Timmy said. 'Going out.'

Sheila looked at me. There was an odd expression on her face.

'What's the matter?' I said.

She shook her head.

'Come on. What is it?'

'Just a feeling. I don't know what it is.'

'About what?'

She shook her head again.

'Look,' she said, 'just in case... just in case anything happens...'

'What happens?'

'If something's wrong when you come, I'll leave the bathroom window open. Wide. You can see it from over the road.'

'And what sort of thing do you think's going to happen?'

'Nothing. I'm just saying. Just in case.'

A warm breeze whipped the dead wasteland grass from side to side. Cloud shadows raced across the earth. Timmy clutched my hand and struggled happily through the tall grass.

Half way across the wasteland I sat down on an old brown drainage pipe and watched Timmy rush about and fetch the ball I'd thrown for him. I lit a cigarette and looked up at the sky and watched the clouds rush across the face of the sun. There was sun all the time in South Africa. But there was no way we could go, not yet. Buying the car had made a hole in the money. It would be another six months before I'd be able to move. Unconsciously I put my hand to my stomach and felt the money belt. Another six months of living like this. But the warm breeze on my face and Timmy's cries made me feel better about things. I'd been lucky so far. Six months wasn't so bad. It would be worth waiting for.

I looked towards the opposite edge of the waste ground. There'd once been a row of houses there but at some time they'd been bulldozed down. I could see the gleaming sunlit road and on the other side of the road a row of shops. The shops were only about a hundred yards from where I was sitting. I stood up.

'Come on, Timmy,' I said. 'Let's go and get some sweets.'

'Sweets, Daddy!'

I took his hand and we walked over to the edge of the waste

ground. The traffic was thin and there weren't many people walking up and down in front of the parade of shops. We crossed over the road and went into the tobacconist's.

The shop was empty except for the man behind the counter. I asked Timmy what he'd like and he pointed to the Smarties. I took a bottle of lemonade from its rack and bought Timmy a lollipop as well as the Smarties and paid the man and Timmy and I left the shop and crossed the road.

When we got back to the drainpipe again I sat down and uncorked the lemonade and took a great swig. It tasted beautiful, and it reminded me how lucky I was.

When we got back to the end of the cut I looked across the road to the house where the flat was. The glance was automatic, without thought, instinctive. I expected to see nothing unusual or startling. Just a glance at the house I lived in, nothing more.

So it took a minute or two for the fact that the bathroom window was open to register on my brain.

When it dawned on me I went cold as ice. The bathroom window. Open. Sheila had said the bathroom window. Eventually I became aware of Timmy pulling on my arm, not realising why I'd stopped in my tracks.

I knelt down and said:

'Timmy, love, just stay here a minute will you? Daddy wants to have a look round the corner.'

'Why, Daddy?'

'I just want to have a look. Now you stay here. All right? Here, here's your lollipop. Have a go at this.'

I unwrapped the lollipop and gave it to him. Then I walked the few steps to the end of the cut and looked round the corner.

The front of the house was clear. Nothing. But down the road, on the same side as the cutting, about fifty yards down, there was a white Zephyr parked by the kerb. There was nothing on it that said it was a police car. But I knew. And because the van was plain I knew it must be Tobin. And Ronnie had given me to him. Tobin was in the flat now, with Sheila, waiting for me.

I turned away from the end of the cut and knelt down and said to Timmy: 'Listen, mate, I want you to do something for me. I want you to cross over the road and go into the house on your own like a big boy. Will you do that?'

'Why Daddy?'

'Because Daddy's forgotten to get something at the shop and he's got to hurry before they close.'

Timmy didn't say anything.

'Daddy won't be long.'

He put his lollipop in his mouth and sucked.

'Can you do that?'

Timmy nodded.

'All right then, son,' I said. 'I'll see you shortly.'

He nodded again and walked across the road. I watched him for a moment then I turned and ran back down the cut.

I looked at the clock on the pub wall. A quarter-to-one. I'd been there since eleven-thirty. After I'd crossed the wasteland I'd hailed a cruising taxi and had the driver bring me here, to a pub in Clapham, behind the common.

Ronnie had put Tobin on to me. And Walter had put the pressure on Ronnie. It was no use getting hard with Ronnie. He'd done all he could. Knowing Walter he'd have used Ronnie's wife and kids as stakes. And Ronnie loved his wife and kids, like I did mine. So it was no use getting hard. And in any case, I hadn't the time. Sheila and Timmy had been taken. Sheila was in line for three years if they decided to stick it on her. I had to think. I had to clear my head and think. They'd taken Sheila.

I went to the bar and bought another drink but that didn't help. There wasn't a thing I could do to help Sheila. All I could do was to concentrate on not getting myself caught. Because there was just a chance, just the one chance: Tobin might not press charges. He might let her go. So that she'd lead them to me. That was the only chance we had. But if Tobin pressed it – three years. She could get three years.

I ordered another drink and went to the phone and phoned the flat. There was no reply. That meant they hadn't got anyone staking it on the inside. They'd all be out in the street and the neighbouring houses, just waiting for me to show up.

I put the phone down and went back to the bar and drank some of my drink. I swore to myself. This was it. If they let Sheila go, then we'd be off. Out of it. Whatever it cost. But to pay for it I had to take a risk. There was no other way. I had to put myself on show.

I kept the Mini garaged in a lock-up a mile away from the flat. When the pub shut I took a taxi to the garage and went in and sat in the Mini and waited for the night. Then, at about seven-thirty, I drove the Mini out of the garage and made for Richmond, stopping on the way to buy an evening paper. I found a nice quiet little pub and bought a drink and phoned Sheila's mother. She told me that she'd got Timmy and he was all right, and that my lawyer had been in touch but as yet he didn't have any news. Before she could get into her diatribe I cut in and I'd told her I'd phone again tomorrow. And I told her to kiss Timmy for me.

Then I sat down and looked through the flats in the evening paper. There were about a half a dozen likely sounding numbers. All pricey, all flash, none of them the kind of place the law would be looking for Billy Cracken.

I made the phone calls and arranged to go and see the four that hadn't already gone. Twickenham, Barons Court, Fulham and Parsons Green.

Three hours later I'd secured two of them. Barons Court and Fulham. The one in Fulham had a fire escape.

Then I drove back to the garage and spent the night in the Mini.

I phoned Sheila's mother at six o'clock the next evening. But it was Sheila who answered the phone.

'Billy! Are you all right?'

'They let you go! The bleeders let you go!'

'It was Tobin. He thinks I'll bring him straight to you.'

'I can't... are you all right. How was it?'

'Not bad. I let Tobin think I was all folded up. Which is what he wanted to think. There's a man outside me Mum's right now.'

'Christ,' I said. 'I was sick. I thought...'

'I know. So did I until Tobin started. He's barmy, Billy. He really wants you and he doesn't care how he gets you. One of the other coppers wanted to do it legal, commit me for trial with a recommendation for a suspended sentence but Tobin said he couldn't wait that long and as far as he was concerned I hadn't even been brought in.'

'Listen,' I said, 'we've got to get out of this lot. We can't last much longer if we don't.'

'But how, Billy? We haven't the money. Especially now, now Tobin's started up again. It'll cost twice as much.'

'Don't worry about the money,' I said. 'I'll see to that.'

'Billy...'

'Listen, love, I've got to take a chance. If I don't then Tobin's going to get us. Sooner or later he'll have us. Do you understand that?'

'Yes. Yes I do. But...'

'So I've got to take a chance. I've got to get us out of it.'

There was a silence.

'What are you going to do?' she said at last.

'I don't know yet. I'll have to fix something up. It might take time. But I'll tell you what I want you to do. I want you to stay put until I tell you. I'll phone you at the weekend. And don't worry. I'll be all right. You'll hear from me at the weekend.'

'For God's sake be careful, Billy.'

'I'll be careful, love,' I said. 'Don't you worry, I'll be careful.'

After I'd phoned Sheila I went and had another drink. This time I actually enjoyed it. Sheila was safe. With Timmy. But I had to get us all out of it if we were to have any chance of ever living properly together again.

I downed my drink and went back to the phone. I dialled a number and waited. At the other end a receiver was picked up and a voice said:

'Yes.'

'Could I speak to Jimmy?' I said.

'Who wants to know?'

'A mate of his.'

'All his mates are here.'

'One of them isn't.'

I heard Jimmy's voice in the background asking what the fucking hell the performance was all about.

The voice told him some joker was on the other end of the line saying he was a mate. Then Jimmy said well for Christ's sake ask him his bleeding name.

The voice came back on the line.

'Now look here, Jokey, let's be having you. Jimmy only talks to names.'

'I'll give you one. Benny Beauty.'

'Do me a favour. Are you out of your tiny mind?'

'Just tell Jimmy Benny'll hear that he wouldn't talk to a mate of his. Benny won't always be where he is now.'

The voice started to explain that bit but Jimmy must have got sick of the game and the next voice that came on the line was his:

'All right, cunt. What's *your* problem?'

'Christ, Jimmy,' I said. 'It was never so difficult to get you in the old days.'

'Who's this?'

'Billy. And don't say my name.'

'Jesus. I've been hearing it all over the place during the last few days.'

'But not reading it in the papers, eh?'

'Hardly surprising.'

'Not really.'

I heard Jimmy clear whoever was in the room with him out of it and then there was a pause while Jimmy frantically tried to work out how to phrase the question that was scurrying around in his brain.

I saved him the trouble.

'Don't worry, Jimmy,' I said. 'I'm not after a bed for the night. There's no danger of you ending up like Ronnie.'

'What do you mean?'

'Leave it out, Jimmy. You know what I mean. I'm not after any embarrassing favours. Except maybe one. But nothing that'll put you out on a limb.'

'What can I do for you?'

'I want putting in something. Doesn't have to be one of your tickles. But it has to be in with a safe firm. No ex-associates of Walter. No arse-lickers. Know what I mean?'

'Yeah, I know what you mean. But everybody's heard about Ronnie. They might not want to wear anything with you.'

'Maybe not. But you know as well as I do, Jimmy, the scene changes. There's plenty of young tearaways out to make a name who don't give a stuff about people like Wally. They'd be glad of the experience of working with Billy Cracken. And you know who they'd be, Jimmy. That's all I want you to do for me: just put me in with a firm that's about to go.'

'You're taking a big chance, Billy. You know that. You can't trust anyone nowadays.'

'Let's face it, Jimmy, I'm taking a chance talking to you. You could do yourself a bit of good here and there if you turned me over.'

'I'm no Walter lover, Billy. You should know that.'

'I know. I know what he did.'

There was another silence. Eventually Jimmy said: 'All right, Billy. I'll see what I can do.'

'Thanks.'

'I can't promise anything.'

'I know.'

'Phone me back Sunday.'

'Thanks, Jimmy. I'll do that.'

I spent the following two days and nights at the flat in Barons Court. It was strange to wake up in a bed and find myself without Sheila and Timmy. The flat was lifeless and depressing. Only the rumpled bed and the few bits of multipurpose crockery gave any sign that someone was living there. I spent my time on the phone to a few contacts I had, getting the current gen on what it would cost to get us out of it and what was available over the next month or so. When I wasn't doing that I sat around reading the papers and when I wasn't doing that I'd break up the monotony of prowling round the flat by doing my exercises. I'd neglected them over the last few weeks.

On Saturday I phoned Sheila. She told me she was being followed everywhere. She wasn't bothered by it. She said she got a lot of satisfaction out of the fact that the law thought any minute she was going to lead them to me.

On Sunday I phoned Jimmy.

'How's the job hunting going?' I said by way of a kick-off.

'Not bad,' Jimmy said. 'I've got something that might interest you. If it's a goer, that is.'

'Tell me all about it.'

There's a firm in Finsbury Park set to go on a Post Office van. Could be worth a few bob.'

'Why shouldn't it be a goer?'

'No reason. I mean, the firm'll take it on.'

'But?'

'Well, you know as well as I do, Billy. Some of these young tearaways... all cock and no balls.'

'I know all that Jimmy,' I said. 'But beggars can't be choosers.'

'Well, it's the only thing I can put you in right at the moment.'

'Have you mentioned me?'

'To one of them. The heaviest of them.'

'And?'

'He gave me some smart talk but he's interested. He wants to meet with you tonight.'

'Whereabouts?'

'Out of town. Pub in Woodford.'

'Woodford? Christ.'

'Well, there you are. I said they were like that. If I were you...'

'What am I likely to make?'

'I'll be honest, Billy I don't think they'll be divvying-up. They know the position you're in.'

'I thought it'd be like that. Just so long as it's worth my while.'

'That I couldn't say, Billy. But they know why you need it. So they must know what you expect.'

'Yes,' I said. 'Anyway, I'll give it a throw. What's the name of the pub?'

I parked the Mini on the pub forecourt and got out.

The pub had a string of fairy lights draped across its mock-Tudor frontage and soft pinks and oranges glowed behind the frosted glass casements. Just the kind of place I'd imagined they'd choose.

I walked across to the saloon bar entrance. I noticed a big

Zodiac parked at the far end of the forecourt. That would be them. Apart from that there was an Eleven Hundred and a Viva and nothing else. There was nobody about. But I was past caring about that kind of scouting. The thoughts of the job and the money and getting Sheila and Timmy out of it made the risks seem light, negligible. In an odd way this biggest risk of all had given me a kind of fatalistic calm. I had a peaceful feeling that I wouldn't be caught, that the job would progress through smoothly, that Sheila and Timmy and me would make it with no trouble. Maybe I had these feelings because I had no choice: that to think the other way would automatically bring everything down on my head. I didn't know. All I knew was that this was what I had to do to clear up the mess we were in. There was no way I could allow myself to fail.

I walked into the pub.

They were sitting in a corner, in one of those booths carved in a phony medieval style. There were only two of them. Both flash, all the gear, beige leather and soft suede and rings and identity bracelets and the hairstyles and the arrogance. Nobody was ever going to put them away. Nobody was smart enough.

I walked to the bar and got a drink and waited for them to come to me. They didn't move for a while. They were playing the same game. After three or four minutes one of them left his seat and came over to the bar and stood behind me. I could tell he was behind me because of his aftershave.

'Evening,' he said.

I turned round and looked at him. He was grinning at me, but I didn't like the grin. It was arrogant, full of condescension.

I nodded in reply.

'You must have missed us,' he said. 'We're over in the booth.'

'Thanks for telling me,' I said.

I walked past him and over to the booth and sat down. The other one watched me all the way. This one wasn't grinning but the same arrogance and conceit were there.

The first one slid into the seat, next to me.

There was a silence.

'I'm Vince,' said the first one. 'And this is Dave.'

I nodded again.

'And you're Billy,' said the one called Dave.

I didn't answer.

'And you want to work,' he continued.

'That's right,' I said.

There was another silence.

'Jimmy tell you what we're on?' Vince said.

'Yes.'

'All we want,' said Dave, 'is some extra muscle.'

I didn't say anything.

'Five minutes work, really.'

I waited.

'Thing is, for five minutes, we can't count you in on the divvy. I mean, we've been sorting this one for a couple of months now.'

'See what we mean?' Vince said. 'We'll be glad to give you the work. But as to the divvy…'

'Did Jimmy tell you I'd expect to be in on the divvy?' I said.

'No, but…'

'Then the conversation we're having's pointless, isn't it?'

'Just wanted to make sure you understood our position,' said Dave.

'Fine,' I said. 'Now you understand my position: I'm working for a grand. Half first, half after. No ifs, no buts. Just tell me what needs doing and I'll do it. But leave out the lip and leave out the clever glances and on Wednesday evening you'll both be a lot better off. Thanks to me. Because you two couldn't knock over my Auntie Nora's karsi on your own. And she's been dead ten years.'

I took a sip of my drink. They both looked at me. After a little while Dave said: 'We don't need you, cunt.'

I smiled at him.

'Then why am I here?'

'We're doing a favour for Jimmy.'

'Don't make me tired,' I said. 'You've never done anybody a favour in your life. You need me. You can't get any of the pros to work with you. It's plain as day. You're only getting me because I want out of my present situation. You're just a couple of wankers. Without me you don't stand a snowball's chance.'

'Listen, clever sod,' Dave said, 'there isn't only you, you know. There's two other geezers in on it. You're just insurance. One more isn't going to make all that much difference.'

'If it's me it will,' I said. Vince began to speak but I cut him off. 'Look, is it on or isn't it? Otherwise I can think of other places to do my drinking.'

They looked at one another, Dave said:

'What makes you think we can put the bread up front?'

'Oh, you can,' I said. 'Couple of affluent lads like yourselves. You'll be able to manage that.'

'Supposing we don't want to?'

'Then you don't want me, do you?'

There was another silence.

'Are we having another drink, or what?' I said.

Dave looked at Vince. Then he nodded.

Vince got up and went to the bar. Neither of us spoke until Vince got back with the drinks. When Vince sat down I said: 'The other two you mentioned. They know I'm in it?'

'Not yet,' Vince said.

'Who are they?'

'What does it matter?'

'I said who are they?'

'George Fulcher and Mickey Reeve.'

I shook my head.

'Don't know either of them.'

'Well, you wouldn't, would you,' Dave said.

I looked at him.

'Well, you know what I mean,' he said.

I left it and took a drink.

'All right,' I said. 'Tell me all about it.'

'Nothing to tell,' Vince said. 'It's a doddle. Just a Post Office van. Ram and scram. Two cars, one posted on the route, one following the van. Once we've stopped the van we take the stuff in the second car, drive two streets and get into the straight cars.'

'A doddle,' I said. 'I've been on doddles before.'

'What can screw it up?'

I scratched my head.

'Well?' said Vince.

'Nothing,' I said. 'Nothing at all.'

I finished my drink.

'And you want me to supply some muscle,' I said.

'You and the other two. Dave and me'll concentrate on the rear doors.'

'Which car am I in?'

'The first one. The waiting car.'

'I take it you don't intend going tooled up.'

'Tooled up? On this kind of job?'

'Just so's I know what I'm into,' I said.

'Christ, we don't want ten-stretches.'

'I thought you were the types that were never going to get your collars felt. I thought that was just for old timers like me.'

'Yeah, well. There's always the possibility. I mean, you have to think of these things, don't you?'

I didn't phone Sheila when I got back to the flat. I felt too tired and depressed.

The two tearaways had put the mockers on me. Had I been like that ten years ago? Christ, I hoped not. I'd hate to have thought I'd been nicked as a result of being as stupid as they were.

I made a cup of tea and put the pot and the milk on a tray and set it down on the bedside table and got straight into bed.

The job had sounded straightforward enough. Even if they screwed it up I reckoned I could get myself out of it without concerning myself with them. And have the half a grand. But the whole thing seemed unreal to me. There was none of the old elation, no excitement at the prospect of action. Maybe the tearaways were right. Maybe I was an old man without any appetite.

I drank my tea and switched out the light. Outside the distant sound of traffic drifted up into the sky. For some reason I thought of myself as a boy, lying in my bed just this way, listening to the noises of the outside world, wondering what was happening out there, inventing stories to fit the sounds of the night.

'Sheila, it's me.'

'Billy, love. I thought something had happened...'

'Nothing's happened, sweetheart. Look. I think it's time for us to get back together. I think it'll be OK now.'

'Billy, that's marvellous.'

'Yeah, well listen. I want you to go to this flat in Fulham. Now you'll be followed, we know that, but don't worry about it. Just go to the flat and go in. The door'll be open. On the hall table there'll be an envelope with the keys to the Mini and the address of where I'm living, right? Don't bother reading it then. Just pick it up and go through the flat to the back bedroom window and out and down the fire-escape. You'll be quite safe because there's a courtyard that can't be seen from the way you go in. Just cross the courtyard and there's a passage under the flats behind, right? Go down the passage and the Mini'll be opposite the passage in the next street.'

'What time shall I come to where you are?'

'About seven o'clock tonight,' I said.

We talked a little while before I put the phone down but I didn't tell her about the job. I'd tell her about that tonight, in the flat, when it was over.

I sat in the car and looked out of the window. The side street was empty. Next to me the driver, George, flexed and closed his hands over the steering wheel, regularly, monotonously. On the corner, about ten yards away from us at the end of the street, Mickey waited for the van to round the corner of the street that formed the junction to the street where we were parked.

I looked at my watch. Approximately two minutes to go. I felt the pick-handle that lay across my knees. Above us light fluffy clouds drifted across the deep blue sky.

Then, at the end of the street, Mickey turned and began to walk towards us. George and I pulled on our stocking masks. George slid off the handbrake and the Jaguar began to move forward. I leant back over my seat and opened the back door for Mickey. Mickey got in and George put his foot down.

'She's here,' said Mickey, putting on his mask. 'Vince and Dave are right behind her.'

George swung the Jag round the corner and there it was, the Post Office van, trundling down the empty street towards us, the Dormobile in tow right behind.

They must have known. The minute the Jag pulled out, they must have known. But there was nothing they were going to be able to do about it.

George wrenched the wheel over and pulled the Jag broadside on in the path of the van. The driver of the van pulled on his wheel, too, but there was no chance. The van hit the Jag between the nearside front door and front wheel. The Jag twisted round, carried on the path of the van, but came to rest when the van ploughed into the side of the empty warehouse. Almost before the van had stopped we were all out of the Jag, making for the driver and his mate. I heard the sounds of Vince and Dave going to work on the van's rear doors.

George and Mickey took one of the front doors. I took the other. As I pulled it open and yanked out the driver I saw his mate anticipate the door opening on the other side: he kicked out at the door with both feet. I heard George cry out as he got the full force of the door in his face, but Mickey grabbed the legs of the mate and pulled him out of the cab so that his head cracked against the bottom of the doortrip and again on the pavement.

My one was easy. I didn't even use the pick-handle. I just dragged him out and slung him against the side of the van and gave him a couple round his head and he sank to the floor, no fight in him. I left him where he was and ran round to the back of the van. Vince and Dave had got the doors open and were already shifting the sacks into the Dormobile. I began to help them. Mickey appeared from the other side of the van, supporting George. George's mask was soaked with blood. Mickey pulled the mask from George's head and almost immediately George sank down to his knees and was sick. The blood was still pouring from his nose.

'Get him in the back, quick,' Vince shouted at Mickey. 'You'll have to drive now.'

Mickey got George to his feet and shepherded him round to the back of the Dormobile and bundled him in.

'Right, that'll do,' Dave said. 'Let's get going, sharp.'

The driver began to get up.

Mickey got in the driver's seat and Dave got in beside him. Vince and I got in the back with George. Mickey reversed the Dormobile and began to swing it out so that we could get past the Jag.

'What did I tell you,' shouted Vince over the noise of the engine. 'A doddle! A fucking doddle!'

I looked through the rear window. There was a car rounding the corner behind us.

It began to slow down. Then it stopped. The driver got out and ran half way to the van and looked at the men lying in the road. Then he looked down the road towards the Dormobile.

'We're spotted,' I said.

Dave twisted round in his seat. The man ran back to his car and got in and reversed back down the road until he got to a spot where he could turn round.

'Fuck him,' Dave said. Then to Mickey: 'Get moving son, we're red hot for the next couple of minutes if that bastard tips the law.'

Mickey put his foot down. He turned right, then left, then left again. Now we were in a main thoroughfare. There was no other way to get to where the clean cars were parked. We only had to be on it for a couple of minutes, but now it was dicey, now we'd been spotted.

The traffic couldn't have been worse. Ahead of us, traffic lights were reducing the flow of vehicles to a snail's pace. Pedestrians were moving faster than we were.

'Fucking Jesus,' Vince said. 'Let's bleeding move it.'

The traffic ahead of us started up and we moved a few more yards before stopping again.

In the opposite lane, traffic going in the opposite direction was flowing much more easily.

'For Christ's sake,' Dave said. 'Make a U-turn.'

'That'll take us away from the cars,' said Vince.

'We can make it another way. Let's for Christ's sake get off this street. We're like fish in a barrel.'

'What do you want me to do?' Mickey said.

'Make the bleeding turn.'

Mickey threw the van into reverse to give him the space to begin the turn. But as he did that the lights changed and the traffic began to move again.

The car behind went straight up the Dormobile's arse.

'You fucking idiot,' screamed Dave.

People on the pavement stopped, staring. The door of the car behind opened and the driver began to get out. Mickey screwed the steering wheel right over and pulled out into the opposite lane. A Cortina, travelling at about thirty, was headed straight for the nose of the Dormobile. The Cortina braked but it carried on skidding towards us. Dave and Vince screamed at Mickey. Mickey put his foot down and tried to complete the turn, get the van straight to avoid the Cortina, but instead of straightening up, the van mounted the pavement and ploughed into a news-stand. Magazines and papers scattered everywhere and slapped up at the front window.

'You cunt!' Dave screeched.

And as he screeched the Cortina hit us, shuddering the rear of the van along in its path until the Dormobile was almost pointing the way we'd been travelling in the first place.

Dave and Mickey slid open their doors. I kicked at the rear doors and smashed them open and slid out over the sacks. Women were screaming and the traffic had stopped completely. I straightened up and found myself staring in the windscreen of the Cortina. The driver was lying back in his seat, stunned, blood pouring down his face. I ran round the corner of the van, on to the pavement, and collided with Mickey.

'George,' he said. 'Help George.'

George had rolled out off the sacks and was leaning against one of the rear doors, looking round him as though he couldn't quite comprehend what had happened. Mickey went to him and grabbed hold of George's lapels and began to shake him.

'Come on, George,' Mickey said. 'Get a grip. We'll get you out of it.'

I looked down the street. Vince and Dave had already taken off, charging away from us down the pavement through the crowds of lunch-time shoppers. I looked at Mickey and George. There was nothing I could do by staying, other than to make sure three of us got nicked instead of just the two. So I took off after Vince and Dave. I ran along the pavement and above the racing wind I could hear Mickey's voice screaming after me to go back.

I didn't know the area. I knew the name of the street where the cars were, but that was all. I had to stick with Dave and Vince if I wanted to make it by car. I could have stayed on my own, tried to make it alone, but making it by car was safer.

Dave and Vince turned right before they got to the traffic lights. I did the same and found myself in a side street similar to the one we'd been in earlier. Dave and Vince were about twenty yards ahead of me. The street was empty but for the three of us. Away in the distance I could hear the hee-haw of police cars. Dave and Vince took a left turn and again I followed. Then left and right again and we were there, in the street where the cars were parked.

The street was a new development. Where there'd once been nineteenth-century workers' dwellings and warehouses, now there were clean new flats down one side and a low modern school on the other. The cars, a Zephyr and a Rover, were parked twenty feet apart, facing in different directions, by the school railings. The playground was full of kids, chanting and running and playing.

Vince reached the Zephyr and Dave carried on running towards the Rover. Vince got in and gunned the engine of the Zephyr. The car began to pull away from the kerb. Dave was almost up to the Rover. Vince's car accelerated towards the Rover but suddenly he slewed the car across the road and jammed on his brakes.

A police van had rounded the corner of the school and manoeuvred itself broadside across the road.

I stood stock still in the middle of the street. Vince jumped out of the Zephyr and began running back towards me. Uniforms began to pile out of the police van. Children were running towards the railings to get a better view. Dave was in the Rover by now and had started the engine. The Rover accelerated forward and made for the gap between the Zephyr and the railings. There was just enough space for the Rover to get through. Vince ran past me, careless of Dave's Rover. Sheer panic was making Vince's decisions for him.

I ran towards the gap between the Zephyr and the railings. Dave would have to slow down as he went through the gap. If he stopped for a second I'd be able to get in. It was a chance I had to take. I'd get nowhere taking off like Vince.

I stood poised by the boot of the Zephyr. Kids were crammed against the railings, eyes wide. One of the uniforms shouted to the kids to get back but they didn't take any notice. The Rover mounted the pavement. But it didn't slow down. I stared into the windscreen. Dave's face was set with concentration. He was going to try and go through the gap without slowing down. I stepped out into the space and waved my arms at him. But the expression on Dave's face didn't change and the Rover didn't slow down. He must have been doing fifty.

I threw myself out of the gap and landed face down by the Zephyr's rear wheel.

Then there was a crash as the nearside wing of the Rover connected with the boot of the Zephyr. I heard the screams of the kids as the two cars hit.

Then I heard another scream and felt a terrible weight crushing down on the small of my back. The weight was only present for a second. Then it was gone. At first I wasn't sure what had happened. I tried to move my head but when I did that I felt the pain and the scream sounded out again. I could see the Rover racing away from me. I swivelled my eyes and I saw the kids regrouping at the railings, staring down at me. And between me and the kids was one of the Zephyr's rear wheels. That was what had happened. The collision had bounced the Zephyr's rear wheel across my body.

I tried to move again and again I screamed. The scream was

echoed in the crowd of kids. There was the sound of footsteps, coming at a run. I thought of Sheila and Timmy on their way to the flat, getting there, waiting. And among the hubbub in the playground I thought I could hear my own voice, as a child, challenging Bas Acker to a fight, to see who was best.

**The story of Ted Lewis carries historical and cultural resonances for our own troubled times**

*Get Carter* are two words to bring a smile of fond recollection to all British film lovers of a certain age.

The cinema classic was based on a book called *Jack's Return Home*, and many commentators agree contemporary British crime writing began with that novel. The influence of both book and film is strong to this day, reflected in the work of David Peace, Jake Arnott and a host of contemporary crime and noir authors. But what of the man who wrote this seminal work?

Born in Manchester in 1940, he grew up in the tough environs of post-war Humberside, attending Hull College of Arts and Crafts before heading to London. His life described a cycle of obscurity to glamour and back to obscurity, followed by death at only 42. He sampled the bright temptations of sixties London while working in advertising, TV and films and he encountered excitement and danger in Soho drinking dens, rubbing shoulders with the 'East End boys' in gangland haunts. He wrote for *Z Cars* and had nine books published. Alas, unable to repeat the commercial success of *Get Carter*, Lewis's life fell apart, his marriage ended and he returned to Humberside and an all too early demise.

*Getting Carter* is a meticulously researched and riveting account of the career of a doomed genius. Long-time admirer **Nick Triplow** has fashioned a thorough, sympathetic and unsparing narrative. Required reading for noirists, this book will enthral and move anyone who finds irresistible the old cocktail of rags to riches to rags.

**Available from noexit.co.uk and all good bookshops**

978-1-85730-341-7                    £19.99